Death, Taxes,
and Sweet Potato Fries

DIANE KELLY

St. Martin's Paperbacks

This is a work of fiction. All of the characters, organizations, and events portrayed in this novel are either products of the author's imagination or are used fictitiously.

DEATH, TAXES, AND SWEET POTATO FRIES

Copyright © 2017 by Diane Kelly.

For information address St. Martin's Press, 175 Fifth Avenue, New York, NY 10010.

ISBN: 978-1-250-09488-9

Our books may be purchased in bulk for promotional, educational, or business use. Please contact your local bookseller or the Macmillan Corporate and Premium Sales Department at 1-800-221-7945, extension 5442, or by e-mail at MacmillanSpecialMarkets@macmillan.com.

Printed in the United States of America

St. Martin's Paperbacks edition / February 2017

St. Martin's Paperbacks are published by St. Martin's Press, 175 Fifth Avenue, New York, NY 10010.

10 9 8 7 6 5 4 3 2 1

$\mathcal{A}$cknowledgments

Many people played a part in making this book happen, and I'm so grateful to all of them.

Thanks to my fantastic editor, Holly Ingraham, who works as hard as Tara but never threatens to shoot anyone.

Thanks to Sarah Melnyck, Paul Hochman, Allison Ziegler, and the rest of the team at St. Martin's who worked to get this book to readers.

Thanks to Danielle Christopher and Monika Roe for creating such fun book covers for this series.

Thanks to my agent, Helen Breitwieser, for all of your work in furthering my writing career.

Thanks to Liz Bemis and the staff of Bemis Promotions for my great Web site and newsletters.

And finally, thanks to you fabulous readers who picked up this book. Enjoy this latest adventure with Tara, maybe with a side of sweet potato fries!

chapter one

$\mathcal{O}$ver the Moon

Half past seven on a Monday night in late June, I sat at a booth in a trendy restaurant in the Uptown area of Dallas, a heaping platter of sweet potato fries on the table between me and my fiancé.

My fiancé!

Twenty-four hours earlier Nick Pratt had merely been my boyfriend. But when he'd popped the question last night, my answer had been a resounding *Yes!* Nick was not the type of guy a woman said no to. And now, here we were.

Betrothed.

Engaged.

Or, as we say in Texas, *fixin' to tie the knot.*

I could hardly believe it! Though I was in my late twenties, it took everything in me not to whip out a ballpoint pen and write *Mrs. Tara Pratt* a hundred times on my napkin. With his tall, muscular build, dark hair, and amber eyes, Nick would make a handsome groom. He had a small scar on his cheekbone and a slightly chipped bicuspid, but these things only made him more attractive to me because

they made him manly and real. Nope, no perfect pretty
boys for me.

At least not anymore.

I'd dated a pretty boy right before Nick, a nice guy
named Brett with an impeccable smile, crisply ironed
shirts, and flawless manners. Brett was a modern-day
Prince Charming. Problem was, I'm no Cinderella, duti-
fully biding my time, waiting to be rescued. *Hell, no.* I'm
a take-charge type of woman, taking names and kicking
ass rather than simply accepting what fate attempts to im-
pose on me. Brett and I had some fun, even developed
some pretty deep feelings for each other at one point, but
we were a mismatch from the get-go. Those days were long
behind me now.

When Nick reached out his fingers to snag one of my
fries, I slapped his hand away. "Hands off!" Okay, so maybe
I had a hard time saying no to Nick in other contexts, but
I could certainly say no to him when it came to my sweet
potato fries. But, c'mon. You can't really blame me. Is there
anything more delicious than sweet potato fries? If there
was, I hadn't found it yet.

Despite my protestation, Nick grabbed my wrist and
immobilized my arm while snatching a fry with his left
hand. "You and I are getting hitched. I put a ring on your
finger last night. Here in the state of Texas, that makes
these fries community property."

"Nice try," I shot back. "We're not married yet. Not
until I'm wearing *two* rings. So that means the fries are
all mine." I twisted my arm out of his grasp and pulled
the platter closer. Selfish, sure. But Nick could be just as
bad when it came to chili cheese fries.

The waitress stepped up to our table. "How we doin'
over here?"

Nick cut me a scathing look before smiling up at the

woman. "I'm going to need my own order of sweet potato fries. Tara's being stingy with hers."

The woman smiled back. "I'll get right on that." She stepped away to turn in Nick's order.

I picked up a fry and ran it along the edge of the plate, gathering some errant sugar crystals. This place served their sweet potato fries with a dusting of granulated sugar rather than salt, essentially turning the fries into a dessert. Not that I was complaining. Still, sweet potatoes were touted as a vitamin-and-mineral-rich "superfood," so I refused to feel guilty for indulging. I think they even had antioxidants. Good thing, because I'd been feeling quite oxidized lately.

"Have you given any thought to our honeymoon?" I asked Nick before taking a bite.

Nick stole another fry from my plate. "Heck, yeah, I've been thinking about our honeymoon. That's about all I've been thinking about." He sent me a sexy smile and a wink. "How about we spend some time on the water?"

"Good idea. A cruise would be fun." Maybe we could go to the Bahamas, or Jamaica. There were several cruises that left from Galveston and sailed to ports all over the Caribbean.

"Forget the cruise," Nick said. "I was thinking we could take my bass boat out to Lake Texoma and do some fishing, maybe catch ourselves some catfish or bluegill."

Catfish? Is he crazy? I pointed a fry at him. "I am *not* spending my honeymoon with a bucket of worms at my feet."

"So I should bring my artificial lures, then?" He arched a brow, his eyes dancing in amusement.

I tossed the fry into my mouth and offered a much better suggestion. "What about Cancún?"

The beautiful Mexican resort town was where Nick

and I had first laid eyes on each other, though it had been under challenging circumstances. Nick and I both worked as criminal investigators for the Internal Revenue Service. When I'd joined the IRS a little over a year ago, Nick's office across the hall from mine sat empty. When I asked about the mysterious unused space, my coworkers told me it belonged to Nick Pratt, a senior special agent who had worked an undercover investigation three years before, targeting a violent criminal mastermind named Marcos Mendoza. Mendoza ran a variety of cross-border criminal enterprises ranging from gambling to credit card counterfeiting. What's more, Mendoza's business associates had a tendency to disappear or meet untimely, suspicious, and gruesome deaths. As the story went, Nick had accepted a multi-million-dollar bribe from Mendoza and escaped into Mexico, living out his days in a beach paradise, out of reach of U.S. law enforcement.

I'd been assigned to reopen the Mendoza case when fresh evidence came to light. The IRS learned that Mendoza had been laundering his money through a local accountant named Andrew Sheffield, who'd been found butchered, his body parts strewn about the state, one foot surfacing in a garbage bin behind the police headquarters in El Paso. *Eek!*

Nick managed to contact me discreetly and implored me to help him. He told me his cover had been blown when he'd been working the case, and the only way he'd been able to save his own life was to pretend to be for sale. He'd been in forced exile ever since, and desperately wanted to come home and clear his name.

I'd agreed—foolishly perhaps—to go to Cancún to meet him. When he'd emerged from the surf wearing only a tiger-striped Speedo, it took everything in me not to shout *Dios mío!* Once he'd convinced me of his innocence, I'd smuggled him back across the border, a border patrol K-9 nearly making me wet myself when he alerted on the truck I was driving. Fortunately, the dog had been more interested in the leftover beef jerky tucked under the seat than the man hidden in the locked toolbox in the truck's bed.

Together, Nick and I risked our lives to nab the murderous crook and the rest, as they say, is history. Of course, being the upstanding guy he was, Nick turned the money Mendoza had paid him over to Uncle Sam. And now, here we were. Totally in love, both with each other and with the sweet potato fries we were eating.

Nick cocked his head. "Cancún would be a great place for our honeymoon. Now that Marcos Mendoza is locked away and he and his henchman aren't keeping their eyes on me, I could enjoy the place as a free man. Eat all the tacos I want and maybe learn to surf or scuba dive."

It was my turn to send him a sexy grin and wink. "Be sure to pack your Speedo."

He groaned. "Forget it. I only wore that skimpy thing back then so you'd know I didn't have a gun or knife in my pocket. I had to make you trust me."

I tossed him a scowl. "Party pooper."

"What kind of dress are you going to get?" he asked. "One of those big ruffled monstrosities that make you look like Scarlett O'Hara?"

I shrugged. "I'm not sure."

While I didn't have a clear vision of what my perfect wedding dress might look like, I wasn't worried. I'd heard that a bride knows when the dress is right once she puts it on. I was meeting my mom and Nick's mother, Bonnie, at Neiman Marcus tomorrow night to start the search. When I'd phoned the bridal department this morning, I'd expected to have to wait weeks for an available appointment. Luckily, they'd had a cancellation. Well, lucky for me. Not so lucky for the bride who'd called things off. But better to break up now than after spending a fortune on a wedding, only to spend a second fortune on divorce lawyers.

The waitress arrived with Nick's platter of sweet potato fries. "Here you go. Enjoy."

He looked down appreciatively at the orange mound in front of him before glancing back up at the server. "Thanks." After she stepped away, he grabbed three fries at once and held them up. "We should serve these at our wedding."

Sweet potato fries weren't exactly traditional reception fare, but Nick and I rarely did what was expected of us. Besides, who didn't love the things?

One hour and approximately five pounds of sweet potato fries later, Nick pulled his pickup into the driveway at my town house. He looked up at the two-story structure. "You and I need to start thinking about where we'll live once we're married."

I hadn't given our living arrangements much thought yet. Heck, I was still giddy from the proposal! "You don't want to move in here with me?" I'd bought my two-bedroom, two-bath town house a few years ago, partly because of the tax benefits, partly because my roommate at our apartment had decided to move in with her boyfriend. My place wasn't large, but it was still spacious enough for two adults, my cats, and Nick's furry mutt Daffodil.

"Your place isn't bad," Nick said, "but I'd like to get something that's *ours*. You've already staked out all the closet and cabinet space here. I'd be lucky to squeeze in a shirt or two or even a single pair of boots."

He had me there. No sense arguing with him. Besides, the idea of Nick and me searching for a home of our own in which to start our life together sounded romantic and exciting. "Maybe we could get a place with a jetted bathtub," I suggested. It sure would be nice to relax in a whirl-pool after those especially hard days at work.

"Sounds good," he agreed. "And we'll need a bunch of bedrooms and a big yard for the kids."

At the word "kids," my uterus sat up and took notice. "How many children are you thinking?"

Nick raised a nonchalant shoulder. "A half dozen ought to do us."

"Six kids?!?" My uterus squirmed inside me as if seeking escape. Not that I didn't like kids. I adored my nieces and nephews. I was just realistic enough to know that, as cute as children could be, they were a lot of work, and it cost an arm and a leg to raise them these days. "I'll give you one," I told Nick. "Two, tops."

A grin tugged at his lips. "All right. So long as they're both boys and I can take them fishing every weekend and name them after Waylon Jennings and Hank Williams Jr."

"What if they're girls?"

"In that case it'll be Reba and Dolly. And I'll still take them fishing every weekend." Nick slid out of the truck, circled around to open my door, and walked me to the front porch. He left me with a deep, warm kiss, calling back over his shoulder as he returned to his truck. "See you at the office in the mornin'."

chapter two

Coyote Ugly

I woke with my sweet creamy cat, Anne, curled up quietly next to me and my furry Maine coon, Henry, repeatedly poking me in the face with his paw. *Poke-poke.* No doubt he'd bring out his claws if I didn't serve his breakfast in the next minute or two. "All right, Henry. You win."

As I sat up, the demanding cat jumped off the bed, casting a glance back to make sure his servant—*me*—was coming. Scooping Anne up in my arms, I traipsed downstairs after him and fed the two their breakfast. *"Bon appétit,"* I said as I set Henry's bowl down in front of him. The ungrateful little twerp responded only with a swish of his tail, telling me I was free to go as my services were no longer needed.

Now that the cats were taken care of, I set about fixing myself a cup of coffee. Fighting white-collar crime takes brains, guts, and quite a bit of caffeine. Maybe Nick and I should register for one of those fancy espresso machines at Neiman Marcus. Of course, Nick would probably prefer to register for tackle at Bass Pro Shops, maybe a his-and-hers set of rods and reels. Despite having worked summers during high school at Big Bob's Bait Bucket, I wasn't much interested in fishing, though I did enjoy sunbathing and reading on the deck of Nick's bass boat.

As the coffeemaker began to gurgle, I scurried upstairs to shower and dress, opting for a standard navy suit today, paired with my cherry red Doc Martens. The shoes were cute and offered great traction for chasing suspects and steel toes that served as either protection for my tootsies or an improvised weapon as the situation fit. If you thought working for the IRS only involved pushing pencils, let me disavow you of that notion, right here, right now. We special agents in the criminal investigations division were financial law enforcement, white-collar crime-fighters, trained in both spreadsheets and weaponry. Heck, having been trained by my gun-nut father from an early age, I was among the best shots at the agency, a virtual sharpshooter. They didn't call me the Annie Oakley of the IRS for nothing.

Back downstairs, I prepared a travel mug of coffee, air-kissed my cats so as not to end up with fur stuck in my lipstick, and headed off to work in my red convertible BMW, a car I'd snagged for a song at a government auction.

As I stepped off the elevator at the office, I spotted my boss standing at her secretary's desk, speaking with a fortyish Latino man sporting some type of olive-green uniform, a tool belt with multiple weapons, and a serious expression. The uniform looked familiar, though I couldn't quite place it. *What is he? Army?* The man's bald brown head reflected the fluorescent lights shining down from the ceiling. Drawing near, I noted that the patch on his shoulder featured the outline of the continental United States and the words "U.S. Border Patrol." Aha. *Mystery solved.*

"Tara!" barked my boss, Luella Lobozinski, aka Lu or the Lobo. She waved me over. "Come join us in my office."

Like Nick, Lu was someone I couldn't say no to, though

for entirely different reasons. She controlled my annual raises and determined which of us agents would get the plum assignments. It was best to stay on her good side. Besides, I respected the old broad. She'd been one of the early feminists, debunking federal agent stereotypes and blazing a trail in her go-go boots. We female agents that came along later had a much easier time of it thanks to the efforts of women like Lu.

I followed her towering strawberry-blond beehive through her door, the smell of her industrial-strength extra-hold hairspray wafting after her like a mild form of tear gas. The man stepped in after me and the two of us took seats in Lu's wing chairs.

"Agent Castaneda," Lu said, gesturing my way, "that's Special Agent Tara Holloway, one of my best investigators."

"*The* best," I joked, giving him both a smile and my hand to shake.

He took my hand and returned the smile. "I have no doubts."

"Tara," Lu said, turning her waggling fingers to the man seated next to me, "this is Agent Robert Castaneda with Border Patrol."

"The BORSTAR Unit, to be exact," he added, though his attempt at clarification only further confused me.

"Forgive my ignorance," I said. "But what is BOR-STAR?"

"Border Patrol Search, Trauma, and Rescue," he replied.

That cleared things up. Though if I'd been in charge of choosing an acronym for the unit, I'd have chosen BOPARAMA. It sounded more fun, like a party.

"Our unit's been around since the late nineties," he said. "Our mission is to prevent injuries to migrants and agents.

We're all trained in general search and rescue, field medicine, that kind of thing. But we've each got our specialties, too. Some do swift water rescues or advanced diving. Some are trained in technical rope rescues. Some have more advanced paramedic training."

While many assumed everyone working for the federal government was a boring bureaucrat, Uncle Sam's payroll included a surprising number of super-staff doing wild and crazy things most Americans only dreamed about.

"What about you?" I asked Castaneda. "What's your superpower?"

"I fly helicopters," he replied. "Black Hawks. I'm also trained in helicopter rope suspension."

He went on to explain that the term meant he was trained to descend quickly from aircraft, a technique he called fast-roping, and in insertions and extractions, which meant quickly putting people into or taking them out of dangerous situations. *Wow.* There was a whole lot more to patrolling the border than I'd realized.

"Jeez," I said, "before meeting you I thought *I* was cool."

He chuckled. "I'm sure you are." He shifted in his seat before continuing. "BORSTAR agents are concentrated along the coastal regions, as well as the southern and northern borders of the U.S. We see a small number of illegal crossings along the northern border, mostly through Glacier National Park in Montana, though the mountains and the grizzly bears serve as a natural deterrent. The southern border is much more problematic."

He proceeded to give me a quick—and quite disturbing— lesson in illegal immigration.

"We still have some Mexican immigrants," he said, "but in recent years we've seen many more people from the Northern Triangle area, which includes Honduras, El Salvador, and Guatemala. Between the political instability, poverty, and gang violence, those countries have become some of the most dangerous in the world."

According to the agent, up to half a million people from Central America fled their countries and hopped rides on northbound freight trains each year. While Mexican police routinely patrolled roads, bus stations, and airports, until recently they'd paid little attention to cargo trains. The trains were known colloquially as *La Bestia*, which translated as "the Beast." Unfortunately, the ride was not the wondrous journey aboard *The Polar Express* or Tom Cruise's thrilling train-top, spy-versus-spy battle in *Mission: Impossible*. Migrants would ride on top of the cars where they faced constant exposure and all manner of physical risks. A fall—*or a push*—could mean the loss of a limb, a permanent debilitating injury, or a painful death. Many people, including children, had fallen asleep atop the trains and rolled off, their lives ended in a real-life nightmare. And if the train ride wasn't awful enough, violent gangs and organized crime controlled the routes, inflicting a multitude of horrors on the migrants. Sadly, it was the poorest who suffered these fates.

Those with more means would often hire a smuggler to get them from one country to another. These migrants encountered their own type of woes. Their "travel agents" charged up to ten thousand dollars for the service. Many of the smugglers never carried through on their promises, leaving their clients without their money, their hopes, or any means of recourse.

Castaneda released a long, loud sigh. "We've had a rash of emergency rescues recently in Big Bend."

Big Bend National Park was named for the sharp curve in the Rio Grande River that formed the southern border of both the park and the western part of the state of Texas. The park, which shared 118 miles of border with Mexico,

sat in the Chihuahuan Desert and was known for its spec-
tacular mountain vistas, river-carved canyons, and beautiful night skies. Despite its natural beauty, it was among the
least visited parks due to its remote location and sweltering
summer temperatures. It was also known for wild javelinas
and both drug and human trafficking. All of this was
common knowledge among Texans. But there was lots I
didn't know about Big Bend and the migrant issues, and
Agent Castaneda was more than happy to fill me in.

"Before 9/11," he said, "Mexicans routinely crossed into
the U.S. to buy milk and gas and sell their wares. Americans went south for *cerveza* and fresh tortillas."

He went on to tell me that Mexicans had often provided
transportation to tourists via boat or burro. Thanks to the
terrorism threat, these cultural and financial exchanges
had all but ceased. Many newly unemployed burros were
let loose and used their free time to copulate and popu-
late, resulting in a virtual explosion of feral donkeys in the
region. Moreover, the fences erected to halt human traffic
also impeded wildlife. Habitats became fragmented, and
any species that slithered, crawled, or walked could not
cross. The harmful effects on populations of bobcats, the
already endangered ocelot, and other species were serious.

Though Agent Castaneda had given me quite a bit of
information, he still hadn't said what any of this had to do
with the Internal Revenue Service.

"What brings you to our office?" I asked.

"This." He reached into an official-looking messenger-
type bag and pulled out a manila envelope, holding it out
to me.

I took the envelope from him, noting the name "Juan
Alonso Alvarez" scrawled across the top of it. Inside I
found multiple copies of a certified birth certificate for a
man who'd been born in 1987 in Sabinal, Texas, a small

town in the southern part of the state, approximately sixty miles west of San Antonio. There were also multiple copies of a social security card in the same name, as well as an Uvalde County voter registration card. In other words, though there was no photo ID, there was sufficient documentation to enable someone to fulfill the requirements of the I-9 Employment Eligibility Verification Form.

I looked up at Castaneda. "Where'd you get this documentation?"

"Same place I got *this* documentation," he said, pulling several more envelopes from his bag and spreading them across Lu's desk in front of me. The names on these envelopes read "Julio Luis Guzmán," "Francisco Arturo Soto," and "Camila Teresa Contreras," among several others. "They contain the same thing. Multiple copies of birth certificates, social security cards, and voter registration cards, all in the name marked on the envelope. A border patrol agent found them early yesterday afternoon, at the Port of Entry in Presidio. They were in the possession of a man named Salvador Hidalgo, a suspected coyote."

I'd heard the term *coyote* before and knew it referred to those who trafficked people illegally across the border in return for money. While some equated the system to an underground railroad for migrants, Castaneda explained that many coyotes were nothing like Harriet Tubman, who escorted her charges to safer, more welcoming territories. Rather, coyotes treated human lives as nothing more than a commodity.

Castaneda pulled another document from his bag. This one was a single page containing Salvador Hidalgo's mug shot and identifying information. The guy had wiry black hair and dark, cavernous eyes. He wore a smug grin that sent a clear message. *Fuck you and the free-range donkey you rode in on.* A pretty bold message for an *hombre* who stood only five feet five inches tall, weighed a mere 135 pounds, and had the alias Sally. Then again, I was only five feet two and could pack quite a wallop when necessary.

"Hidalgo has dual citizenship," Castaneda said. "He was born in the U.S. and has a home in Dallas now, but he lived in Mexico for several years during his childhood and teen years and became a naturalized citizen there. He routinely crosses the border by car in Presidio or on foot at the Boquillas Crossing Port of Entry, in the southeastern part of Big Bend."

He went on to tell me the latter port was established just a few years ago to reinstitute and encourage cross-border commerce between Mexicans and park visitors, and was named for the town of Boquillas del Carmen, which sat on the banks of the Rio Grande. Before this entry point was opened, the closest port was the one in Presidio, a hundred miles to the northwest. Not exactly convenient.

With no roads or large bridges at the Boquillas site, the crossing handled foot traffic only, no vehicles, and was open only during daylight hours. The crossing was an unmanned station equipped with twenty-four-hour surveillance cameras monitored by staff at the Border Patrol Station in Alpine, Texas. Though it was the first unmanned station along the southern border of the U.S., unmanned stations had been in operation for years along the northern border with Canada.

All of this was news to me. "If there's nobody working the crossing," I asked, "how are people processed?"

"By computer," Castaneda said. He explained that computerized kiosks were used by visitors to present passports or other acceptable forms of identification required by the Western Hemisphere Travel Initiative, such as Trusted Traveler Program cards or military ID cards for those traveling on official business. The travel documents were sent via cyberspace to Border Patrol agents in El Paso. When the Boquillas Crossing was established, some expressed concerns about security risks, but these concerns were addressed by staffing a substation in Big Bend, along with National Park Service rangers. "The officials in the park's substation can respond quickly to anyone attempting to cross the border illegally or to perform physical inspections when necessary."

Sounded like a reasonable arrangement to handle crossings in such a remote area.

Castaneda's expression became somber. "Besides the emergency rescues I mentioned, there've recently been numerous deaths. Sad business. Coyotes sometimes abandon people miles from the nearest town. We found several members of an extended family who'd succumbed to dehydration. Only their toddler survived. They must have given the last of their water to the child. Fortunately, I spotted him from the air when I saw buzzards circling and went to investigate." He shook his head. "Poor kid. He was terrified and traumatized."

My heart went out to the child. As a young girl, I'd been lost once for only a minute or two when I'd strayed away from my mother, who'd been looking at vacuum cleaners in a department store. I still remember the panic I felt when I looked around and couldn't find her. My pulse still went into overdrive just thinking about it, even though the whole ordeal had been decades ago and lasted only a short time.

"These stories are all too common," the agent said. "The most notorious was the one about the Yuma fourteen. Smugglers abandoned them in the Arizona desert, promising to return with water. The smugglers never went back. Some of the group became so desperate and sunburned they sought out help, even knowing it would mean their journey had been for naught. Fourteen of them died of heatstroke." He shook his head. "People have no idea what they're getting themselves into."

He said there'd also been numerous reports of women and girls being sexually assaulted. Even if the migrants were lucky enough to find a place to live and work in the U.S., they had to live a clandestine life under constant worry that they'd be caught and deported. Some employers lacking in ethics used these fears against them, paying less than minimum wage, threatening to turn them in if the workers made a report. "Some become modern-day slaves."

The better life these people sought often eluded them. What's more, immigration was an extremely controversial subject among Americans, and many immigrants found themselves shunned or persecuted or blamed for everything from declining wages to unemployment rates. Others, however, saw many migrants as refugees and believed humanitarian concerns should prevail, that families should be reunited. The federal government had attempted to institute compromises through programs such as DACA (Deferred Action for Childhood Arrivals) and an expansion of DAPA (Deferred Action for Parents of Americans). However, these plans had been challenged in the Supreme Court by none other than the State of Texas. While *mi casa es su casa* might be the philosophy south of the border, it didn't extend into the U.S.

"To put it mildly," Castaneda said, "the past few years have been a real shit storm. Border Patrol is caught in the middle, not only of the government battle I just described, but in the middle of citizens, too. On one side, we've had pastors and concerned citizens establishing watering stations along some of the more heavily traveled migrant routes. On the other side, we've had the Minutemen."

The Minuteman Project was an anti-immigrant movement of unofficial, self-appointed, and heavily armed
people who performed patrols along the border. Chris
Davis, a commander of a Minuteman unit in Texas, had
been featured in a YouTube video instructing members of
the organization how to handle a confrontation with an
undocumented migrant. *"You see an illegal, you point your
gun right dead at them, right between the eyes, and say,
'Get back across the border, or you will be shot.'"* He also
instructed members that if law enforcement gave them any
flak, they should respond by saying the land belonged to
them and was their birthright. Davis should have paid more
attention in his high school history class. The U.S. Con-
stitution said we were entitled to life, liberty, and the pursuit of happiness, but there was nothing in the document
guaranteeing anyone land.

Given that the Minuteman group attracted extremists,
who are prone to disagreement and irrational behavior, the
movement imploded, with many of its members ending up
dead or imprisoned for their actions. Shawna Forde, one
of the Arizona activists, turned to crime to fund the operations and was convicted of murdering a man and his
nine-year-old daughter after a botched armed robbery of
the victims' home. Another problematic member was J. T.
Ready, a neo-Nazi Marine veteran who'd been court-
martialed twice and discharged from the military for bad
conduct. Ready murdered his girlfriend and three of her
family members at his home in Gilbert, Arizona, before
committing suicide.

"At the time of Ready's death," Castaneda said, "an FBI
domestic terrorism investigation had been looking into his
connection to a number of dead migrants whose bodies
had been found in the Arizona desert."

I swallowed the lump of emotion that had formed in

my throat. I'd faced a lot of ugly things during my time at the IRS. Con artists. Killers. The mob. I'd seen elderly people lose their retirement savings in investment scams and families lose their homes in mortgage schemes. But it never seemed to get easier and this situation had my insides squirming. "My, my," I said in reply, attempting to mask my horror with humor. "You're just a ray of sunshine, aren't you?"

Castaneda offered a mirthless chuckle. "I hate to tell you, Agent Holloway, but I'm just getting started."

chapter three

*H*eld for Ransom

Agent Castaneda pulled another manila envelope from his bag and handed it to me, his expression pensive and pained.

My stomach shrank into a hard ball as I opened the clasp and pulled out the contents. Inside were photographs of three young women who bore a strong resemblance to each other. All had dark hair, brown skin, dainty noses, and warm, innocent smiles. The oldest appeared to be in her early twenties, the middle around eighteen, and the youngest fifteen or so. I looked from the photos to Castaneda, my eyes asking the questions my mouth was too afraid to ask. *Who are these young women and what's happened to them?*

"Those girls are sisters," he said. "Nina, Larissa, and Yessenia. Yessenia is the oldest. They're from San Pedro Sula, one of the most violent cities in Honduras. The leader of one of the gangs had set his sights on Yessenia and wouldn't take no for an answer. Other gang members had begun to harass the younger sisters. Their aunt lives here in Dallas with her husband. They came here from Honduras two years ago and are undocumented. They'd hired a coyote to get themselves into the country, and they hired the same man to bring their nieces here. They thought they were getting their nieces out of danger."

His intonation told me the danger wasn't over yet and my stomach clenched even tighter. "But something happened, didn't it?"

"Yes." He exhaled a sharp breath. "The girls left Honduras three weeks ago. They contacted their aunt every two or three days along the way until last night. That's when Yessenia called in tears and told her aunt they'd been kidnapped by two armed men."

Lu and I gasped in unison. "Kidnapped?" Lu squeaked out.

Castaneda's jaw flexed as he nodded. "I'd like to tell you this is an isolated event, but I'd be lying. We've seen multiple cases where migrants are kidnapped for ransom. In some cases, the kidnapping is staged by the smugglers themselves in an attempt to extort money from the victims' families in the United States. I suspect that's what's happened here, that Hidalgo and his men are behind this kidnapping. In these kidnappings, the families are in extremely vulnerable positions because they feel they can't go to the authorities for help. These girls were lucky their aunt is willing to risk deportation to try to help them."

Though I understood the point he was making, it was hard to see anyone in this situation as *lucky*.

Castaneda filled us in on the rest of the events. "After Yessenia told her aunt they'd been taken, a man got on the phone and told the aunt she had one week to pay the kidnappers five thousand dollars or they'd never see the girls again. She was told she would receive a phone call next Monday with instructions, that she'd be given the name of the bank and the account number for making the deposit. She also was told if she contacted authorities, the girls would be killed. They said they'd have someone watching her and her husband to make sure they didn't speak to law enforcement."

How could the smugglers do such a thing? I glanced down at the photos again. These young women should be shopping for shoes at the mall, taking in a movie, giggling about boys. Not being held somewhere for ransom, living in terror, wondering if their days were numbered. "This is all so . . ." I couldn't decide which word to use. *Horrifying? Heartbreaking? Disturbing? Unconscionable?* None seemed adequate.

He didn't wait for me to come up with a word, but dipped his head in acknowledgement of my unnamed emotion.

"So Hidalgo was the aunt's coyote?" I asked. "And the one who was smuggling the girls?"

"It wasn't Hidalgo himself," Castaneda said. "The aunt said the man she hired went only by the name Zaragoza. But she said he regularly checked in with another man via cell phones and radios, and that the other man seemed to be the one in charge. We believe Hidalgo's got several men working under him, and that Zaragoza is likely part of Hidalgo's network. Unfortunately, she never heard Zaragoza identify the man by name, and we can't seem to get enough information to make a direct link between this Zaragoza and Hidalgo."

I took it the two weren't Facebook friends, hadn't posted photos of themselves taking in the scenery of Big Bend together. "How'd their aunt get in touch with you?" I asked.

"The aunt used her phone to get onto the Border Patrol Web site and sent an e-mail. She figured that would be the most private way to contact us. She and her husband don't have the money to pay the ransom. They spent every last cent when they made arrangements with the coyote to transport their nieces. To make things worse, they have no way of getting in touch with the kidnappers to see if they can negotiate more time."

"They weren't given a phone number?"

"No, and no one is answering the cell phone the girls had with them, either."

"Any idea where the girls might be?"

"The last time the girls phoned their aunt before the ransom demand, Yessenia said they were in Mexico, but not far from the U.S. border. We're not sure whether they made it across before they were kidnapped. Mexican authorities attempted to ping the phone but had no luck. We've tried the towers along the border here, too, but got nothing. The battery could simply be dead or the phone may have been intentionally disabled or discarded."

Lu cocked her head, her beehive tilting to the right at approximately a two o'clock position. "Is Hidalgo still in custody?"

"Yes," Castaneda said. "We're holding him on suspicion of human trafficking. The envelopes with the birth certificates and social security cards were hidden inside the spare tire in the trunk of the car he was driving. The car was a rental he'd picked up in Mexico. He claimed he had no idea the documents were in the car and that they don't belong to him."

Yeah, right. And all those potheads who claimed to be holding for a friend were telling the truth, too. "Did you ask him about the girls?"

"Not yet," he said. "We didn't want to tip him off that the aunt had reported the kidnapping to law enforcement. We're afraid he'd make them disappear."

The strategy made sense. "So long as he and the men in his network think they might receive the ransom, they'll keep the girls alive."

"That's what we assume," Castaneda concurred.

I glanced down at the photos still clutched in my hand, taking another look at the innocent faces of Nina, Larissa, and Yessenia. *If he hurts any of you,* I vowed silently to their pictures, *I'll make him pay.* I looked back up at the agent. "Did he have any weapons on him when he came across the border?"

"No, and he has an aggressive attorney working on his release. Unless we can convince the judge we have solid evidence against Hidalgo and that he's a danger to others, we'll be ordered to let him go."

The general rule of thumb for holding a suspect without charges was seventy-two hours, and the clock had already begun to count down the instant Hidalgo was arrested yesterday. We had a mere two days to come up with good evidence against the guy or he'd be turned loose. In other words, we'd better bust our asses.

"Why was he in a Mexican rental car?" I asked.

"He'd flown from Dallas to Chihuahua, Mexico, purportedly to visit relatives. He says he decided to drive to Big Bend to do some stargazing. He had a book on astronomy with him and a cheap telescope, but the story seemed flimsy. He hadn't made reservations at a hotel or lodge in the area and didn't seem to have a concrete plan. Our guess is that he was planning on meeting up with someone in his trafficking network to supply the papers. Or maybe he'd dropped some of the migrants just south of the border, gave them instructions on where to cross, and told them he'd meet them on the other side. We're not entirely sure." He exhaled sharply and sat back in his chair. "That's the problem with this guy. He's back and forth across the border dozens of times each year, and we've encountered him before not far from where we've picked up undocumented immigrants. We suspect he's to blame for some of the deaths, including that extended family I mentioned, but we've never been able to prove any clear link to human trafficking."

"That's where we come in," I supplied for him. "You want us to see if we can come up with evidence to link the guy to smuggling activity." It wouldn't be the first time another agency had come to the IRS for help.

"Exactly. The last thing I want to do is put Salvador Hidalgo back out on the streets where he can lure desperate, unsuspecting people to risk their lives while he pockets their hard-earned cash."

"I can check the W-2 filings for people working under the names and social security numbers from the documentation you found in Hidalgo's car. With any luck, one or more of them will have settled in the north Texas area."

Castaneda somehow managed to look both encouraged and skeptical at the same time. "I'm hoping that will be the case, though I'm not holding my breath that they'll cooperate. The undocumented migrants might be too afraid to talk, or they might simply disappear once law enforcement comes sniffing around. I see it all the time. But this plan is our only chance for nailing the guy. This is the third time we've arrested him. Both times before, we had to release him for lack of evidence."

That explained the smug expression on Hidalgo's face in his mug shot. But as they say, the third time's the charm. I wasn't about to let him leave another person to die in the desert. We'd get him this time, come hell or high water.

Lu turned toward her open doorway and called for her secretary. "Viola? Could you come make us some copies?"

Viola appeared in the doorway, her gray curls bouncing as she dipped her head. "Whatever you need, boss."

Lu gestured for Agent Castaneda to give Viola all of the

envelopes he'd brought with him. "Make a copy of each set of documentation for Tara, please."

"You got it." Viola took the stack of envelopes from the man and carried them out the door.

We discussed our strategy further while Viola was preparing the copies. I hadn't handled a human trafficking case before, but Lu had seen a few come through the office over the years and knew what to look for.

"Once Tara gets her hands on Hidalgo's bank records," my boss told Castaneda, "the activity will likely tell us whether he's engaged in human trafficking. People who do that kind of thing make regular cash deposits in large amounts. They'll also deposit checks where the payee line was clearly completed by someone other than the person who signed the check. Often there will be cash deposits made at banks or ATMs by the families of the person who's being trafficked. The ones who've made it to the U.S. will pay to have the coyote transport other family members here, like the situation with the three missing girls. And if Hidalgo's illegally trafficking humans, it's a safe bet he's not reporting the income. We'd be able to tack on some tax evasion charges."

"Great," Castaneda said. "The more charges we can throw at the guy and the longer we can keep him locked up, the better."

chapter four

$\mathcal{U}$p, Up, and Away

After Viola brought me copies of the relevant documentation, I walked Agent Castaneda to the elevators. "What's it like to ride in a helicopter?" I asked as we waited for the car to arrive.

"I could tell you," he said, arching a brow. "But I'm guessing you might be the type of woman who'd like to find out for herself."

He'd pegged me. I wasn't a mere idle observer of life. I was an active participant, grabbing life by the horns and hanging on for a wild ride, whooping all the while. I gave him a smile. "What gave me away?"

"The gun at your waist and your steel-toed shoes."

"Any chance one of my coworkers could come along?" A particularly sexy one with dark hair and amber eyes?

"So long as he can come now," Castaneda said. "I've got to get back to Big Bend by the end of the day. My wife promised to make my favorite enchiladas for dinner."

I wondered what Nina, Larissa, and Yessenia would be fed for dinner. *Ugh.* Pushing that awful thought from my mind, I pulled my cell phone from my pocket and dialed

Nick. When he answered, I said, "You've got ten seconds to meet me at the elevator if you want to ride in a Black Hawk helicopter."

The only response was a *click* as he ended the call. A moment later, he careened around the corner of the hall, his boots sliding across the industrial carpet.

With a *ding,* the elevator car arrived and Agent Castaneda and I stepped in, Nick rushing to jump in just as the doors began to close.

"Where's your helicopter?" I asked Castaneda.

"At the city heliport at the convention center on South Lamar."

In other words, within easy walking distance. That meant there was no need to get a car to drive over. I jabbed the *L* button to take us down to the lobby and turned my attention back to the men. "Nick," I said, holding out a hand to indicate Castaneda, "this is Agent Robert Castaneda with the Border Patrol search and rescue." I swung my hand the other way. "Agent Castaneda, this is Senior Special Agent Nick Pratt."

The two exchanged handshakes as the car descended.

Nick eyed the border patrol agent. "Search and rescue, huh? I'm guessing that means you work in a remote area?"

"Big Bend," Castaneda replied.

"My parents took me out to the park once as a kid," Nick said. "Beautiful place, though I have to admit I was disappointed not to see a mountain lion. Saw a rattler or two and some roadrunners, though."

I fought the urge to say *meep-meep.*

"I've spotted a cougar or two from the air," Castaneda said, "but they tend to avoid humans when possible."

A smart decision on the cat's part. Encounters with humans often weren't a good thing for wildlife.

We stepped out into the lobby and exited the building. Castaneda stopped and glanced around, as if trying to get his bearings.

"This way," I said, gesturing to the left.

The half-mile walk took us only ten minutes, during which the agent regaled me and Nick with stories of harrowing rescues he'd performed.

"The worst was during a flash flood," he said. "Several people were trapped in a canyon, clinging to the walls, trying to fight the current. I went down on my rope but the wind was so strong it kept slamming me into the canyon wall. When it was all over I was one big bruise, black and blue from head to toe. It was a wonder none of my bones was broken."

My exploits had caused me injuries, too, ranging from minor burns and a broken tooth to a major concussion. Besides having one target plant an explosive under my car and another try to trap me in a burning building, I'd been shot at, hit in the head with a baseball bat, plunged into a vat of melted chocolate, and stabbed by an armed rooster at a cock fight. No matter where I went, or how hard I tried to avoid it, trouble just seemed to find me. But maybe this case would be different. Maybe this one would be uneventful.

Heh, I mentally scoffed. Even I didn't believe myself.

The men being, well, *men,* compared the size and power of their equipment on the way over.

"How fast can your helicopter fly?" Nick asked.

"Top speed is a hundred and fifty-nine knots," Castaneda said. "That's one-hundred and eighty-three miles an hour. Cruising speed's around a hundred and fifty-three knots or a hundred and seventy-three miles per hour."

"I've got me a bass boat," Nick said. "Three hundred horses in the engine."

"That'll get the job done."

"Sure will."

I was tempted to toss out some exciting facts about my 2200-watt hair dryer and four-slot toaster, but I doubted they'd be impressed.

Minutes later, we stepped up to the Black Hawk helicopter, which despite its name, was actually gray in color. The aircraft was much larger than I'd expected, with a huge propeller on top of the main body and another at the end. With its wide windshield wrapping around the sides, it looked like an enormous metal dragonfly.

As we climbed in, I motioned for Nick to take the front seat.

Excitement gleamed in his eyes. "Really? You sure?"

"I'm sure," I said. "I figure it might make up for not sharing my sweet potato fries last night."

"We'll call it even."

Nick took his seat up front, while I strapped myself into a canvas fold-down seat behind them. All around me was equipment used in the search and rescue missions. Ropes. Harnesses. Cables. All manner of hooks and straps. Even a couple of those basket-type things used to raise injured people up into the chopper.

Once I was secured, I glanced into the cockpit. There seemed to be no end of switches and buttons and dials on the control panel, which took up not only the dash but also the center console and part of the ceiling. How anyone could make sense of it all was beyond me.

Agent Castaneda sat straddling the enormous control stick. He donned a pair of padded headphones and handed me and Nick each a pair for ourselves.

"Ready?" he called though his microphone.

"Ready!" Nick and I called back.

Castaneda flipped a series of switches, and the long

blades began to move overhead, slowly at first but rapidly speeding up until they morphed into a mere blur through the upper part of the window. When we lifted off, my stomach forgot to come with the rest of me, seemingly dropping down into my lower abdomen to keep my reproductive organs company. I breathed through my mouth, hoping that would prevent me from getting motion sickness. I wasn't usually prone to it, but the aircraft was vibrating much more than an airplane and had an entirely different feel to it. I felt like a can of paint in one of those automated mixing machines at the hardware store.

A moment later, the upward movement turned into forward movement, and we swooped up and over the Dallas skyline. In my excitement, any discomfort I'd been feeling was totally forgotten. Seeing the city from this angle gave me an entirely different perspective. The people walking around the city below looked like ants in an ant farm. I'd never realized there were so many rooftop gardens, and the tall construction cranes, which normally loomed far overhead, were at eye level now. Oddly, though we were only at a higher elevation and hadn't grown, of course, I got the sense of being a giant. Nick glanced back my way, the broad grin on his face telling me he was having a heck of a time, too.

Castaneda made three wide circles around the city. We could see the smaller skyline of Fort Worth to the west, as well as the roller coasters at Six Flags and the enormous Dallas Cowboys stadium in the nearby city of Arlington. To the south loomed the Cotton Bowl and the Ferris wheel in Fair Park. To the east lay White Rock Lake. Being able to take all of this in at once was amazing, and made the city seem much smaller.

On our last go-round, Castaneda drew close to Reunion Tower, which resembled a handheld microphone, tall and narrow on the bottom with a big glittering ball on top. Nick and I had spent New Year's Eve there, though he'd been exhausted and jet-lagged from traveling internationally on two big cases. Such were the lives and sacrifices of government agents.

Castaneda came in for the landing and expertly set us back down. Our ride over now, my stomach ascended to its appropriate place behind my belly button.

Nick and I climbed out of the helicopter and thanked Castaneda.

"That was incredible!" Nick said.

"Glad you enjoyed it," the agent said. He turned my way, reaching into his breast pocket and pulling out a business card, which he held out to me. "Let me know what you can find out. The sooner the better."

I ducked my head in acknowledgement as I took the card from him. "I'll get right on it."

chapter five

Form over Substance

Nick and I returned to the IRS office, parting ways in the hall as he turned left into his office and I turned right into mine.

Though my desk sported a tall, off-kilter stack of pending files roughly the size of the Leaning Tower of Pisa, I ignored them and honored my word to Agent Castaneda, making his case a priority. After all, the clock was ticking. Unless I could find some hard evidence to implicate Salvador Hidalgo within forty-eight hours, the killer and kidnapper would be released.

A search of tax filings showed Hidalgo had filed no returns. Although State Bank of Dallas had reported some interest income in his name, it was not enough to give rise to a filing requirement. Did he have unreported income from his trafficking activities? I suspected he did. Now, I just had to prove it.

I turned my attention to the names on the social security cards, birth certificates, and voter registration cards Agent Castaneda had given me, the ones that had been found hidden in the rental car. I searched the W-2 wage filings first. *Whoa.* The name and social security number for Julio Luis Guzmán turned up on no less than seventeen W-2s for the preceding year. According to the forms, Julio allegedly lived in as many different places, ranging from as far west as Santa Monica, California, to Jacksonville, Florida, in the east. Twelve W-2s appeared in the name of Francisco Arturo Soto, while nine included the name and social security number for Camila Teresa Contreras. I searched the other names with similar results.

Due to the fact that the tax returns filed by the real Julio, Franciso, Camila, and others did not include all of the wages reported by the employers on the W-2 forms, the taxpayers had received notices of the discrepancies and either a bill for the revised amount owed or a refund when the amount of income tax withheld from the numerous payments exceeded the revised amount due. In each instance, the taxpayer had filed a Form 14039, Identity Theft Affidavit, informing the IRS that incorrect information had been reported under his or her name and tax ID number.

"What a mess," I muttered at my computer screen.

Knowing I had neither the time nor authorized budget to travel far from the Dallas–Fort Worth Metroplex, I culled through the W-2s for addresses in the north Texas area. If I could track down some of the immigrants nearby, maybe I could get Agent Castaneda the information he needed to nail the coyote Salvador Hidalgo once and for all.

One of the Julio Guzmáns—whom I dubbed Julio Número Uno—lived in Euless, one of what were often called the "mid-cities" that sat between the larger cities of Dallas and Fort Worth. Per his W-2, he worked at a Mexican restaurant called El Loro Loco. I knew the word *loco* meant "crazy," but *loro* was a new one for me. After running it through a Spanish to English translation tool I found online, I learned that *loro* meant "parrot." Another of the Julio Guzmáns—Julio Número Dos—lived in South Dallas, his W-2 issued by Saint Lucia Catholic School. A third Julio Guzmán—Número Tres—lived in Garland, which sat to the northeast of Dallas. His W-2 had been issued by Ellington Nurseries Inc.

Holy guacamole.

Ellington Nurseries was owned by Brett Ellington, a successful landscape architect to whom I'd once given my heart, along with occasional other body parts. He was the guy I'd mentioned earlier, the twenty-first-century Prince Charming. I'd once thought Brett could be *the one,* but then Nick came along . . .

Though our breakup had been mutual and amicable, I wasn't particularly interested in seeing Brett again. The one time we'd run into each other since had been awkward. Nick had been working an undercover narcotics case with Christina Marquez, my good friend from the Drug Enforcement Administration. Feeling lonely, I'd decided to treat myself to a nice dinner at one of my favorite restaurants. Unfortunately, Brett had been there with his new girlfriend, Fiona. He'd come over to say hello when Fiona left their table, and explained that the two had gotten engaged and were expecting a baby. *He certainly hadn't wasted any time, had he?* The fact that he'd moved on so quickly made me wonder whether what we'd shared had truly been as meaningful and special as I'd thought. While I wished both Brett and Fiona all the best, seeing someone you used to date is always awkward. You can't help but picture them naked and remember all of the secrets they'd told you, and you knew they were having the same thoughts about you. It made you feel exposed.

But just because one of the Julios worked for Brett didn't

mean I had to pursue that avenue, right? If the other Julios could give me the information needed to help Castaneda nail Hidalgo and locate the missing girls, there'd be no need for me to venture out to Ellington Nurseries. I mentally crossed my fingers that would be the case.

I continued on with my searches. One of the women named Camila popped up on a household employer tax form filed by Trent and Kendall Oswalt. Judging from the hoity-toity address in the Bent Tree neighborhood as well as the seven-figure income reported on the couple's tax return, I surmised "Camila" worked as either a live-in housekeeper or a nanny for the wealthy family.

Unfortunately, the three tax reports were the only ones with addresses within reasonable driving distance of the office, other than several others issued by Ellington Nurseries. In addition to Julio Guzmán, Brett also employed workers going by the assumed identities of a Pablo Perez, a Miguel Gallegos, and a Diego Robles. Digging a little deeper, I could see that all four men who worked for Brett had started at the same time, their first withholding paid in November two years earlier. If I had to hazard a guess, the men had entered the United States together, or had known each other back wherever they'd come from. Maybe both. Perhaps they were even related, brothers or cousins, maybe.

I'd certainly do whatever it took to help those poor girls, but I'd visit Brett's business only as a last resort, if the other leads didn't pan out. It was a logical plan. After all, Brett's nursery was farther from the office than the other employers. But I had to admit that part of the reason for my hesitation was that seeing him might be a little awkward and uncomfortable. What's more, Nick was sure to get upset. Nick had many good qualities. He was generous, down-to-earth, and hardworking. But he tended toward excessive possessiveness and jealousy where I was concerned. Absolutely unnecessary, because my heart fully belonged to him, but his knowing that Brett and I had shared an intimate relationship didn't help matters. When Nick thought of Brett, he, too, probably pictured Brett and me rolling around naked. Besides, the four men who worked for Brett might stick together and refuse to speak to me. Strength in numbers. A lone undocumented migrant would probably feel more defenseless and be more likely to give in to my requests for information.

Knowing Agent Castaneda was still in the air on his flight back to Big Bend, I shot him a quick e-mail to update him on what I'd found. *Several people working under the subject names and social security numbers are in the Dallas area. Off to speak with them.*

I stood and was sliding the documentation into my briefcase when the Lobo trotted into my office.

"Got another one for ya." She held the file out to me. "One of the victims has raised a big stink, got his congressman involved. Make it a priority."

"You tell me to make all my cases a priority," I replied, taking the file from her. "How am I supposed to do that? There are only so many hours in a day."

She narrowed her eyes, her false eyelashes coming together to form a thick line of fringe. "Are you talking back to your boss?"

"No," I said. "I'm asking a real question." I gestured to the stack of files on my desk. "Every one of those files is urgent, too. I feel like I'm in over my head." How the heck was I supposed to find time and energy to plan a wedding with all of this work to do?

Lu scowled for a moment before her face softened. "Sorry, Tara. I'd love to offer you a solution, but all I can offer right now is encouragement." She raised her arms as if shaking pom-poms, the flabby flesh underneath her arms jiggling with the movement. "Go, Tara! Go!"

"No cartwheel?" I teased.

"Cartwheel?" She lowered her arms. "You trying to kill me?"

I sat down to take a quick look at the file. "I take it there's still been no word on hiring more agents?" Lu had a perpetual request in with those up the chain to expand the department. Unfortunately, the powers that be had repeatedly said there wasn't room in the budget for more agents. They treated us like taffy, stretching us so far we threatened to snap.

"No," she said. "No new agents. But on a bright note, they just approved Eddie and Nick serving as co-directors of Criminal Investigations."

I bolted upright in my seat. "That's fantastic!"

Lu planned to retire soon, and had first offered her position to Eddie Bardin, my training partner and the most senior agent in the office. When Eddie hadn't jumped on the opportunity, she'd offered the job to the second highest-ranking agent, which was Nick. Like Eddie, Nick hadn't been entirely convinced he wanted the job. While it came with higher pay and a much nicer office, it also came with a lot of headaches and red tape and tied the person in the position to their desk. Besides, despite the heavy workloads and personal risks that came with working as a special agent, the job got us out of the office and the work was interesting and challenging. For all the jokes people make about accountants and their dull work, financial sleuthing was actually a lot of fun, exciting, and even dangerous on occasion. Neither Eddie nor Nick was ready to turn his back entirely on fieldwork.

I stood from my desk. "Have you told Nick yet?"

The Lobo shook her head. "I peeked in his office on my

way in here, but he was on his phone. You're the first to know."

"This is big news. We should round everyone up to tell them all at once."

I jumped on my phone and buzzed each agent in the office. Fortunately, all of them were in. "Come to my office," I told them. "Lu's got some important news to share."

A glance across the hall told me Nick was now off his phone. "Nick!" I waved him over. "Lu's got something to tell us."

He stood and moseyed over, leading a virtual parade of special agents as the others stepped in after him. Josh Schmidt, the geeky office tech guru, with his boyish blond curls, baby blue eyes, and standard blue button-down. Hana Kim, a Korean-American agent with straight black hair, a direct demeanor, and an athletic build that made her one of the best players on the IRS softball team. William Dorsey, a relatively new addition to the criminal investigation team, having worked his way up through the collections department. Senior Special Agent Eddie Bardin, who, like Will, was dark skinned and determined but, like me, was at the smart-ass end of the personality spectrum. With so many people in my office, we were surely violating the fire code. Everyone looked expectantly at Lu.

"Agents," Lu said, taking Eddie and Nick by the wrists and raising their arms as if they were prizefighters who'd just won a bout. "Let's hear a big round of applause for the new co-directors of Dallas Criminal Investigations!"

The room erupted in excitement and applause, as well as a loud whistle, the latter coming from me. *Twee-eet!* High fives were exchanged all around. *Slap-slap-slap.*

Lu released their arms and looked from Eddie to Nick. "I suppose the two of you will have to draw straws to see who gets my office."

Nick put a hand on Eddie's shoulder. "You can have it, bro. I happen to like the view from the office I've got now." He shot me a wink. Sitting directly across the hall from him, *I* was his view.

Eddie turned to the Lobo. "When does this go into effect?"

"August first," Lu replied. "That gives me a month to get you boys up to speed."

This announcement marked the beginning of a new era and, while I was glad to see Eddie's and Nick's careers advance to the next level, I also knew things would be very different without Lu. I'd miss her barking orders, her colorful sixties-era outfits, her surprising moments of vulnerability when her facade of toughness fell and she showed just how much she cared about those who worked under her.

Melancholy tears pricked at my eyes. "We're going to miss the heck out of you, Lu."

The others murmured in agreement.

Lu's blue-lidded eyes met mine and misted up, too. "Don't get me started!" she said, her voice choked with emotion. "If I cry my eyelashes will fall off." She fanned her eyes with another file to dry them.

I stepped over and enveloped her in a big hug that broke all sorts of protocols on physical interactions and maintaining a professional distance in the office. She hugged me back, but when she released me she wiped her eyes and gave me a soft whack on the back with the file. "For now, I'm still the boss. I want all of you to chip in and help Tara. She's got two urgent cases and needs some help. Got it?"

The agents murmured their assent.

"Great," Lu said. "Get back to work, everyone!"

chapter six

Winners and Losers

Josh, Will, and Hana made their exits, but as Eddie turned to the door, Nick stopped him with a hand on the shoulder. "Got a second, Eddie? There's something I wanted to ask you."

Though Nick and I hadn't directly discussed the matter, I had a feeling I knew what was coming. Before I'd come along to the IRS, Nick and Eddie had partnered on several cases. When Nick returned from Mexico, they'd handled a couple of big ones together. As the most senior agents in the office, they'd essentially grown up here together, career-wise. And it was clear that, despite their superficial differences in dress and musical tastes, they shared a mutual respect and the admirable traits of dedication and determination. Plus, Nick knew Eddie meant a lot to me. When nobody else would step up to train the scrawny rookie, Eddie had offered to take me on. Eddie and I had been through a lot together, too. Shootings. Explosions. Various other near-death experiences. Nothing like almost dying with someone to make you appreciate having him or her in your life.

Eddie seemed to know what was coming and broke into a wide grin. "Sure, Nick. I'll be your best man."

Nick chuckled. "I was going to ask to borrow a hundred bucks," he teased, "but best man works, too."

Eddie gave Nick's shoulder a jab, a sign of manly affection. "You know you wouldn't have it any other way. Neither would I."

I chimed in now. "Me, neither. You do realize we're going with powder blue tuxedos with ruffled shirts?"

Eddie took my joke in stride. "Sounds good to me. I'll look like one of the Temptations from back in the day." He turned sideways and swayed front to back, snapping his fingers and launching into an off-key rendition of "My Girl." He continued singing as he left my office, the strains drifting down the hall behind him.

After my coworkers vacated my office, I sat back down to take a quick glance at the thick file Lu had just brought to me. A thick stack of documentation was contained therein. The top page was official correspondence from the office of Ernest Perkins, a United States senator from Texas who'd been known to use his position to further the special interests of his biggest donors. Among "Ernie's Perks" was a multi-million-dollar flood control project awarded to a cement company owned by a major contributor.

The senator's letter demanded we take quick action to assist a constituent named Thomas Hoffmeyer who'd complained that the IRS had sent him an erroneous bill for over $250,000. I rolled my eyes. Senator Perkins had voted against more funding for the IRS. If he wanted us to do our jobs quicker, he needed to fund more staff rather than spending Uncle Sam's money to line the pockets of his supporters.

Underneath the senator's letter were copies of 1099-MISC forms reporting large amounts of alleged prize winnings to more than a dozen people, five of whom lived in the Dallas area. The amounts ranged from a low of $100,000 to a high of $3 million. The payments were purportedly made by Winning Tickets Corporation, which was based in Kalamazoo, Michigan. However, when the auditor had contacted the payees, everyone said they were not aware of winning any prize. The auditor later spoke with the chief financial officer at Winning Tickets, who'd informed her that, while the company had contracts with various states to print scratch-off lottery tickets, the company itself paid no prizes. They had not issued the bogus 1099s, and had no idea who might have done so.

Hmm. What an odd situation. Had someone been asleep at the proverbial wheel and issued the payments in error? Maybe made some typos? Had a programming glitch in computer software caused these incorrect 1099s to be issued?

Given more time, the auditor could have answered these questions. But when the letter from the senator's office arrived, the head of the audit department had apparently determined the better option would be to take the heat off his department and punt the case over to Criminal Investigations. *Yep, the buck stops here.*

My first action was to call Senator Perkins's office. Of course, I didn't expect to speak directly to Perky Ernie. A rank-and-file government agent like me would warrant only an aide. "Hello," I said to the youngish male voice who answered the phone. "This is Special Agent Tara Holloway with the IRS. I just wanted to let the senator know I've been assigned the Thomas Hoffmeyer case and will be getting on it as soon as possible."

"Hoffmeyer?" the guy repeated. "Hold a moment please."

The hold music was a version of "God Bless America"

sung by a woman with a shrill trill that made my eyeballs vibrate. Fortunately, another male voice came on the line before my retinas exploded.

"Agent Holloway," said the man. "Senator Perkins here."

Wow, I'd been transferred right to the top. If that didn't put the *special* in *special agent,* I didn't know what did. "Good morning, sir."

"My man tells me you're working the Hoffmeyer complaint. I trust you'll be getting right on that."

"I certainly will," I replied. "As soon as I resolve a more pressing matter."

He scoffed. "What's more pressing than a personal request from a sitting U.S. senator?"

"Three girls have been kidnapped," I explained. "Rescuing them depends on me tracking down recent immigrants who might have knowledge about their suspected kidnapper and their whereabouts."

"Are the girls immigrants, too?" he asked.

My blood began to warm. *How about a little sympathy here? Some empathy for their plight?* "Yes. The girls are immigrants."

"*Legal* immigrants?"

My hemoglobin was simmering now. "What does that matter?" I said. "Their lives are at stake either way." *Seriously? This guy could turn his back on three young women in danger?*

When he spoke again, his words bore a haughty tone that said he considered me too stupid to live. "It matters, Agent Holloway, because illegal aliens are not my constituents. My duty and yours is to the *American* people. I expect you to fulfill that duty."

I'd never been more glad I hadn't voted for the jerk in the last election. "I'm curious, senator," I snapped, my blood on full boil now. "How much did Thomas Hoffmeyer donate to your campaign?"

"That's beside the point!" he snapped back.

"Is it?"

While the senator ranted about my insubordinate tone and disrespectful behavior, I crossed my fingers that I hadn't just gotten myself fired and ran a quick search on my computer. Campaign contributions were a matter of public record. Sure enough, Thomas Hoffmeyer had not only donated the maximum legal amount to Senator Perkins's campaign, but he had also supported a number of political action committees and super PACs with known ties to the senator.

"And furthermore—"

"Sorry," I lied. "Getting another call. I'll be in touch later. Gotta go." With that, I hung up on the man and dialed Eddie's office.

He answered with a casual "Yeah?"

"Got some time to accompany me in the field?" I figured I'd better be ready with backup in case Julio Número Uno attempted to flee when I approached him for information. Two agents would have a better chance of catching him than one.

"Sure," he said. "Give me twenty minutes to wrap something up and I'll come down."

I was gathering up the paperwork when Lu stuck her head in the door. "Senator Perkins just called. He said you hung up on him."

I bit my lip and grimaced. "Any chance you would believe it was an accident?"

"No," she said, "and it wasn't an accident when I hung up on him, either. But what's he going to do, fire me? I've already tendered my resignation."

Lu's unwavering trust and support was among the many reasons her agents adored her.

"I'm on my way out of government service," she said, pointing a finger at me. "But this agency needs you. Let *me* take any heat, okay? If you need to communicate with the senator's office, let me handle it."

I gave her a salute. "Aye-aye, captain."

While waiting for Eddie to join me, I found the phone number of Winning Tickets Corporation's chief financial officer in the file and dialed it. When she answered, I identified myself. "Hello, this is Special Agent Tara Holloway with Dallas IRS Criminal Investigations. I understand you spoke with an auditor previously about erroneous 1099s purportedly issued by Winning Tickets. The situation has been escalated to our department and my boss told me to make it a priority." *Along with the other fifteen investigations I'm working on.* "I have some follow-up questions."

"Shoot."

I liked this woman. She got right down to business and didn't waste my time or her own. "What kind of internal investigation did your company perform to ensure the reports weren't issued by an employee? It's possible a staff member made an error, or maybe issued the false reports intentionally."

The woman's tone was slightly annoyed when she responded. "I went through the files myself with the help of our IT specialist. We even checked the computer backup to see if one of the employees had screwed up and deleted the forms to cover it up. We found nothing."

In other words, I could cross *internal error* and *inside job* off my list. "Who processes your tax reports? Do you take care of them in-house, or do you have a CPA firm or outside service file for you?"

"We do it here in the office," she said.

That ruled out an error by a contractor.

"What about your accounting and tax software? Any glitches?"

"Nope. The software works like a charm."

Hmm . . . "Have any of the alleged winners contacted you?"

"Several," she said. "They wanted to know why they'd never been notified they'd won a prize and what happened to their winnings. I explained that our company only prints lottery tickets and doesn't award prizes, and that we had no idea who issued the 1099s. One woman threatened to sue us for fraud if we didn't pay her the hundred grand that was reported to her."

"Did she follow through with her threat?"

"She went so far as to have an attorney send a demand letter offering to settle for 10 percent of the alleged winnings. Our lawyers wrote back and questioned whether the woman and her attorney were attempting some type of extortion scheme. Our lawyers also threatened to countersue on our company's behalf if they went through with litigation."

"And?"

"And that seemed to shut 'em up."

I pondered the information for a moment. "Do you think that could be true? That the woman was trying to scam your company?" Maybe the woman hoped the lawyers for Winning Tickets would offer a small settlement simply to dispense with the matter quickly and cheaply. She wouldn't be the first person trying to make a living from bogus threats of legal action.

"Who knows?" the CFO said on a sigh. "I just want this to stop. I've got enough on my plate without something like this to deal with."

You and me both, sister. "Will you send me copies of

the correspondence between you and the woman who threatened to sue?"

"Sure. Anything that will put an end to this nuisance."

I rattled off my e-mail address and we ended the call. As the correspondence traveled through cyberspace between Kalamazoo and Dallas, I mulled things over. Was this a case of attempted fraud/threat of a nuisance suit, or could this situation involve a more sinister plot in which someone was using the IRS as a means to harass others? The agency sometimes found itself used as an unwitting pawn in someone else's dispute. Couples getting divorced routinely reported their ex's suspected financial indiscretions, sometimes without bothering to get their facts straight first. Often, these reports came back to bite the whistleblower on the butt given that those who filed joint returns during their marriage were generally on the hook for any unpaid taxes, interest, and penalties brought to light.

I quickly looked over the returns for the victims, hoping something might provide a clue, maybe indicate a pattern. While most of the victims were female, there were three males in the bunch. Most of the victims were single, though a small number filed married joint or married separate returns. Their incomes varied drastically, from the low twenty thousands to the high three hundred thousands earned by Thomas Hoffmeyer and his wife. Their addresses were spread all over the Dallas area.

I eyed the paid preparer section of each return. After all, some unscrupulous tax preparers had been known to use their clients' personal information in illegal refund ploys, or had included false information on their clients' returns in the hope of gaining a reputation as the person to hire if you wanted a big refund. But no. Such was clearly not the case here. Some of the returns had been prepared by H&R Block, others by Jackson Hewitt. A few of the returns had been prepared and filed by the taxpayers themselves using tax software. The Hoffmeyers' married joint return had been prepared at a CPA office. *Hmm.* There appeared to be no link between the preparers.

As I stared at my computer screen, the CFO's e-mail popped up with two documents attached. The first was the letter from a local law firm written on behalf of a woman named Bethany Flagler. The letter noted the erroneous 1099 for $100,000, described the audit and "severe emotional distress" that resulted, and demanded ten grand in compensatory damages. The response letter, written by an attorney from a firm in Kalamazoo, was scathing. Not only did it threaten a counterclaim for fraud and the referral of the matter to law enforcement as attempted extortion, it suggested that, at the very least, Ms. Flagler had failed to properly safeguard her social security number. Both sides were pointing more fingers than John Travolta in *Saturday Night Fever.*

A quick search told me that no other 1099s had been filed in Bethany Flagler's name. If she were running an extortion scheme, Winning Tickets appeared to be her only target. Or at least the only target in which a fraudulent 1099 was involved.

Next, I ran a criminal background search on Bethany Flagler. *Aha!* She'd been charged two years ago with three counts of theft by check. Though the charges had later been dismissed, the dismissal didn't necessarily mean exonerating evidence had been provided. She might have paid the victims or worked out some type of settlement with them or the district attorney's office in return for them dropping the charges.

Hmm . . .

I wasn't sure what to think. Given that Bethany wasn't

the only one named on the false 1099s, my gut told me she wasn't trying to pull a fast one. On the other hand, she'd faced bad check charges. Apparently, she wasn't a saint, either.

While I could phone Bethany, in my experience in-person interviews yielded more and better information. Even if the person said no more than he or she might have over the phone, speaking with a person face-to-face allowed me to evaluate the demeanor and body language, those subtle signs that might tell me whether the interviewee was telling me the truth or whether he or she was lying or holding something back. Avoiding my eyes. A nervous nose twitch. A defensive posture. A handwritten confession wadded up in their wastepaper basket.

The W-2 filings for the preceding year told me Bethany Flagler had been employed by Sweet Melody Music Company in Hurst. I found the company's number online and dialed it from my office phone.

"Sweet Melody Music," said the male voice that answered. "How can I help you?"

"Is Bethany Flagler in?"

"Just a moment," he said, "I'll transfer you."

When the line went to waiting music, I hung up. The fact that the man attempted to transfer the call told me Bethany was still employed there.

I moved on to map out a route for the day. I'd just finished when Eddie appeared in my doorway, gun on his hip and briefcase in hand, the odd mix of weaponry that exemplified the unusual skill set of an IRS special agent. "Let's rock and roll."

I grabbed my things and out the door we went.

chapter seven

*H*itting a Sour Note

Given the stops we planned to make, it seemed to make the most sense to start to the west and then head back east. Our first stop would be Sweet Melody Music. Well, make that our *second* stop. Our first stop was at Smashburger where I picked up two orders of sweet potato fries and Eddie got a burger and onion rings to go. It was lunchtime now, and we special agents needed sustenance in order to fight tax crime. Besides, I'd kind of become addicted to sweet potato fries and boy did I need a fix.

As we waited for our order, I filled Eddie in on the details of both cases and showed him the photos of the three girls.

He groaned. "You didn't tell me there was more than money or our safety at stake."

"It wouldn't have changed your mind. You still would've agreed to help me."

"That's true." He sighed and scrubbed a hand over his pained face. "We live in a messed-up world, don't we?"

I was forced to agree. "But at least you and I are doing something about it."

"But what if—" He stopped himself, as if afraid to complete the sentence and thought.

I finished for him. "What if we can't help find these girls in time?"

"Yeah," he said softly.

"The answer is simple," I told him. "That's not an option."

We ate our lunch on the road, Eddie filling me in on his twin girls' latest shenanigans as we rode along. "They keep dropping hints that they want to take a beach vacation. I took them to our neighborhood pool the other day, and they said the cement hurt their feet and that they wished they could swim somewhere where the ground was softer, like sand." He chuckled. "They're so obvious."

They might be obvious, but they also had their dad wrapped around their adorable little fingers. "So which beach are you going to and when?"

He scoffed. "They're not the boss of me."

I cut a look his way. "Yes, they are. So which beach and when?"

He turned to look out the window and put a hand over his mouth, mumbling, "Galveston. End of July."

I snorted. "Well, at least you'll get to be the boss at work soon."

I finished the last of my fries just as we pulled to a stop in the parking lot of Sweet Melody Music. The business was located in an enormous warehouse with musical notes and symbols painted on the outside. Half note. Quarter note. The notations for sharps and flats. A musical staff.

We stepped through double glass into a small customer service area. Over the speakers came the sound of a marching band playing an instrumental version of the Survivor classic "Eye of the Tiger." A young, skinny guy sat on a stool behind the counter, eating a peanut butter and jelly sandwich and drinking a soda. Not a health nut, clearly, but lucky enough to still have a fast metabolism. He washed down his bite with a swig from the can and stood. "Hi, there. What can I do for you?"

"We're looking for Bethany Flagler," I said.

"Are you the one who called earlier?" he said. "The line went dead. Sorry if I accidentally disconnected you."

While it was tempting to let him take the blame, my personal moral code wouldn't let me do that. "It wasn't your fault. I went into a dead zone and my cell phone dropped the call." Okay, yeah, my moral code only went so far. I wasn't above a little white lie when it would further my purposes. I couldn't very well tell this guy I'd hung up on him on purpose or he'd wonder what was up. "Is she around?"

"Let me check. She might be at lunch." He picked up a walkie-talkie. Apparently they used them to communicate inside the vast warehouse. He pressed the talk button. "Bethany, there are two people here to see you."

When she replied, "Who?," he eyed us and raised a brow in question.

"Tara Holloway and Eddie Bardin," I said, purposefully neglecting to offer our titles or the fact that we were from the IRS. No sense letting her know—*yet*—that we were special agents here to interrogate her, to determine if she was the mastermind behind the fake prize reporting scheme. If she knew, she'd only have extra time to come up with a story and compose herself, or maybe even to flee out the back door. With my stomach full of sweet potato fries and Eddie loaded down with a burger and onion rings, we were in no mood for a foot chase.

The guy repeated our names into the radio. "Tara Holloway and Eddie Bardin."

There was a moment of silence as Bethany tried to place our names. When her voice came back, it was tinged with irritation. "I'm on my lunch break in the kitchen. Can someone else help them?"

Again the guy looked to me for an answer. I shook my head. "It's personal."

He pushed the talk button again. "She says it's personal."

Another pause. "Okay," came Bethany's voice, tentative now, but still irritated. "Send them back."

He stepped out from behind the counter and opened a door for us. "The kitchen's at the back of the warehouse. Just follow the scent of microwave popcorn and burnt coffee."

We walked into the long, wide, and tall warehouse. Towering metal shelves held every type of musical instrument imaginable, housed in standard black cases. Tubas. Clarinets. Saxophones. The long cases with the bowl-shaped end had to contain trombones. There might have been seventy-six trombones in the big parade, but there were thousands of them here. This place must supply instruments to most of the junior high and high school bands throughout north Texas. There were also shelves with books of sheet music, everything from Sousa marches to orchestra pieces to jazz standards.

We continued down a long aisle until we reached the back of the building. His and her restrooms flanked a door marked STORAGE. To the right of the storage closet was an open kitchen. The smells of various microwaved cuisine wafted out, as did rapid-fire Spanish that sounded as if it were coming from a television.

We stepped to the door to find a thirtyish woman with dark blond hair pulled up in a ponytail. Fortunately, Bethany was the only person in the room. We'd be able to speak privately. Her attention was glued to a TV mounted on a bracket in the back corner of the room. A telenovela played on the screen, the actors engaging in emphatic *es-*

pañol, while subtitles in *inglés* played across the bottom of the screen.

The camera zoomed in on a woman who, judging from her glamorous dress and perfectly coiffed black locks, must be the female lead. The woman had many things going for her. Long lashes. Smooth, café au lait skin. Full ruby-red lips and a thousand-megawatt smile that lit things up like a neon light. Beautiful actresses were a dime a dozen, but an exceptional smile like that? Rare. Surely that dazzling smile is what landed the actress the part.

A handsome man in a business suit took the woman's hand, tipped with blood-red nails. He gently kissed the back of it and asked, *"¿Ahora? Por favor, dime sí."* This appeared in the subtitles as *Now? Please say "yes."*

"Hello, Miss Flag—"

"Shush!" She shrieked, raising a hand as well to silence me. "Ah ee vay is on!"

Eddie and I exchanged glances. *Ah ee vay?* What the heck was she talking about?

On the TV screen, the woman withdrew her hand from the man's grasp and clapped it to her heart, plastering the back of the other hand to her forehead. She looked directly into the camera, her smile disappearing, her brown eyes burning bronze with fire. *"¡Nunca!"* she cried. *Never!* echoed the translated subtitle below.

Jeez. Talk about melodrama.

The show broke for a commercial, a logo of a red heart with a knife in it popping up on the screen, the words *Amor y Vengaza* appearing below it. The announcer said something that translated as *Stay tuned for more* Love and Vengeance *after these words from our sponsors.*

Okay, now I got it. *Ah ee vay* was Spanish for *A y V,* a shortened term for the show.

Bethany turned to me, standing from her seat, her tight face and rigid posture revealing her impatience. Clearly she wasn't happy about us interrupting her lunch hour or the show.

I held out a hand. "I'm Special Agent Tara Holloway from the IRS." I angled my head to indicate Eddie. "This is Senior Special Agent Eddie Bardin."

She cautiously took my hand. "Okaaaay," she said, the elongated word telling me she was questioning why Eddie and I were here.

"We're investigating the false 1099s that were purportedly issued by Winning Tickets Corporation."

"I thought the IRS closed the case."

Is that what she'd been hoping for? That the investigation had been terminated? "The audit department went as far as it could." I watched closely to gauge her reaction. "They turned it over to Criminal Investigations. That's our department."

"Good. I hope you can make some headway."

Instead of looking concerned or guilty, she appeared relieved, her face and shoulders relaxing. *Huh.* Of course, it could be an act.

"We'll try our best," I said. "Why don't you give us your take on things." I'd learned from experience that open-ended questions could yield juicy tidbits of information that more direct questions would not.

"My take?" She rolled her eyes. "It's been an absolute mess. When I got the notice from the IRS telling me I owed money on prize winnings, I got all excited. I thought I'd won something. Then I come to find out it was someone's idea of a joke."

"You were disappointed?"

"Who wouldn't be?" she replied. "I figured whoever played the joke had to work for Winning Tickets. How else would they know the company's name and address and tax ID number to put on the tax form?"

I knew it was not an employee who had issued the reports. Besides, it was common knowledge among those in financial professions that tax ID numbers for businesses could easily be found online. Corporations were required to register with the secretary of state in their state of incorporation. The tax ID number would be in the public files along with information about the officers and directors. Once the culprit decided to run a phony prize scam, all the person had to do was search the state databases for companies that sounded like the type of business that would award prizes, maybe try keywords like *winner, prize,* or *award*. Winning Tickets Corporation would clearly fit the bill.

"Actually," Eddie explained to Bethany, "it's fairly easy to get tax ID numbers for corporations online if you know where to look."

"It is? Well, I wouldn't know anything about that."

Is she telling us the truth? Or is she actually a clever extortionist?

"Anyway," she continued, "my cousin's a lawyer and he said he'd write a letter for me and see if he could get some type of settlement from Winning Tickets. But they wouldn't offer me anything. They even threatened to sue me back! Can you believe it?"

After all the crazy things we'd seen on the job, Eddie and I would believe just about anything. All we could do was offer her a pair of sympathetic shrugs.

"Do you think you'll figure out who sent in the fake reports?" she asked.

Was it you, Ms. Flagler? "I won't stop until I exhaust every lead," I said, knowing I could make neither threats nor promises.

She frowned. "So no guarantees, huh?"

"Nope. But I'm hoping you can help me." I cocked my head. "Any idea who it might have been?"

She raised her palms. "None. I told the auditor as much."

As I asked the next question, a commercial for laundry detergent came on. If the ad was any indication, its fresh lavender scent could inspire a person to dance around in the grass in their freshly laundered clothing. Maybe I should buy some. My current detergent was entirely uninspiring. "Are you aware of anyone who'd want to make things difficult for you?"

Bethany scoffed. "Hell, yeah, I know someone who'd want to make things hard on me."

"Who?"

"My former roommate. We shared an apartment for six months. She stole my checkbook, wrote bad checks all over town, wiped out my bank account, and ruined my credit. I hardly ever write checks so it was weeks before I realized my checkbook was missing. She picked up our mail from the box every day. I didn't know it at the time, but she was throwing away collection letters sent by the places where she'd bounced the checks. The cops came here one day and arrested me. I told them I had nothing to do with the bad checks, but they hauled me off anyway. In handcuffs! Most embarrassing day of my life. I was lucky I didn't lose my job. The prosecutor eventually realized I was innocent and that my roommate was the one behind it. By then she'd stolen my jewelry and my boyfriend, too. I don't miss the boyfriend, he was lazy and not going anywhere with his life, but there were a couple of bracelets I would have liked to hold on to."

Interesting . . . "What happened to your roommate?"

"She spent a month in jail and was ordered to perform community service. Last I saw her she was on her knees in the mud pulling weeds in one of the city parks. Serves her right."

Perhaps the experience would set the wayward woman straight. At any rate, my suspicions about Bethany had been put to rest. She was a victim, not a lawbreaker.

"Your roommate sounds horrible," I said in empathy. "Do you think she's the one who issued the fraudulent 1099 in your name?" After all, if she'd taken Bethany's checkbook, she might have also searched the apartment until she found Bethany's social security card, too.

Bethany's expression was skeptical. "As awful as she was, she wasn't very smart. She probably doesn't know the first thing about tax forms. I doubt she's ever even filed a return."

It was a good point. Whoever had done this presumably had at least a minimal level of knowledge about tax filings. But perhaps someone else had given her the idea or provided assistance. I'd be able to determine whether she was the likely culprit if she had a link to the other victims, too.

"What was her name?" I asked.

"Robin Beck." Bethany eyed the TV, which was currently in the middle of a commercial for auto insurance. Why humans should take advice from a gecko who'd never once driven a car or purchased an insurance policy was beyond me, but I had to admit the little green guy was cute and his Australian accent was adorable.

I made a note of the name. "Any idea where Robin is now?"

Bethany scoffed. "Probably mooching off another friend, sleeping on their couch and eating all their food and not chipping in for the bills."

"What about a job?" I asked. "What did Robin do for a living?"

"Mostly retail work," Bethany said. "She never seemed

to keep a job for more than a few weeks at a time. She'd just gotten fired from a shoe store right before they sent her off to jail."

"Got a cell number for her?"

Bethany pulled her phone from her back pocket, brought up her contacts list, and rattled off the number.

"Thanks." I took note of the number and looked back up at her. "Anyone else who might have a vendetta against you for any reason?"

"I can't think of anyone."

The commercial ended and a quick Spanish guitar riff played as the station segued back into *Amor y Vengaza*. Bethany seemed to instantaneously forget that I was even there. She stared up at the screen, her mouth slightly agape. On the screen, a different handsome man in a business suit walked past a group of women seated in front of computers, typing. *"¡Ponte las pilas!"* he barked, the translation reading *Put in your batteries!* Judging from the context, the phrase appeared to be an idiom for "hurry up." Whaddya know? I'd learned something new. I gave myself a mental pat on the back.

"Bye," I said to Bethany. "Thanks for the information."

She made a soft grunt of acknowledgement but didn't look my way. That Mexican soap opera sure must be addictive. Eddie stuck out his tongue, put his thumbs in his ears, and waggled his fingers. Still she didn't turn our way. She was mesmerized by the drama.

Eddie and I ventured back through the building and bade farewell to the friendly guy working the front desk. Unlike Bethany, he actually said good-bye.

Back in the car, I fished my cell phone out of my jacket pocket and called the number Bethany had given me for Robin Beck. An annoying series of shrill tones followed by a computerized voice told me the number was no longer in service.

Eddie ran a quick search on his laptop. "Robin's driver's license is expired. So is her vehicle registration. Both show an address in Cypress, Texas."

Cypress was one of the many suburbs north of Houston. There was no telling where Robin might be now, and it didn't seem like much of a lead anyway. Bethany hadn't thought Robin was the guilty party. Barring another victim of the 1099 scheme telling us that he or she knew Robin, we didn't see much point in putting more time into chasing her down. Besides, getting evidence against Hidalgo and trying to help the Border Patrol find the three kidnapped girls was much more important.

I started my engine, pulled out of the lot, and aimed my car for El Loro Loco.

chapter eight

*R*unaround

As we pulled to a stop in the parking lot, I closed my eyes for a brief moment, imploring the good Lord Almighty with a silent prayer that Julio Número Uno would give us the information we needed to save Nina, Larissa, and Yessenia. When I opened my eyes again, I caught Eddie doing the same thing.

El Loro Loco was housed in a stucco building painted a terra-cotta orange with green cartoon parrots in sombreros gracing the outside walls, the words in their speech bubbles promising "The best beans north of the border!" and "Salsa so fresh you should slap it!"

We stepped through the front door and found ourselves face-to-face with an oversized green and yellow mechanical macaw sitting on a wooden perch. Our movements having activated its motion sensors, the bird tilted its head first one way, then the other, his eyes sliding around in their metal sockets. He flapped his wings and opened his beak, squawking so loud it threatened to burst our eardrums. *"SQUAWK! Welcome to El Loro Loco!"*

Grinning mischievously, Eddie gestured to the raspy-voiced parrot. "How about I get you a bird like that for your wedding gift?"

"How about I buy your daughters a couple of them for Christmas?"

That shut him up. My eyes scanned the room. The hostess stand was unmanned for the moment, the hostess evidently taking care of another task. The lunch crowd was dwindling, many settling their tabs and leaving their tables, some with to-go boxes. The smell of onions and green pepper permeated the air.

As the door opened behind me to admit a patron, the macaw flapped his wings again and repeated his greeting. *"SQUAWK! Welcome to El Loro Loco!"*

Eddie grabbed a paper delivery menu, wadded it into a ball, and shoved it into the bird's gaping beak. "Maybe that'll shut him up."

It didn't. As a trio of men walked past us to leave, the bird flapped his wings and opened his mouth again, the wadded menu falling out and dropping to the floor. *"SQUAWK! Welcome to El Loro Loco!"*

Eddie cut the bird a dirty look. "Stupid bird. They're leaving, not coming in."

Undaunted, the bird emitted another *"SQUAWK!"*

Eddie glanced around and, seeing nobody in authority in the immediate vicinity, edged toward the bird. In a clandestine move, he stepped onto the electric cord with one foot to hold it still, while he hooked the opposite ankle around the cord and yanked the plug out of the wall socket. *"SQUA—"*

The bird silenced, we stepped up to the hostess stand, where a woman in an apron was approaching.

"Table for one?" the grandmotherly Latina woman asked in a heavy Spanish accent.

"Actually, we're looking for Julio Guzmán," I told her.

I pulled out a business card and handed it to her. I found the cards gave me just as much legitimacy as flashing my law enforcement badge but freaked people out less, kept them more at ease. "I understand he works here?"

Eddie offered his card, too. "I'm Eddie Bardin."

Her face clouded as she read our cards. *So much for keeping her at ease, huh?*

"Julio works the early shift," she said. "Five in the morning until two in the afternoon. But he's off until Thursday." Her eyes narrowed as she looked from me to Eddie and back again. "Why are you two looking for him?"

"He's not in trouble," I told her, hoping to alleviate any concerns. "We think he might have some information about a case we're working on."

She said nothing in return, just continued to stare at me through her eye slits. *Okay, then.*

"Are you the manager?" I asked.

"Manager and owner," she replied with a mix of pride and pensiveness.

"You're not in trouble, either," I assured her. After all, the documentation Salvador Hidalgo had provided to the people he'd smuggled into the U.S. appeared to be valid documentation that would allow a person to work here. Presumably the man going by the name Julio Guzmán had given this woman the same set of documentation to prove his eligibility for employment. She'd have no reason to question the validity of the documents. "Could you give me his home address?" I asked. "I could speak to him there so I don't have to interrupt him here at work later in the week."

She took a deep breath as she thought things over, but eventually motioned for me to follow her. She led me to a hallway at the back of the restaurant and stepped into the small office at the end. Walking over to a filing cabinet, she opened a drawer, rifled through the files therein, and pulled one out. I stood in the doorway as she dropped into her chair and opened the file on the desk. She proceeded to give me an address in Hurst, where Eddie and I had been before heading here. *So much for using our time efficiently, huh?* I entered the address into my phone's GPS.

"Thanks," I told her. "Enjoy the rest of the day."

As we exited the restaurant, the parrot once again raked our nerves with his grating mantra. *"SQUAWK! Welcome to El Loro Loco!"* Looked like an employee must've plugged the annoying bird back in.

Leaving the macaw to his sentry duties, we set off to the mobile home park where Julio Guzmán Número Uno lived. The female voice of the GPS led us back onto Highway 121 for just under three miles before directing me to exit. A couple of turns later and we were pulling into the mobile home park. Though the homes were modest and set fairly close together, they were well kept and clean. Ditto for the yards. The place had a small neighborhood pool where children played and splashed about and shrieked with glee. As sweltering hot as it was outside, I was tempted to get out of my car and perform a cannonball in my clothing.

My eyes sought the lot numbers on the mailboxes. Twenty-five. Twenty-six. Twenty-seven. *There it is. Lot twenty-eight.* An ancient blue Buick Riviera sat in the driveway.

I pulled to a stop behind the Buick, and we climbed out of my car, taking the two steps up to the porch. Eddie rapped three times on the glass storm door. *Rap-rap-rap.*

A moment later, a Latina woman who appeared to be in her mid-thirties opened the door. Her hair was pulled into a loose pile on her head. She wore a tank top, denim shorts, no shoes, and an uneasy expression. *Is she undocumented, too?*

A young boy, maybe four or five years old, scurried up behind her, latching onto her leg for comfort and looking up at us with big brown eyes, a small stuffed dog with long floppy ears clutched in his hands. From how worn and old the dog appeared, I guessed it must've served as the boy's security blanket, his velveteen rabbit. I gave the kid a smile and he flashed me a shy grin back. *Adorable*.

"Hi," I said to the woman. "I'm looking for Julio Guzmán. I understand he lives here?"

She looked me up and down, then did the same to Eddie, as if her response depended on her assessment. "No. No Julio here," she replied in a thick Spanish accent. "Wrong house."

From behind her, I heard the same guitar strain I'd heard at Sweet Melody Music. This woman was also watching *Amor y Vengaza*. It sure seemed to be a popular show.

"Mr. Guzmán's not in trouble," I said, telling her the same thing I'd told his boss. "I just need to ask him some questions about a man named Salvador Hidalgo."

She sucked in a quick breath of air—*uh!*—and her eyes flashed in alarm. These two things told me two other things. One, this was not the wrong house as she'd just suggested. And two, she was familiar with Salvador herself. Maybe he'd arranged to get her into the U.S., too.

"No," she said, beginning to close the door. "No Salvador here. Wrong house."

I wasn't quite buying her act. "Are you the wife of the man who is working under the name Julio Guzmán? Maybe his sister?"

She shook her head again. "No Julio here."

She went to shut the door, but I stuck my steel-toed shoe in the space before she could get it closed. "I'm trying to help, ma'am. We believe Hidalgo is responsible for the deaths of several people in the desert in west Texas. But we can't do anything about it until someone gives us information." I pulled the photos of Nina, Larissa, and Yessenia from my briefcase. "We also believe he's involved in the kidnapping of these three girls. They're missing." I let that sink in for a moment.

She said nothing. I wasn't sure if she hadn't understood me or was simply refusing to speak to me. I looked past her into the house but saw no one else inside. If Julio lived here, he didn't appear to be home at the moment. Maybe he worked a second job or was out running errands. Or perhaps he was holed up in a bedroom or closet. I returned my attention to the woman and looked her in the eye. Or as much in the eye as I could given that she repeatedly cast her glance downward.

"We are trying to help people," I told her, speaking slowly. "To keep desperate people from paying a lot of money to someone who is not going to keep them safe. And we've got to find these girls right away. If we don't, they might disappear forever."

Still she said nothing, though the anxious look on her face indicated that, despite the language barrier, she understood the gist of what I was saying to her.

"We really need someone to talk to us. I can get a translator if necessary. Would you like me to do that?"

"No." She shook her head frantically, her eyes clouding in fear.

I realized that part of the reason she might not want a translator is because she didn't want to speak about the unspeakable things that had happened to her and Julio on their journey to America.

"Did Salvador hurt you?" I asked gently. "Or maybe someone he is working with?"

She gulped back a sob. "Wrong house," she said again, though this time she had to choke the words out.

"Ma'am," I tried again, taking a different tact that I thought might hit home with her, convince her to help. "A Border Patrol agent told me they recently found a child in the desert in west Texas. He was the only survivor. His parents died of heatstroke and dehydration and we believe Salvador Hidalgo is responsible." I gestured to the little boy. "A little boy like him will grow up without a family now. We can't let there be others. We need Julio's help. *Your* help. For that little boy's sake. For the girls' sake."

My heart and gut both squirmed. I didn't want to pressure this woman. Clearly, she was distraught. But if nobody would give us information Hidalgo would only rack up more victims.

When she shook her head again, I pulled out one of my business cards and handed it to her. "Please have Mr. Guzmán call me, okay? Or if you change your mind and would like to talk you can call me, too."

She blinked back her tears, nodded, and took my card. I removed my foot, and she closed the door.

Strike one.

Eddie and I exchanged looks of frustration. It sucked when a case depended on the cooperation of witnesses, which wasn't always easy to get. It was much easier when we had numbers and financial records to rely on.

"Think we should wait around?" I asked Eddie. "See if Número Uno might show up?"

He shook his head. "I don't think that's the best use of our time." He gestured at the door to indicate the woman inside. "She probably texted or phoned him the instant she closed the door and warned him to look out for us."

Eddie was probably right. Besides, if Uno decided to cooperate, he had my card and phone number and could get in touch with me.

As we climbed back into the car and headed out, I cast a final wistful glance at the children playing in the swimming pool. *Oh, to be so carefree, unencumbered by the shackles of the world's complex and emotional issues.* I heaved a loud sigh.

Our next destination was Saint Lucia Catholic School, where the second as-yet-unidentified man working under the name of Julio Guzmán was employed. I drove east, back to Dallas. The school was located in Cedar Crest, a neighborhood in the southern part of the city known for low-cost housing and high crime. Property values and crime were two variables that tended to run in inverse directions.

I pulled into the parking lot. While the lot was open, the remainder of the school grounds was surrounded by eight-foot wrought iron fencing, to keep the students in and sin out. Given that school was out for the summer, the teaching and administrative staff were on vacation and sin had to seek the children elsewhere. Only two cars, an older model plain white pickup and a deep purple Honda CR-Z coupe, sat in the lot. I pulled into a space one row over.

As if he'd read my mind, Eddie said, "I'll check the car. You run the truck."

I ran the truck's license plate through the system. Sure enough, the truck was registered in the name of Julio Guzmán. *Good.* At least I knew the man using that alias was on-site. Julio Número Dos. "The truck is registered in Guzmán's name."

"The Honda belongs to a woman named Mary."

I climbed out of my car with a file folder containing a copy of the documentation in hand. Eddie fell into place beside me as we made our way up to the double iron entry gates. I put my hand on the lever and pushed down on it. It wouldn't budge.

"Locked?" Eddie asked.

"Yes, dang it." Still, a locked gate had never stopped me before. Heck, I'd once sneaked into an enclosed area guarded by three drooling Dobermans. I'd been armed only with fried baloney sandwiches and had come within inches of being torn to shreds. But, hey. Such was my duty to the American people. I took that duty seriously.

No reason to climb a gate if I didn't have to, though. The push broom leaning against the brick building told me my quarry might be working outside.

"You see anyone?" I asked Eddie.

"Not a soul," he said.

While Julio Dos might not be in sight, there was still a chance he was in earshot. "Mr. Guzmán?" I called through the fence, glancing left and right along the front of the building. "Julio?" Too bad I didn't know the guy's real name. When there was no response, I upped my volume to the maximum my lungs and vocal chords could muster. "Mr. Guzmán? Julio? Anybody?"

No one appeared, though a squirrel on a nearby oak chattered at me in a scolding manner. *Chit-chit-chit!*

Eddie put a finger in the air and made a twirling motion. "Let's walk the perimeter. You go right. I'll go left."

I turned to the right and proceeded to walk the fence, continuing to call out all the while. "Mr. Guzmán? Julio? Hello? Anybody here?"

Eddie and I crossed paths at the back of the building.

"See anyone?" he asked.

"Nope. You?"

"Nope."

"Keep going," he said. "We can meet up out front."

After completing a full circle around the compound, my brain came to the conclusion that either the guy was somehow evading us or he was working inside the building where he couldn't hear me hollering for him.

"I'll try calling," Eddie said. He looked up the school's phone number and dialed it. He held up a finger to indicate each ring. One. Two. Three. Four. Five. "I'm getting a voice mail," he said. "Should I leave a message?"

"Not yet," I said, looking up at the oak from which the squirrel had chitted at us. As a girl growing up in the piney woods of east Texas, I'd spent many a day climbing trees. Time to put those climbing skills to use once again. I returned to the oak, received another scolding from the angry squirrel—*chit-chit!*—and reached up to grab a limb that extended over the top of the fence. I could barely reach it, my body stretched as far as it would go.

Eddie made a stirrup with his hands. "Need a heave-ho?"

"You calling me a ho?" I teased as I lifted my right food and stuck it in his hands.

"One!" he called out. "Two! Three!"

chapter nine

All Abuzz

Eddie's heave-ho packed much more power than either of us had anticipated. While I'd expected him to merely hoist me up, instead he sent me sailing over the fence as if I'd been shot from a cannon. "Aaaaah!"

Unfortunately, unlike cats with their propensity to land on their feet, I flailed in the air, inverted with my legs above me, seemingly destined to dive headfirst into the grass. If my neck didn't snap, my brain was sure to be concussed. I did the first thing that came to mind. Curl up in a ball, tuck my head in, and prepare to roll.

Luckily, my instincts served me well. My shoulders hit the grass and I somersaulted three times before coming to a stop on my back under the tree. The snarky squirrel stared down at me from his perch on a branch. I swear he rolled his eyes before giving me a *chit-chit-chit-chit!* The translation, in this instance, being *what a dumb ass*.

"Holy crap!" Eddie hollered from behind the fence, his hands reflexively grabbing his skull. "Are you okay?"

I sat up. Despite Eddie's inadvertent attempt to kill me, nothing seemed to be broken. "I'll live," I told him as I stood and brushed leaves and dirt from my clothing. "You been taking steroids or something?"

"Nah," he said. "Just working out with Nick. We've been focusing on our biceps. I guess he knew he'd be proposing and wants to be ready to carry you over the threshold."

"That won't be a problem for him." Nick had played high school football and, though his playing days were long behind him, he was still ripped.

Eddie snorted. "It'll be a problem if you keep eating double orders of sweet potato fries."

I responded with a raspberry. *Pfft.* My inelegant retort delivered, I made my way to the main walkway, where a large statue of the blessed mother greeted students with an implicit welcome and reminder to safeguard their virginity. Though I was a backsliding Baptist, I nonetheless gave in to the urge to genuflect and cross myself. *When in Rome, right?*

"What are you doing?" Eddie called from the front gate, where he stood with his hands wrapped around two posts now. "You're not Catholic."

"I don't know," I called back. "It just seemed like the right thing to do."

The statue stood behind a small water garden, the angels at Mary's feet playing trumpets that, unlike the real trumpets at Sweet Melody Music, spewed liquid streams that fell among the water lilies topping the shallow pool. The sound of the moving water both soothed me and gave me the instant urge to urinate.

Walking past the statue, I clenched my bladder and stepped up to the double front doors. The sign read WEL-COME TO SAINT LUCIA CATHOLIC SCHOOL. ALL VISITORS MUST PRESENT IDENTIFICATION AT OFFICE.

I pulled on the doors. Like the gate, they were locked. I yanked again, half hoping the force would set off an alarm. That would bring Julio Dos running. Probably the cops, too. To my disappointment, the alarm didn't sound. I figured it must be disengaged.

I tucked the file folder under my arm, cupped my hands around my eyes, and put my face to the glass. I could see down a long hallway all the way to the double doors at the back. A series of narrower hallways extended to each side. To the immediate right sat an office with a plate glass window looking out onto the foyer.

From inside, over the sounds of the trumpeting angel fountains behind me, a faint sound could be heard, a mix of a hum and a whine. The sound grew louder, and as I watched through the glass a Latino man emerged from a side hallway pushing a floor polisher.

"Hey!" I hollered, pounding an open palm on the glass. *Bam-bam-bam!* "Mr. Guzmán!"

He neither saw nor heard me, continuing in a straight path out of sight, leaving a strip of gleaming tile floor in his wake.

"Dammit!" I cried, looking back over my shoulder and adding "Sorry, ma'am," to the statue of Mary. *Had it been my imagination or had she tossed me a disappointed look?*

"He's in there?" Eddie called.

"Yeah!" I called back. "He's polishing the floors."

I backed away from the front doors and trotted around the side of the building, hoping to catch Julio Número Dos as he approached one of the glass fire doors along the side. I reached the first door just as he turned around to head back down the hallway in the other direction. He didn't see me waving my arms behind him, and my knocking fell on deaf ears. *Bam-bam-bam!*

Eddie had followed along outside the fence. "Any luck?"

"No. He didn't hear me."

I ran back around the building to the other side and

stood in wait at that door. I had to give the guy credit. He took his job seriously, kept his eyes on the floor in front of him, occasionally pulling the machine backward to go over a particularly stubborn spot of the floor a second time. Heaven might have pearly gates, but Saint Lucia Catholic School would have the shiniest floors God had ever seen. *Is it true that cleanliness is next to Godliness?* If so, I should be having an ethereal vision right about now.

As I stood under the overhang, waiting, my ears clued in to a steady sound overhead. *Bzzzz.*

Uh-oh . . .

Glancing up, I found myself standing under the largest paper wasp nest in the history of mankind. *Whoa!* The thing was the size of a piñata. What seemed to be hundreds of wasps were working to build the nest. A wasp who'd flown in to report for work hovered an inch from my face as if questioning the presence of this oversized intruder. Apparently, the wasp determined that I was a threat and made a beeline for my nose, his stinger at the ready.

While my dedication to duty had led me to face many dangers without complaint, my natural instincts again took over. I swatted at the wasp with the file folder and screamed. "Aaah!"

Unfortunately, while instincts could often protect us from harm, they could also sometimes get us into more trouble. As I flailed around, I inadvertently whacked several wasps who'd been hovering about the nest. They turned their attention from their residential construction project to yours truly.

Bzz! The first sting I felt was just below my ear. *Zing!* I shrieked again, clawing at my neck with one hand while trying to fend the wasps off with the folder. *Bzz!* The next sting I felt was on my left cheek. *Zing!*

Damn, that hurt!

"Tara!" Eddie cried from his place behind the fence twenty feet away. "Are you okay?"

"No!" I screamed, swatting randomly in every direction. "I am most definitely NOT okay!"

Bzz! Bzz! Bzz! When more of them came for me, I realized that office supplies were no defense against this squadron of stingers. I turned and ran for my life, the buzzing growing softer behind me as I left the wasps in my dust.

Eddie ran along with me, removing his suit jacket and waving it over the fence in a desperate attempt to dissuade the wasps from following me. He was too far away to have any effect, his efforts thoughtful yet futile.

As I rounded the building, I backed up to the wall and stopped to pull the stinger out of my skin. Feeling nothing but a welt, I remembered that, unlike bees, wasps did not leave their stingers behind when they struck. In other words, their stingers weren't single-use weapons. They could be used over and over again. *There's a cheery thought . . .*

The wasps seemed to know this fact, too. Instead of giving up or being confused by my evasive tactic, they continued to come after me with a vengeance. *Bzzzz! Bzz! Bzz!*

I took off running again, the persistent pests in hot pursuit. *Bzzzzz!* The squirrel chattered again, this time seemingly cheering the wasps on. *Chit-chit! Chit-chit!*

What an asshole.

I ran to the exit, where Eddie was yanking on the gates with all his might but to no avail. The lock held firm and all my partner managed to do was make a racket as the metal clanged. *Clang-clang-clang!*

The iron fence had trapped me inside the school grounds. If I stopped to climb the fence the wasps could complete their aerial assault, most likely targeting my ass as it would be the largest, most exposed area. *How many stings does it take to kill a person?* I feared I'd find out. Or, more precisely, Nick and my parents would find out when the coroner issued my official death report.

But no. I'd faced down a drug cartel, terrorists, and the mob, and they hadn't been enough to put an end to me. No way would I let myself be taken down by a swarm of inch-long insects, no matter how pissed-off and persistent. This would not be how I'd die. *Hell, no!*

My wounds throbbing, I ran toward the statue of Mary. I supposed on some instinctual level I wanted my mommy and, given that she wasn't available at the moment, had decided that any mother would do, even one made of stone. I stopped at the edge of the pond and turned to face the swarm flying after me. I tossed the file folder aside and reached down to my holster, yanking my Glock from its sheath.

Unfortunately, the weaponry issued by the federal government was intended for use on humans, not insects. Though I had quite a few bullets in my magazine and impeccable aim, a gun wasn't the right weapon for close combat with tiny targets. Besides, the gun didn't even act as a deterrent. While a human target might dive for cover at the sight of the gun, the bugs just kept coming in a sky-darkening cloud, a wasp Luftwaffe.

Still, while the gun itself wouldn't scare the wasps off, maybe noise would. I raised my hand over my head and fired a shot into the air. *Bang!* To my dismay, the sound only seemed to fuel their fire and I felt a trio of stingers sink into my flesh, one on my forehead and two on my raised hand. *Zing! Ouch! Zing! Ouch! Zing! Ouch!*

"Stupid mother—" I caught myself just in time. Cursing was sinful enough without doing it under the watchful eye of Mary Immaculate.

Eddie was trying his best to climb over the fence to help me, but with horizontal bars only on the bottom and top of the fence there was no way for him to get leverage. "Try your pepper spray!" he shouted.

I returned my gun to my holster and reached for my pepper spray. It wasn't intended for use as an insecticide, but I wasn't going to let the product labeling stand in the way of defending myself from these insistent insects.

I closed my eyes, held my breath, and pushed the button, waving the canister around in the air over my head. *Psssshhhh!*

I turned again to run, hoping to leave a trail of retreating wasps in my wake. To my dismay, the spray only seemed to piss them off and renew their determination. They came after me with fresh vigor, two stinging the back of my neck before I could take a single step. "Ow!"

I twirled around, flailing my arms, my eyes burning and watering from the spray. Through the haze, I saw Mary standing in front of me, her arms spread in welcome, as if she were inviting me to dive into the shallow pond at her feet.

Smart idea, Mary! No wonder God chose you to bear his only son.

Smack! I belly flopped into the pond, doing my best to submerge as much of myself as possible in the twelve inches of water available to me. Too bad I didn't have a reed to breathe through.

I rolled onto my back and flattened myself against the bottom, snorting bubbles and occasionally lifting my head to gasp a quick breath before going back under. I suffered two more stings, one on my lip and one on my ear before the wasps decided they'd taught me my lesson. They began to retreat and return to work.

I floated on my back in the pond, my body throbbing

in pain, my brain delirious from lack of oxygen, pepper spray, and the poisonous wasp venom. An image appeared to me then, much like the image that had appeared to the young girls in Fatima. I looked up at the visage, at a peaceful woman's face, a glowing light encircling her head.

Holy mother of God! Am I a chosen one?

"Mary?" I croaked.

"Sister Mary Margaret," the fortyish nun corrected me, reaching out a hand to help me out of the pond and putting an end to my narcissistic fantasy.

So I wasn't chosen. *Bummer.* The glowing light behind the woman's head was only the afternoon sun, not an aura of holiness. Too bad I hadn't been wearing a habit like hers. It would've protected my neck from the wasps.

I took her hand and together we dragged my soaking body from the water.

"What brings you to Saint Lucia today?" the woman asked calmly, seemingly unfazed to find a woman in a business suit floundering around in the fountain. "Were you only interested in gunplay and ridding the school of wasps, or did you and the gentleman at the gate have other intentions?"

I squeezed water from my clothes as I explained our reasons for coming to the school. "We're not interested in prosecuting Mr. Guzmán," I assured her. "We're only trying to get information to stop a coyote from leading people to their deaths."

"I see," she said, her expression concerned and conflicted. "And how did the IRS get involved in this matter?"

"Two reasons," I said, pulling off my right shoe and holding it over the pond to dump water out of it. "The only evidence we have linking Hidalgo to human smuggling is the documentation found in the car he was driving. Those W-2s and social security cards are what we've used to locate the people using the false documentation." I put my right shoe back on and pulled off my left, dumping water from it into the pond, too. "The IRS often gets involved in the investigations of other agencies. Where there's any type of illegal activity going on, there's likely to be a tax crime. Income going unreported or money being laundered."

"I see." She mulled my words over for a moment before walking over to the gate, pulling a set of keys from her pocket, and unlocking it to let Eddie in. She motioned with her arm. "Follow me, please."

The two walked back toward me, coughing and blinking and waving their hands to dissipate the cloud of pepper spray still hovering about.

Sister Mary Margaret led us inside and parked us in the teachers' lounge while she went to round up the staff member posing as Julio Guzmán. My soaked clothes felt cold now that I was inside in the air-conditioning. I dried myself off as well as I could with a stack of napkins I found on the table and sat in one of the plastic chairs, water dripping from the hem of my pants onto the floor.

Eddie sat in another chair, watching me with a half-pained, half-amused expression on his face. "How do you get yourself into these things?"

I shrugged. "It's not like I try. They just happen."

"But they only happen to *you*," he said.

It was true. I had an uncanny ability to create chaos.

A man in his early thirties appeared in the doorway. He looked very anxious and sheepish when he entered the room. He slid tentatively into a seat across the table from me. Sister Mary Margaret took a seat next to him.

I explained to Número Dos and the nun that those of us in law enforcement were far more interested in taking action against Hidalgo than any of the Julio impersonators.

"Salvador Hidalgo is a danger to others. He's been linked to multiple deaths in west Texas." I pulled the photos of the girls from the file and laid them side by side on the tabletop. "We also believe he's responsible for the kidnapping of these sisters. He must be stopped."

Despite my words, his expression was skeptical.

"Without your help," I told him, "more people could die. Fathers. Mothers. Children. We need you to testify that he is the man you paid to smuggle you into the United States. That he is the man who gave you the papers identifying you as Julio Guzmán. We also need you to tell us anything that might help us locate the girls."

The janitor hesitated a long moment, his expression both anxious and anguished, before issuing a long sigh. "I am Julio Guzmán," he said in heavily accented English. "My paper say it. That me."

I tried my best not to sound accusatory. "I'm sorry, sir, but I don't believe you are. There are seventeen men working under the same name and social security number as you. I can understand why you are afraid to tell us the truth, but we need you to be honest, to tell us everything you know about Salvador Hidalgo." I paused a moment, imploring him with my eyes. Though I didn't know much Spanish, anyone growing up in Texas couldn't help but pick up some basics. "Please, sir. *Por favor, señor.* For the girls."

As neither I nor the man said anything for several long moments, the nun's gaze went back and forth between the two of us and Eddie. "Looks like he's not talking. We're done here, then?"

I turned to her, hoping maybe she could help me convince the man to do the right thing. "Can you help me? Try to convince him?"

Her face was stern, her lips pressed into a thin line. "This is his decision to make."

"You aren't concerned that one of your workers isn't who he says he is?" I argued, frustrated. "That your school, which has hundreds of children entrusted to its care, has someone unknown on staff?"

"We run fingerprints on every potential employee," she snapped back. "This man has no criminal record. Besides, he doesn't work during school hours. During the academic year, he's only on campus nights and weekends. I'm much more concerned that an employee who has worked harder than any janitor we've ever had is going to end up in hot water."

I couldn't blame her. And I didn't want to see the poor guy end up in hot water, either. There'd been enough people ending up in water today, myself being Exhibit A.

"I understand," I told the woman, raising my palms is resignation. I stood from my seat. "If either of you change your mind," I said, "please give me or Eddie a call." I pulled two soggy cards from my jacket pocket and handed one to the man, the other to the nun. Eddie did the same. "But please call us soon. If we don't get any real evidence against Hidalgo, he'll be released in less than forty-eight hours and these three girls"—I picked up their photos from the table and held them up—"could disappear forever."

As the two walked me and Eddie back to the front doors, I left a wet trail behind me, like a human-sized slug. Along the way, the man stopped at a janitorial closet for a mop, cleaning up the mess I'd made on his freshly waxed floors.

"Sorry about the *agua*," I told him as we stopped at the front doors.

He nodded in acknowledgement, even offering a small smile. The nun must have told him about my impromptu dip in the pond out front. "Is okay."

As Eddie and I turned to go, the man grabbed my arm and said, *"Cañón de teléfono."*

"Excuse me?"

"Telephone Canyon," he repeated. *"Las muchachas.* Girls. Maybe they there. I only say this. *No más."*

No more. In other words, he'd told me all he was willing to. Still, it was a start. I gave him a smile and put my hand over his on my arm, giving it a grateful squeeze. *"Muchas gracias, señor."*

While Julio Dos returned to his work, the nun walked me and Eddie past the Mary statue and pond to the gate, using the key to let us out again. The chattering squirrel was on the walkway now, batting around the spent bullet casing. Much to his disappointment, I picked it up and tucked it into my pocket.

"Bye," I told the nun. Eddie gave her a nod.

"Peace be with you," she said.

Peace? If only.

chapter ten

*H*ide and Seek

Back at the car, I immediately phoned Agent Castaneda.

"Got something for me?" he asked.

"My partner and I spoke with one of the Julios," I told him. "He wouldn't implicate Hidalgo or tell me his true identity, but when I showed him the girls' photos and told him their lives could be at stake he said they might be in Telephone Canyon. Does that mean anything to you?"

"It does," he replied. "Telephone Canyon is in the southeastern part of the park, not far from Boquillas. It's a remote area with rough terrain. Few people venture there, especially in summer."

Rough terrain and few people meant less chance of being spotted. That could explain why Hidalgo used it as a smuggling route.

Castaneda went on to explain that the site's moniker was derived from a failed government project from World War I to string telephone cable through the canyon. "It's an ironic name, really," he said, "because the plan was never executed. There's no telephones, poles, or wires there.

No cell service, either. The only phones that work out there are satellite phones."

Perhaps they should consider renaming it No Reception Canyon, instead.

Castaneda thanked me for the information. "I'll get agents out there right away to take a look."

In the meantime, I'd keep my fingers crossed they'd find the girls there.

Our final stop in my quest to find someone—*anyone!*—willing to point a finger at Salvador Hidalgo was the home of Trent and Kendall Oswalt. Well, anyone other than one of the men who worked for Brett. I was still hoping not to have to go that route.

It was almost five o'clock when we pulled into the Bent Tree neighborhood. I turned onto Club Hill Drive and stopped at the home. Though the neighborhood was built back in the 1970s, the beautiful, classic French design of the house would never go out of style. The circular drive curved gracefully in front of the single-story ivory brick house, which featured arched floor-to-ceiling windows. The glass gleamed, as if the windows had just been cleaned. If Camila worked as a housekeeper here, she was doing a damn good job.

I parked at the curb and climbed out of my car, grabbing my jacket from the backseat and wringing it out one last time, a few drops of pond water that had accumulated at the hem dripping to the pavement. I donned the damp, wrinkled blazer and walked up the driveway to the front door, Eddie following alongside me. *Ding-dong!*

We waited for fifteen seconds or so after ringing the bell. As I put my finger to the doorbell again, I heard the sound of a female voice calling "I'll get it!" A moment later the voice was followed by the sound of the dead bolt releasing.

The door swung open to reveal a woman with golden blond hair draping to her shoulders in a chic, blunt cut. Her makeup was impeccable, her physique the perfectly trim silhouette that comes with lots of free time and an expensive personal trainer. Her designer jeans, sandals, and summer blouse were casual yet clearly costly.

Her demeanor was wary as she looked me up and down, taking in the chestnut locks glued to my head, my smeared makeup, and my clammy clothing, not to mention the lovely red welts all over my neck and face courtesy of those stupid wasps. The woman's nose twitched in repulsion. Perhaps I should've changed and cleaned myself up before coming here. But with the clock ticking until Hidalgo's release and the three girls missing, I had no time to spare. She gave Eddie a once-over, too, but seemed to find the well-dressed man in the nice suit much more acceptable.

"Hello," I said, foregoing a handshake under the circumstances. "I'm Tara Holloway with the Internal Revenue Service."

Eddie stuck out his hand. "Agent Bardin, also with IRS."

After the two exchanged a handshake, I asked, "Are you Mrs. Oswalt?"

She tilted her head, her hair swaying with the movement. "Yes?" It was as much a question as an answer.

"I understand you employ a Camila Contreras in your home. We need to speak with her, please."

She tilted her head in the other direction. "About . . . ?"

About something that's none of your business. "About an urgent, private matter."

"A tax matter, I'm guessing?"

Sheesh. This woman was relentless. I understood that this was Kendall Oswalt's home and that Camila was her employee, but we were federal agents on official business and she had no right to question us or dig into her employee's personal business. "We'd prefer to discuss the matter directly with Ms. Contreras." Or the person posing as Camila Contreras, whoever she was.

"Camila . . . isn't here right now," Kendall said, stepping onto the porch and pulling the door closed behind her.

Eddie and I exchanged glances. We didn't believe this woman for a second. I'd bet my firstborn—Waylon or Hank or Reba or Dolly—that Camila was inside as we spoke.

I made a show of checking my watch. "The workday's not over. It's not yet five o'clock."

"She came in early today so I let her go home early, too."

Came in early? I fought the urge to scoff. The woman lived with the Oswalts. Whether or not she was on duty at the moment, she woke up here each day. "The W-2 you filed to report her wages listed your address," I pointed down to the ground on which we stood, "*this* address as the home address for Ms. Contreras." *Gotcha, you pretty little liar.*

Kendall's eyes blazed. "If you leave me your contact information, I'd be happy to give it to Camila next time I see her."

"Are you saying she doesn't live here anymore?" Hey, I could be just as pushy as she could. And, frankly, my patience was gone. I felt like I'd been playing a warped game of hide and seek all day and I was tired of it. Three girls had been kidnapped and I needed information to rescue them and nail their kidnapper, dammit!

The woman spoke deliberately now, enunciating each word as if spitting them at me. "I'm saying I will give your contact information to Camila the next time I see her."

Eddie joined the conversation. "Where does Camila live? We need her address. It's urgent."

"I . . . I can't tell you that."

"Because you won't?" I snapped. "Or because you don't know?"

"Because . . . I'm not sure where she stays."

Short of calling this woman a liar outright, we were out of options. I tried to look at the situation from her point of view. A little empathy couldn't hurt, and it might help us get the information we sought. If I were in her shoes and employed a live-in nanny or housekeeper who did a good job and who I was fond of, and if a federal agent showed up at my door asking questions, I'd probably do what I could to make sure she didn't end up in trouble or, even worse, being deported.

"What about her phone number?" I asked.

Kendall hesitated. "Look," she said finally. "I think whether she talks to you is her decision to make, not mine."

Finally, some honesty. I pulled another soggy card from my jacket pocket. "I can understand your concern, Mrs. Oswalt," I said, handing her the card. "But I assure you we're not here to harass Ms. Contreras. We have reason to believe she has information about a wanted criminal who's been responsible for the deaths of numerous people. We also believe he's responsible for the kidnapping of three sisters who are missing. We have to stop this guy before he kidnaps or kills again."

Kendall looked taken aback now, her mouth gaping and her eyes wide. Obviously, she'd expected this to be something more routine. She was probably wondering whether her family was in danger.

I retrieved the photos of the girls from my folder and showed them to her. "These are the girls who are missing. Their names are Nina, Larissa, and Yessenia. They fled Honduras when a violent gang member attempted to force Yessenia into a relationship." I paused a second or two to let that information sink in. "The girls were kidnapped along their way to the U.S. Their aunt was told if she didn't pay their ransom in just a few days she'll never see them again."

The woman swallowed hard, as if forcing down a lump in her throat.

"Time is critical," I said. "The man is in custody, but he'll go free on Thursday if we can't get some concrete information before then to warrant his continued confinement." I drove the nail home. "Camila may be our last hope for saving lives. You wouldn't want someone to perish, for these girls to end up dead, would you? Because you were hiding your housekeeper or nanny from us? Do you want that on your conscience for the rest of your life?"

She gnawed her lip and clutched my card to her chest, still looking uncertain. "Isn't there someone else you can talk to? Someone else that has the information you need?"

I hated to lie to this woman, but if I told her the others wouldn't talk to me about Hidalgo, either, I might lose what little leverage I had. "Camila's all we've got," I said, twisting my words so that they wouldn't be a total fabrication. She was all we had, here at this house anyway.

The woman looked down at my card again, then glanced at the photos of the girls I was still holding. "We'll be in touch," she said finally.

"Thanks. We'd really appreciate it."

With that, Eddie and I returned to my car. I fought the urge to claw at my wounds. The swelling had made them tender and itchy. Luckily, there was just enough time to run by the minor emergency clinic and shower before my appointment in the bridal department at Neiman Marcus.

Half an hour later, after dropping Eddie back at the office, I was seated on a paper-covered examination table. Doctor Ajay Maju was repeating Kendall Oswalt's head-tilting

performance, looking first at the stings on one side of my
head, then angling his head to look at the other. On his
feet were a pair of black Converse high tops, and underneath his white lab coat he wore a T-shirt that featured a
cartoon drawing of internal human anatomy. While his
look might not be perfectly professional and his bedside
manner ran to snarky, he was nevertheless a good doctor.
I'd trusted him with dozens of injuries I'd incurred while
with the IRS. I'd also been the one to introduce him to
Christina Marquez, a DEA agent I'd worked with on one
of my first major cases and who had become one of my
closest friends. Ajay and Christina had hit it off instantly
and were now engaged. Seemed all the single people I knew
were pairing up and settling down. But we were at that
age, I suppose.

Ajay reached out a gloved hand and poked one of the
welts on my forehead.

"Ow!" I cried. "What did you do that for?"

"The fun of it." His lip curled up in a mischievous smile.

"Sadist."

"You'll live." He reached into a drawer and pulled out
a small bottle. "Take this Benadryl. It'll help with the itch-
ing."

I took the bottle from him. "Thanks."

He made a note in his computer file. "What are you and
Nick doing this weekend?"

"No plans yet. Why?"

"Christina and I are flying to Vegas to tie the knot."

I virtually leaped off the table. "What?!? Why didn't she
tell me?"

"We just decided late last night," he said. "Her parents
are insisting on a big Catholic church wedding and my
family wants to do a traditional Indian wedding. There's
no way we can make everyone happy. So we figured

we'd do what's fair and piss off both families equally by eloping."

I couldn't much blame them. Weddings could be both happy occasions and cause for contention. Eloping seemed like a good option under the circumstances. "Count us in!"

"Great," he said. "I'll let her know. She's going to book everyone on the same flights and get a room block at Caesars Palace. We were able to snag a time slot for the ceremony early Saturday afternoon."

On the way out of his office, I texted Nick. *Pack your bags. Christina and Ajay are getting married in Vegas this weekend.*

He texted me back a moment later. *How about we make it a double wedding? Elvis can officiate.*

As tempting as it was, I couldn't deny my mother this rite. With me being her only daughter and her being the Martha Stewart type, she'd been looking forward to my wedding since the day I'd been born. If I didn't give her this, I'd never hear the end of it.

I texted Nick back. *Nice try. You're not getting off that easy.*

My next text went to Christina. *Heard the great news! Can't wait!* By that point I was at my car. I slid inside, opened my Internet browser, and began searching for something fun we could do in Vegas Friday night for a last-minute bachelorette party. The Thunder from Down Under all-male dance review would fit the ticket, and they had a late show at eleven o'clock. *Perfect.*

Christina's reply came a minute or so later. *Thanks! Would've told you myself but we just decided last night and I've been on a stakeout all day. Will you plan a girls' night for Friday?*

I chuckled. *Already on it.*

chapter eleven

$\mathcal{B}$ustles and Trains and Ruffles and Lace

Back at my town house, I showered and shampooed and did my best to conceal the swollen stings with dabs of makeup. Unfortunately, my best wasn't good enough. My skin appeared to have sprouted miniature volcanoes all over the place. It was as if God had plagued me with boils for going after someone who worked at one of His schools. Oh, well. There was nothing I could do about it.

As I headed back out to my car, my cell phone rang with a call from a number I didn't recognize. I accepted the call. "Hello. Special Agent Holloway."

A woman's voice with a thick accent came over the line. "The girls," she said, "maybe they in cave in Telephone Canyon."

"Is this Camila?" I asked.

"All I say," the woman replied. "Girls maybe in cave. Telephone Canyon cave."

"Thank you, *señora*," I told her. "*Gracias*. Would you be willing to tell me about Salvador Hidalgo?"

"No. All I say is girls maybe in cave."

"If you change your mind," I said, "and are willing to

tell me more about Salvador Hidalgo, please call me back. Okay?"

She hung up without responding to my question or saying good-bye.

I immediately phoned Castaneda again. "I've spoken with a woman using the alias Camila Contreras. She mentioned Telephone Canyon, too. She said the girls might be in a cave there."

"Thanks for the information," he said. "After you called earlier, I flew out to the canyon with a couple of agents. We didn't spot anyone, but there's lots of brush and washes and boulders out there and it's easy for people to hide. Plus, we can't exactly sneak up on them in the Black Hawk. You can hear that thing coming for miles. But we'll try again tonight with the infrared cameras, and we'll send agents out in the morning to check the caves."

"Good luck," I told him.

"We'll need it," he said. "Time's running out, both for keeping Hidalgo in custody and for finding the girls alive."

My insides twisted at the thought.

"Any chance the woman is willing to provide testimony against Hidalgo?" he asked.

"At this point, no," I said. "She said the information about the caves was all she'd say."

"Damn!" he spat. "But at least if we find the girls, maybe they can provide testimony against Hidalgo."

If. For a word of only two letters, it sure could pack a powerful, terrifying message.

We ended the call, and I set off to deal with something much more pleasant. Dress shopping!

I arrived at the Neiman's bridal salon to find my mother and Bonnie already looking over a sampling of dresses. With her chestnut hair and petite build, my mother was essentially an older and slightly heavier version of me.

Bonnie, on the other hand, was tall, with dark hair like Nick, though hers contained a gray strand here and there. Unlike Nick's amber eyes, Bonnie's were blue.

"Tara!" my mother cried, rushing forward to embrace me. She'd driven three hours from our hometown of Nacogdoches in east Texas to be here for my dress appointment. I was lucky to have such a devoted mom, and I knew she'd help me pick the perfect dress.

As my mother grabbed me in a bear hug, Bonnie caught my eye over my mother's shoulder. The wide smile she bore turned into an open-mouthed shriek. "My lord, Tara! What happened to you?"

My mother released me, pushing back but holding me in place by my shoulders to get a good look. "Have mercy! Are those boils on your face?"

"Nothing so Old Testament, thank goodness. I had a run-in with some wasps."

"Wasps!" my mother cried, yanking me back into the hug. "Oh, my poor baby! Can I do something?"

I squirmed in her arms. "You can let me go so I can breathe."

She released me again, shaking her head. "How do you always manage to find trouble?"

Jeez. There's that question again. "I don't find trouble. Trouble finds *me*."

The clerk stepped over. "Is this the beautiful bride?" she asked, though the look of barely masked horror on her face belied her words. I was anything but beautiful at the moment. She probably wondered who in his right mind would agree to marry me looking like this.

I explained the situation. "I upset a swarm of wasps and they let me know it."

"Wow," she said. "That had to hurt."

"Like heck." Fortunately, the Benadryl that Ajay had

given me had kicked in and my stings no longer felt so itchy. My skin still throbbed and felt tender, though.

The clerk turned to the long racks of wedding dresses behind her. "What kind of dress did you have in mind? Traditional? Contemporary? White? Ivory?"

"I have no idea," I said. "Other than that I want something that's not too froufrou."

"A simple dress," she said, nodding in agreement. "That's perfect for someone with your petite frame. Too many ruffles and poofs can swallow someone your size."

She stepped over to a rack and slid several aside before pulling out a strapless mermaid style made of white satin. She held it up.

I looked it over. "Maybe," I said. "It's pretty and I like the style." Of course, I'd have to see it on to be sure. I knew from years of cruising the clearance racks that some things looked better on the hanger than they did on me and vice versa.

She carried the gown over to a large dressing room and hung it on a hook inside before returning to the dresses. "When is the wedding?" she asked.

"We haven't set a date yet," I replied. "We've got to check with the churches and reception venues first. But we're aiming for sometime this fall." Or at least that's what I had in mind. I was ready to begin my life with Nick *now*. Nick was an easygoing guy, and he felt the same way I did. We'd agreed to get hitched. Why wait any longer than we had to?

"A fall wedding," she said. "Maybe something with a longer sleeve would work then." She pulled out a dress with a round neckline, full-length sleeves, and a lace overlay.

I reached out to touch the fabric. A little scratchy, but none of the lace would be touching my skin. "This one's pretty, too."

By the time we'd looked over the selections, I had a dozen dresses to try on, ranging from a slinky and sophisticated halter style to a bohemian number with long flowing sleeves to another with cap sleeves, a lacy beaded bodice, and a handkerchief hemline that looked like something from a medieval fairy tale. Perhaps I could convince Nick to get a tux made of chain mail to wear as the perfect complement. He could ride down the aisle on a black steed and sweep me up in his arms like a marauder. That would be romantic and make the wedding memorable, huh?

Bonnie and my mother sat on chairs outside the dressing room, sipping the champagne the sales clerk had offered and chatting excitedly while the woman expertly helped me in and out of each dress.

I tried the mermaid style first. Frankly, the tight fit made it feel as if my thighs were trapped together. I could only move the bottom half of my legs, which made walking awkward. I wasn't sure I wanted to go down the aisle in little baby steps. It would take me half an hour and a thousand steps to get from one end to the other. And how would I be able to dance the two-step, schottische, or cotton-eye Joe, not to mention the chicken dance, if I couldn't move my legs independently?

"What do you think?" I asked my mother and Bonnie, hoping they wouldn't like it. I didn't want to insult their taste.

There'd been no need to worry. They both gave the dress a thumbs-down, too.

"It's not you," my mother said.

"It looks confining," Bonnie added. "You want to be comfortable on your big day, especially if you'll be dancing."

Oh, I'd be dancing, all right. No way would I throw a party without giving the guests the opportunity to get their groove on.

I tried on the next gown, which was the round-neck with the longer sleeves.

My mother scrunched her nose. "That one looks . . ."

Bonnie found the word my mother was searching for. "Prudish."

"Yep." Overly sexy wedding dresses always struck me as being in poor taste, but I didn't want to look frigid, either.

Back into the dressing room I went.

The halter style seemed better suited for someone with a larger bust, while the bohemian model reminded me too much of Lu's sixties-era wardrobe.

But the medieval fairy-tale dress? The instant the fabric slid over my body I knew.

This is it! This is the one!

A glance in the mirror confirmed it, as did the nodding head and smile on the attendant. The dress was a size larger than what I normally wore, so the clerk grabbed a few fabric-covered clips to cinch the dress up in the back and give us a better idea how one in my size would look.

I opened the door to the dressing room and stepped out. Both my mother and Bonnie rose instinctively from their seats.

"Tara!" my mom cried, tears welling in her eyes as she rushed over. "That's it! That's the dress!"

Bonnie, too, had grown misty. "You look beautiful, honey! Nick's eyes are going to fall out of his head."

While the dress was perfect, I didn't want to go bankrupt paying for it.

"How much does this one cost?" I turned to the three-way mirror, reaching back awkwardly to try to find the price tag.

My mother gently pushed my hand away. "Don't you worry about the price, Tara. Daddy and I will take care of it." She consulted the tag. "Apparently by selling a couple of kidneys."

"I can keep looking, Mom."

"You'll do no such thing," she said, running her gaze over me again and smiling from ear to ear. "This dress is absolutely perfect. And your wedding is the last chance I'll get to splurge on my only daughter."

"If you insist," I said, grinning back at her. *Do I have the best mother or what?*

I made arrangements with the clerk to have the dress ordered in my size and made a later appointment for a fitting. She brought out several pairs of shoes for us to try with the dress, and we all agreed the lacy pair with the medium heel looked the best with the dress and would be comfortable enough for me to stand in for an extended period.

Our work done, I suggested we go out for dinner and drinks to celebrate. A half hour later, we were seated at a nearby Chinese restaurant, sipping green dragon cocktails and eating egg rolls and lo mein.

My mother took a dainty sip of her bright green drink and dabbed at her lips with a cocktail napkin. "Have you thought about where you want to have the wedding? Will it be here in Dallas, or do you want to have it in the church back home?"

Nacogdoches was a nice town situated in the beautiful piney woods of east Texas. But given its small size and limited tourist attractions, it was hardly the kind of place where you'd plan to have a destination wedding. Still, it was my hometown and I couldn't imagine anyone other than Pastor Beasley officiating at my wedding. He'd been the pastor at our Baptist church since I was a kid. He promoted a loving, laid-back version of our creator in which the almighty expected little more from us humans than for us to be kind to each other and avoid being assholes. Not hard to get on board with that.

"Back home," I said, turning to Bonnie. "You think Nick would mind that?"

She smiled. "Nick will want whatever you want, Tara." She raised her glass. "You know how that boy is. He'll be happy if all he has to do is show up. He'd gladly leave all the planning up to us women."

We shared a chuckle and clinked our glasses together conspiratorially before taking another sip of our drinks.

"What about the reception?" my mother asked, a hopeful expression on her face as she squirmed in her seat.

She was so obvious it was all I could do not to laugh. "Any chance Holloway Manor is available?"

She squealed and clapped her hands in delight.

When my parents had bought the dilapidated Victorian farmhouse I grew up in, my cash-strapped yet clever mother had named the house Holloway Manor, had it designated as a mixed residential and commercial property, and obtained a grant from the local economic development bureau to help finance the renovations. Soft blue paint graced the exterior, with the shutters and trim in a contrasting ivory. The roof was shiny tin, classic though quite loud on rainy days. The wide front door bore a welcoming floral wreath, and each window was adorned with curtains of Battenburg lace. The mismatched wooden rockers that lined the front porch gave the place a comfy, folksy feel.

My mother regularly rented out the downstairs for teas, bridal and baby showers, and wedding receptions. It seemed only natural the house should host the reception for one of its former inhabitants.

"What about food?" Bonnie asked. "Have you given any thought to the caterer or menu?" Bonnie was an excellent cook, and she made the best peach sangria on earth. It was no wonder food was one of the first things on her mind.

"We haven't discussed the menu yet," I said, fighting the urge to remind them I'd been engaged for only two days. Really, I was ahead of the game, having already found my dress this quickly.

My mother toyed with her napkin. "What kind of cake do you want? And what about the groom's cake?"

There was no time for me to reply before the two went into overdrive, peppering me with questions to which they supplied their own answers.

"I know you'll want Jesse to be your flower girl," my mom said. "What kind of dress should she get? I'd advise against lace. If the dress is itchy she'll stand up at the altar scratching herself the whole time."

"What about music?" Bonnie asked. "Do you want a deejay or a live band?"

"We could get that band that always plays at the honky-tonk up the road," Mom said.

"Good idea," I said. "Just don't let 'em drink. Too much beer and they forget the words to the songs." Once they'd even trapped themselves in a continuous loop, evidently having forgotten how to wrap up Willie Nelson's country classic "Whiskey River." As the lyrics said, the whiskey river must have taken their minds.

"I'd keep an eye on the band," Mom promised. "I've been looking for an excuse to put air-conditioning and a new floor in the barn. It'd be a perfect place for dancing."

"It sure would," I said before polishing off the last egg roll.

My mother whipped out a pen and began writing on her napkin. "We'll need to think about the dinner menu, drinks, bridesmaids, and groomsmen. Do you want to send out those 'save the date' cards or just invitations? I'm thinking we should do one of those photo magnets with the date on it. That way people can put it on their fridge as a reminder."

"Don't forget flowers," Bonnie said. "We'll need bouquets and boutonnieres."

Mom nodded. "We'll need a few floral arrangements for the church and house, too. We could go with traditional roses. Or maybe we could try something different, mix it up a little."

I sipped the sparkling wine in my glass and eyed the two women. Maybe it was wrong of me to attempt to foist the planning on them, but they seemed to be eating this stuff up. Besides, as excited as I was about marrying Nick, I was too worried about Nina, Larissa, and Yessenia to put much thought into my wedding at the moment. "You two seem really on top of things. Any chance you want to work together on the planning?"

The two exchanged thrilled looks, their eyes wide, brows lifted.

"You'd let us take charge?" my mom asked, incredulous but overjoyed. "Really?"

I nodded. "I'm swamped at work," I said. "It would be a huge relief to me, and you two seem like you'd enjoy it."

"We would!" Bonnie cried with glee. "I just never thought I'd get a chance to plan a wedding, what with not having a daughter."

"Well, you've got one now," I said, giving her a smile. "Besides," I looked from one of them to the other, "I trust

you two. Y'all know Nick and me better than anybody else.
You'll make it a day to remember."

"We sure will." My mother picked up her glass and
tossed back the remaining cocktail. "Finish that drink,
Bonnie! You and I have got a wedding to plan."

chapter twelve

$\mathcal{TV}$ Addiction

My mother had planned to spend Tuesday night at my town house, but once I'd asked her and Bonnie to plan the wedding the two had been so eager to get started they'd tossed me aside like a bridal bouquet. She'd ended up staying at Bonnie's house so they could set right to work on the details.

I woke Wednesday morning, disappointed my mother wasn't there to make me biscuits and gravy. But given that she was hard at work pulling my wedding together, I supposed I had no right to complain. Instead, I fished around in my purse, found the fortune cookie I'd tossed in there when leaving the Chinese restaurant last night, and cracked it open. I ate the crunchy bits while removing the slip of paper inside. It read, *A smile can hide a thousand feelings*. So true. A smile can also reveal fortune cookie remnants stuck between a person's teeth. Better go brush and floss, huh?

I fed my cats, got myself cleaned up and dressed for work, and headed out.

Given that I'd gotten nowhere yesterday on the Hidalgo

case, I knew I had to go out to Ellington Nurseries today and speak with Brett and the workers using the borrowed documentation. While I often took another agent with me to assist with interviews and to provide backup, Eddie had to attend a deposition and couldn't accompany me today. I supposed I could've asked Josh or Hana or Will to come along but, to be honest, I didn't want the fact that I was at Brett's business to get back to Nick. He wouldn't like it one bit. No sense getting him riled up over nothing. Besides, if Nick knew I was going out to Brett's business, he'd insist on going with me. How awkward would that be, my former and current boyfriends going head-to-head, while I stood by trying to act nonchalant? No thanks. I also planned to make a quick stop on the way at Metal-Masters, a company that, per my Internet search, manu-factured household hardware items, such as doorknobs and drawer pulls and hinges and faucets. *Really exciting stuff, huh?* According to information contained in their tax records, two of the prize scam victims worked in the company's billing department.

As I pulled up to a red light, my cell rang. It was the Lobo calling.

I jabbed the button to put her on speaker. "Hi, Lu."

"Senator Perkins's office called again this morning. Thomas Hoffmeyer phoned them wanting answers, and now the senator's chief of staff is breathing down my neck demanding them. Little twerp. I know you've got a full plate and then some, but have you made any progress on the fake prize case yet?"

I told her that I'd gone to see Bethany Flagler and that the only lead she'd given me was her former roommate, Robin Beck. "I plan to interview the other victims who live in the area. When I do, I'll see if they know Robin."

"Any idea when that will be?"

"I'm on my way to speak with some men about the Hidalgo investigation." It was clearly the more critical matter. The fake prize scam was a nuisance, no doubt, but nobody's life was at stake. "But I'm going to stop and see a couple of the 1099 victims on the way. After that I plan to check in with some of the others."

"Is Thomas Hoffmeyer one of them?"

"He can be." Though Hoffmeyer was the one who'd sicced the senator on us, instinct told me he'd be the least likely to provide useful information. He seemed like an anomaly, an outlier. While the majority of the other prize scam victims were female, he was male. And while most of the other victims were in the twenty-five to thirty-five age range, he was in his sixties. I'd thought I could learn more by speaking with the typical victims first, figure out what the common denominator was between them before trying to figure out how he fit in to the equation. I explained my rationale to Lu.

"That's a reasonable approach," she said, "but how 'bout you at least call Hoffmeyer to schedule your meeting? That'll give me something to tell Perkins's pushy little pinhead. If he knows you're scheduling the interview, maybe he and Hoffmeyer will stop complaining."

They might also stop complaining if I stuffed socks in their mouths. Unfortunately, such tactics weren't allowed. I supposed I should be more patient, but the problem was that those who complained the most about us agents not doing our jobs fast enough were often the same ones who complained that tax rates were too high. Without those taxes, there'd be even less money to fund the IRS, which meant it would take even longer for us agents to get around to helping them. Their arguments were logically inconsistent and there was no possible way to make them happy. *Ugh*. Besides, it's not like the auditor hadn't tried to figure things out. She'd done her best. These types of white-collar crimes didn't leave DNA or a set of fingerprints that could lead investigators directly to the lawbreaker. Our cases could be very complex, with clues hard to pinpoint.

The light turned green as I promised to call Hoffmeyer right away. "Be careful out there," she admonished me at the end of the call.

"I will."

Sliding my phone into the cup holder, I drove ahead and hooked a right into the next parking lot. I pulled under a tree for shade, looked up Thomas Hoffmeyer's contact information in the file, retrieved my phone, and dialed the number.

After three rings, a man answered, his voice gruff and growly. "Hello?"

"May I speak with Thomas Hoffmeyer, please?" I asked.

"That depends," he snapped back. "Who's asking?"

"Special Agent Tara Holloway," I said. "From the Internal Revenue Service Criminal Investigations Division."

He barked a humorless laugh. "I knew it'd light a fire under you lazy government folks if I got my senator after you."

Lazy? LAZY?! If I were lazy would I have climbed over a locked fence yesterday to track down a witness? Would I have worked untold hours of unpaid overtime in my quest for financial justice for Americans? Would I have wrestled and wrangled with crooks, enduring untold injuries and risking my life to do my job? *Lazy?* Not hardly. His nasty comment stung worse than those wasps. It took everything in me not to hang up on the guy. I settled for pulling the phone from my ear and giving it the finger. It was little consolation.

Having delivered my crude and silent retort, I put the phone back to my ear. "I need to meet with you to discuss your case." Normally, I asked a victim or witness when he or she was available, checked my calendar, and attempted to find a mutually convenient time. But this jerk could work around *my* schedule. Given that I wasn't exactly sure where things might take me, I pulled a day and time out of my ass. "I've got an extremely tight schedule the next few days, but I can squeeze you in at four o'clock tomorrow."

"That doesn't work for me. I golf on Thursdays."

"All right, then," I told him. "I'll let the senator's office know we offered you an appointment and you declined in order to play games. Good—"

"Hold on!" he said. "I suppose I can make that work if that's the only time you've got."

"It is. I work an extremely heavy caseload." I was tempted to make him come to my office, but I feared he'd be one of those difficult people who I'd have a hard time booting out. "I'll come to your home. See you then." With that, I hung up, not bothering with good-bye this time.

I took a deep breath to calm myself. Hoffmeyer wasn't the first jackass I'd encountered on the job, and no doubt there were more like him to come.

After texting Lu to let her know I'd scheduled a meeting with Hoffmeyer for the following afternoon, I drove out to MetalMasters and checked in with the receptionist in the foyer. She called up to the billing department where the two victims worked and got the go-ahead to send me up. "Second floor," she said, gesturing to the elevator. "Last door on the left."

I rode up to the second floor and stepped out into the hall. While the hallway was flanked on the left with offices, the right side of the hall was plate glass that looked out over the manufacturing floor. Below, workers moved about the assembly line equipment. A machine spat out a nickel-plated interior doorknob, then another, then another, all of them exactly the same. *And I'd thought depreciation computations had been mind-numbing.*

As I approached the last door, I heard a familiar voice. It was the dramatic woman from *Amor y Vengaza.* I stepped to the door to find two young women inside, a tablet situated between them playing the telenovela on the Telemundo app.

I rapped on the door frame and the two women looked up. One was Asian, with dark brown hair and delicate features. She must be Amelia Yeo. The other had brown hair, too, though hers was a lighter shade. She was Caucasian, though on the short and slim side, like her coworker. I pegged her as Gwen Rosenthal. Both appeared to be in their mid-to late twenties, roughly the age of Bethany Flagler. *Could that be a clue?* Maybe. Maybe not. Unlike Bethany and these girls, Thomas Hoffmeyer was in his mid-sixties. If there was a pattern, he didn't seem to fit it.

"Come in," Amelia said.

Gwen stood and rounded up a spare stool for me.

After we exchanged introductions, I gestured to the tablet. "What's the deal with that show?" I asked. "Everyone seems to be watching it."

Gwen shrugged, smiling sheepishly. "We're hooked on it. I know it's crazy. I mean, the show's totally unbelievable and over the top. But it sucks you in! There was another girl who worked here a year or two ago and she introduced us to it."

"She was a huge fan." Amelia raised splayed hands and arcing them in opposite directions to indicate just how huge a fan the young woman was. "She even dyed her hair black and dressed like Isidora."

"Isidora?" I asked.

"The female lead," Gwen clarified. "Isidora Davila."

Amelia chimed in again. "I DVR the show every day and watch it first thing when I get home." She lifted her chin to indicate the tablet. "This episode is a rerun from last week."

The scene moved to a hospital room. The glamorous, fiery-eyed woman was on the screen, adorned in a scarlet dress that seemed more appropriate for singing sultry songs in a lounge than visiting someone in the hospital. She stood at the head of the bed, on which lay a blonde, a wide white bandage wrapped around her skull. A handsome man sat next to the injured woman, grasping her hand as if their very lives depended on it.

"What's going on?" I asked, pulling my stool closer to take a better look.

Gwen rolled her chair over. "Isidora—she's the one standing next to the bed—is visiting her 'friend' Violeta in the hospital." She made air quotes around the word friend. "Violeta was pushed down a staircase and hit her head. She has amnesia and doesn't know who did it, but it's pretty clear it was Isidora. Isidora is in love with that guy," she said, pointing at the screen. "His name is Juan Carlos. He and Isidora were on the verge of something before Violeta came along."

"Ah."

Amor y Vengaza. "Love and Vengeance." The title seemed fitting. Still, how could intelligent people spend their time watching these silly melodramas? Didn't they have better things to do? Oh, well. Whatever makes the workday go by faster, right? Not everyone was lucky enough to have a job as interesting as mine. Rather than criticize their choice in workplace entertainment, I asked about their jobs.

Gwen answered for both of them. "I'm accounts payable," she said. "Amelia handles accounts receivable."

"I see. Do either of you handle any tax reporting?"

"No," Amelia said. "Just everyday payables and receivables. Regular, routine stuff."

I moved on to the 1099s. "Any idea who might have filed them? Maybe someone from your past who's trying to get back at you? A friend or neighbor or coworker?"

"No one that I can think of," Amelia said.

"Me neither," said Gwen. "Both of us get along with pretty much everyone."

I wasn't surprised. They seemed friendly and down to earth from what I could tell so far.

"Did you two know each other before you started working here?" I asked.

"We both took a bookkeeping course at a training center here in Dallas," Amelia said. "That's where we originally met. The career office at the center got us the jobs here."

Hmm. "Was there anyone in the class that seemed strange to you?"

The two exchanged glances, their expressions thoughtful as they considered their classmates.

"I can't think of anyone," Amelia said finally. "Can you, Gwen?"

She shook her head. "Everyone seemed normal."

Their response didn't surprise me. Accounting and business courses didn't exactly attract nonconventional, outside-the-box types.

"Do you two see each other primarily at work?" I asked. "Or are you friends outside the office, too?"

"We're friends, too," Amelia said.

Gwen agreed. "We do stuff together nearly every weekend."

Hmm. I didn't know where to go next with my questions, but I figured it couldn't hurt to see if Bethany

Flagler's former roommate could somehow have a link to these two. "Does the name Robin Beck mean anything to you?"

"Robin Beck?" Gwen repeated, tilting her head, her eyes narrowing as she seemed to be going through names in her mind. "No. Doesn't ring a bell."

"It doesn't sound familiar to me, either," Amelia added. "Why?"

"The name was a potential lead I got from another victim." Looked like it was the weak lead I'd suspected it to be. None of what I'd learned so far would get me anywhere or score the IRS any brownie points with the insistent senator. I pondered things another moment. *Hmm.* I had to consider all potentialities here. "What about the name Bethany Flagler?"

Both of the women shook their heads.

"That name doesn't ring a bell, either," Gwen said.

Amelia murmured in agreement.

So much for my thought that Bethany might have issued one of the false 1099s in her own name to throw suspicion off herself. Of course, one of these women might have done the same thing. Perhaps one of them was only pretending to like the other, was not truly a friend but rather an enemy in disguise, much like Isidora was to Violeta in the telenovela now paused on the tablet.

Might as well cover all my bases and ask whether they knew the other victims. "What about Jocelyn Harris or Thomas Hoffmeyer?"

They shook their heads again. *Darn.*

"I'm in a bit of a rush," I told them. "I've got an urgent matter I need to attend to. But I need some more information from you. I need to figure out what the connection is between you and the other victims. It's possible you victims were chosen at random, but I think it's more likely the person who issued the 1099s knows all of you some-how, or at least obtained your information from a common source. This situation seems more personal, a targeted scam." Of course, I could be wrong about that. Who knew? "I'd like you to e-mail me some additional information. Got something you can make a list on?"

Amelia pulled up a new Word document on her com-puter screen, while Gwen went for good old-fashioned pen and paper.

"Okay," I told them. "I need to identify every place where someone might have had access to your name and social security number two years ago when the 1099s were issued. Tell me where you've lived the past few years and the names of your landlords. Your doctors and dentists. The schools you've attended. Where you bank. Where you bought your cars and what institutions financed them."

Amelia finished tap-tap-tapping on her keyboard and looked over her shoulder at me. "I had to give my social security number to my gym when I joined a few years ago. Should I include that?"

"Definitely," I replied. There was no telling what the common link could be.

"I used a payday advance place once," Gwen said. "I had to get a loan to cover some unexpected car repair bills."

"Give me that information, too," I told her. "While you're at it, tell me what restaurants you went to regularly, what church you attended, your veterinarian's information if you have a pet." Okay, so I was grasping at straws. But you do enough grasping and one of those straws could lead to something. "Basically tell me everywhere you go and what you do."

I'd collect the same information from the other victims and compare notes. Maybe something would pop out at me.

"You can e-mail me the information." I handed each of the women one of my business cards and stood. "Thanks for your time. When and if I find anything out, I'll let you know."

The two issued good-byes and turned their attention back to the telenovela and the stack of paperwork in front of them.

As I rode down in the elevator, I racked my brain, trying to piece together any similarities between these two young women and Bethany Flagler. All were around the same age, and all seemed to enjoy the *Amor y Vengaza* telenovela, but that didn't give me anything solid to go on. *Darn.* I wanted to get this case solved quickly, to impress the pesky senator's office, to show that the IRS was doing its job and helping his constituents resolve their tax issues. There must be something that the victims and I were overlooking.

But what?

chapter thirteen

*T*he Old Flame Flickers

As I walked out to my car in the parking lot, a gust of hot, moist wind hit me, blowing up the flaps of my blazer and infiltrating my hair. The humidity would turn my locks into a frizz-ball in five seconds flat. I blinked against the breeze and glanced up at the sky. Billowy clouds were gathering on the horizon and the sun was only a hazy glow. Looked like a thunderstorm was coming our way. I only hoped it wouldn't hail. My plain G-ride was an ugly enough car without adding hail dents to the mix.

I set back out on the road, aiming for Ellington Nurseries, feeling a twinge of guilt. Was it wrong of me to hide this visit from Nick? *Maybe.* But do two people have to tell each other everything? *Maybe not.* Would I be angry with him if he didn't tell me about a visit to an old girlfriend, even if it was strictly for business purposes? *Hell, yeah, I'd be furious!* Was I being a total hypocrite here? *Yep. No doubt about it.*

The drive out to Brett's business took nearly an hour, but that gave me time to prepare myself, both physically and mentally. The physical part involved swiping on a

fresh coat of plum-colored lipstick and trying to tame my
hair with my fingers and saliva. I had no romantic interest
in the guy anymore, but I didn't want him to take a look at
my colorless lips and tumbleweed hair and think he'd
dodged a bullet. The mental part of my preparation involved reminding myself that this was business, that I
was visiting him as a law enforcement professional, not a
former lover, and that there was no need for my insides to
feel so squishy and squirmy.

I debated phoning him to give him a heads-up, but decided not to. If he said something to his workers, they might
worry that I was coming to arrest them and scatter. Then
I'd never get the information I needed to help Agent Castaneda find the kidnapped girls and keep Salvador Hidalgo
behind bars where he belonged. Nope, looked like my visit
would have to be a surprise.

On the long drive out, I figured what the heck. Why not
see what all the fuss was about? I downloaded the Telemundo app to my phone and pulled up the episode of *Amor
y Vengaza* that Amelia and Gwen had been watching earlier, starting it at the beginning. Normally, I wouldn't do
such a thing, but the roads out here were virtually empty
and, with the phone situated in my dash-mounted holder,
I could cast an occasional, careful glance at the screen
without taking my eyes off the road and posing a danger
to others. Besides, I was only trying to follow the general
gist of the story, not read all the subtitles.

As I drove and listened, the introductory music kicked
in, a longer version of the Spanish guitar riff that an-
nounced the cut to, and return from, commercial breaks.
One by one, the characters were introduced, the shots'
overly dramatic angles showing each actor's back first,
then swinging around to catch the actor from the front. A
mustached male lead in his late forties standing in an

elegant office. A young woman with flowing blond hair standing on a beach in a bikini. An artsy looking guy with a short ponytail working behind a coffee bar. Things went on until, at last, the queen of the telenovela was presented. The camera traveled up a curved staircase until capturing the scooped back of a red satin evening gown. This time, instead of the camera swinging around to catch the actor's face, Isidora Davila twirled on her own to face the lens, coming to a quick, dramatic stop, her ruby lips parted in a broad, friendly smile. When the camera zoomed in on her eyes, however, they flashed with fire. The camera angle widened to catch her sweeping boldly down the staircase as if she owned the world and everyone in it.

The intro complete, the episode began with Isidora Davila stopping in a dark hallway and pulling a ski mask over her face. She tiptoed to an office at the end of the hall, where an unsuspecting blonde stood at a file cabinet, rifling through the contents. Isidora slunk silently into the room, sneaked up behind the woman, and grabbed a lamp from the woman's desk. Moving quickly, she wrapped the electrical cord around the blonde's neck, pulling with all her might. Choking, the blonde clawed at the cord, desperate for air.

Whoa! That was some pretty dramatic stuff. Especially for daytime television. And, of course, the entire scene was punctuated with music that enhanced the mood, minimal at first, but building to a loud crescendo.

Things only got more dramatic from there. Isidora dragged the blonde to a staircase and gave her a forceful shove, sending her careening headfirst down the steps. *Thump-thump-thump-thump!* The camera panned from the blonde's lifeless body on the landing up to Isidora's wide smile, evident even behind the ski mask.

After a quick commercial break, the screen showed the

lead actress now lounging on a chaise, furiously scribbling in a journal with a fancy silver pen, the subtitles revealing the woman's innermost thoughts. *If anyone ever figures things out, I'll be ruined! But I refuse to feel shame. That thief stole a heart that belonged to me. She got what she deserved!*

Good thing people didn't act like this in real life, huh?

Rather than continue with this episode, I figured it made more sense to start at the beginning. When I was forced to stop for a long train at a railroad crossing, I backed out of the program and pulled up the pilot episode of *Amor y Vengaza.*

The story began with Isidora, dressed in a gauzy sundress and stiletto heels, her makeup perfect, standing in the office with the fortyish man. The dialogue in the subtitles told me the man had just recently become her husband. His custom-tailored business suit and the diamond ring logo on the wall behind his desk told me he was a busy man who ran a large, successful chain of high-end jewelry stores.

"You know I adore you," he barked impatiently. *"I didn't just marry you for your family's gold mines."*

Her narrowed eyes said she wasn't so sure. Maybe he'd married her for the family discount. I supposed I couldn't much fault him when I'd been thinking of ways to leverage my relationship with Nick into perks at work.

When Isidora's husband excused himself to take a phone call, she chastised him for not giving her the attention she needed and flounced out of the room.

Ay yi yi, I said to myself. *Such melodrama!*

After a commercial for laundry detergent, the show resumed. An angry Isidora left the office building and stormed across the busy street, where she yanked open the door of a coffeehouse. Inside, she saw something she couldn't resist. No, it wasn't a caramel latte. It was the artsy barista. When their eyes met, she gave him a coy smile, dipping her head and looking up at him from under her long, dark lashes.

She stepped to the counter and placed her order with the girl working the register.

"Your name?" asked the clerk.

"Isidora," the star replied.

She waited patiently until the barista called her name in a warm voice that could melt icebergs faster than global warming.

"Isidora?" His eyes met hers over the counter as he handed her a big cup of coffee, his sexy smile full of suggestion as he spoke, his dialogue translated across the bottom of the screen. *Just the way it should be. Hot, steamy, and only for you."*

The scene continued with the barista's fingers brushing Isidora's as he handed her the cup of coffee. When the caboose rumbled by, the crossing arm lifted, and the warning lights stopped flashing. I drove on. The episode ended with a cliffhanger, the barista stepping over to wipe a ring of moisture from Isidora's table and leaning in close to whisper in her diamond-studded ear. *I can fill your cup like no other. Do not deny me, or yourself.*

The innuendo and double entendre were laughable but, as the closing credits and romantic guitar music played, I found myself wondering. *Will she deny him? And herself?* She had so much to lose if she gave in. Her beautiful home. Her jewelry and clothes. Her share of her husband's fortune. But if her husband didn't truly love her, had married her only for her family's resources, should she be forced to live a lie? To deny herself the love she could find elsewhere?

By this time, I was nearing my destination. I paused the show so that next time I watched I could pick up where I left off.

Brett's nursery and landscaping business sat on a thirty-acre parcel of land several miles beyond the northeast Dallas suburbs. A white wooden fence ran across the front of the property, looking as fresh as the daisies dotting the letter *I*s on the green sign identifying the place as Ellington Nurseries.

I pulled into the asphalt drive. A cute little Mazda Miata and Brett's black Navigator were parked to the right of the metal prefab building that housed the offices and an expansive warehouse. Through the open doors, I could see pallet after pallet of organic compost, soil, and mulch in a variety of wood and color varieties. Beyond the metal building were rows of greenhouses in which plants, shrubs, and trees could start their lives in a protected environment under Brett's nurturing care.

Though Brett owned the operation, his background and education were in landscape architecture, not business, and he preferred to spend his time schmoozing new clients and working on designs. To that end, he'd hired another man to run the day-to-day operations. The guy had worked for several years as an assistant manager with one of the big home improvement chains, but he'd been ready for more responsibility and jumped on the opportunity to be in charge of Brett's nursery and the landscaping crews. I could see the guy now making his way among the greenhouses. A Latino man—perhaps one of the men I was looking for—followed him.

I glanced around for Brett. Not seeing him out and about, I figured he must be inside. Taking a breath to steel myself, I climbed out of my car. The temperature had dropped at least ten degrees since I'd left MetalMasters. A fresh gust of wind pushed me along as I walked to the door and pulled it open.

To my surprise, I found myself face-to-face with Fiona,

Brett's fiancée. Scratch that. Fiona was now his *wife*. The thick band on her left ring finger told me they'd sealed the deal. Her beach-ball-sized baby bump told me that it had been none too soon. It also told me that she'd soon have to replace that cute little two-seater Miata with a mom-mobile.

Fiona looked up from her seat behind the natural wood desk, her reddish-brown hair swaying as she tilted her head. The slightly puzzled look on her fair-skinned face told me she found me vaguely familiar, but couldn't quite place me. "Hello," she said, standing. "How can I help you?"

Before I could answer, two distinct barks sounded at the closed door to Brett's office behind her. Brett might not yet know I was here, but his Scottie Napoleon and his pit bull mix Reggie had scented me and wanted to say hello. Looked like they hadn't forgotten the girl who'd rubbed their bellies and made them fried baloney sandwiches. With Fiona being a chef, I could only imagine what kind of gourmet treats the two were enjoying these days.

The door opened and the dogs bolted out. They rushed over to me and I crouched down to pet their wriggling bodies. "Hey, boys! Good to see you!"

Reggie gave my cheek a lick and Napoleon gave me an *arf-arf* in greeting before I stood to greet Brett. His green eyes met mine, sparking with surprise and—*dare I think?*—a hint of excitement. I had to admit I felt a little flutter in my belly, too. Nick was definitely the right and only man for me, but despite that fact, the undeniable chemistry Brett and I had once shared seemed to still be reactive. And, after all, it's not like we'd broken up because we no longer had feelings for each other, because the physical attraction had died. We'd both simply realized we'd also been attracted to other people, and that we owed it to ourselves to see where those attractions might lead.

Brett wasn't tall, but his lean, muscular build, sandy hair, and toothpaste-commercial smile could certainly turn a girl's head. They'd once turned mine, and I had to admit they'd do it again if I hadn't already been there, done that, so to speak. Like Fiona, he now bore a look that was mostly puzzled, though his befuddlement had nothing to do with trying to place me. He just didn't have a clue why I'd driven all the way out to his business to see him.

"Hey, Tara!" he said, stepping closer. "What brings you out this way?"

"Work."

He laughed and shook his head. "I should've known. It's always work with you."

My dedication to my job had been a sore spot in our relationship. More than once, my work had gotten in the way of our romantic plans. But such is the life of a special agent.

I wasn't sure whether to give Brett a hug or merely shake his hand given that his pretty new bride was standing five feet away, watching us. I decided to let him choose. Apparently he couldn't make up his mind either, at least not quickly, as he came at me with both a hand and an arm outstretched. We engaged in an awkward half-hug handshake combo before separating.

Brett turned to his wife. "Fiona, this is Tara Holloway."

A series of emotions played across her face. Surprise. Suspicion. Jealousy. Acceptance. I supposed the same emotions had played across mine when I'd walked in the door and spotted her at the desk. Silly, really. Brett and I had willingly separated so that he could pursue a relationship with Fiona and I could pursue one with Nick. We'd made our choices and never looked back. And, really, we were all adults here, right? Of course, we were also human. And humans aren't always prone to rationale behavior. Still, once the emotions played out, Fiona gave me a sincere smile and stepped over to shake my hand.

"It's nice to meet you, Tara."

"Same," I said. "You're looking better than last time I saw you."

The puzzled expression returned.

"At Chez Michel," I said, "a few months back. The appetizer made you queasy."

"Oh, right! Those first few weeks, nothing seemed to agree with this little guy." She smiled, pointing both index fingers at her belly to indicate the tiny person growing therein. "I had morning sickness all day long. That's why I'm here, in fact. It's impossible to work as a chef if you can't look at food without—" She stopped herself, put a hand over her mouth, and whispered. "You know."

Such a lady. Being less genteel, I would've just put it out there. *Tossing my cookies.*

I cocked my head. "You couldn't work at the restaurant, but the smell of composted manure doesn't bother you?"

She laughed at that. "Oddly, no."

"You said 'little guy.'" I looked from her to Brett. "So it's a boy, then?"

Brett beamed. "That's what the doctor tells us."

"Picked out a name yet?" You could bet your ass it wouldn't be Hank or Waylon. Unlike Nick and me, Brett wasn't a big fan of country music.

"We're thinking Evan," Brett said.

"Or Spencer, maybe," Fiona said. "We haven't decided for sure."

"Wait a second." Brett reached out and took my left hand, just as he had so many times when we were dating. "What's this?" He held up my hand to show my engagement ring.

I shrugged and grinned. "I'm getting hitched, too."

"To Nick?"

"Yep."

Brett dropped my hand but gave me that easy, boyish grin that used to melt my heart. While my heart wasn't exactly melting now, it had nonetheless grown soft and warm. "He knows what he's getting himself into, doesn't he?"

I couldn't help but laugh. "Yeah. He does."

When Brett and I had dated, he'd routinely expressed concern about the dangers of my job, even going so far as to suggest I return to my safer tax preparation job at Martin & McGee, the CPA firm where I'd worked before joining the IRS. I'd downplayed things so he wouldn't worry. How could I quit the job I felt tailor-made for? There weren't many people out there who could handle both a spreadsheet and a Glock with equal skill.

Nick, on the other hand, fully understood why I loved my job, why I willingly assumed the risks, why I couldn't turn my back on the work that made me feel so satisfied. He understood the desire to seek justice, especially in cases where innocent people had been deprived of their hard-earned savings by unscrupulous bastards. He worried about me, sure. But he knew I'd never be happy doing anything else. Neither would he. Nick and I were cut from the same cloth, two peas in a pod, two sides of the same coin, and a dozen other such clichés.

Niceties complete, Brett got down to business now. "Uncle Sam need some landscaping? Maybe a hedge maze in the shape of a dollar bill?"

"I'm actually here to talk about a tax matter that involves your business."

He stiffened, the easy smile disappearing. "Uh-oh. That doesn't sound good. Am I in some trouble here?"

chapter fourteen

$\mathcal{W}$ho We Are

Was Brett in trouble? Honestly, it depended on how he answered the questions I planned to ask him. If he'd taken the birth certificates, social security cards, and voter registration cards at face value and assumed his workers had the right to accept the jobs, he'd be in good shape. But if he had reason to believe the documentation was fraudulent, it would be a different story. I assumed it would be the former. Brett had reported all the income he'd paid the men and collected all withholding taxes due. That was a sign of good faith, right? Besides, everything I knew about the guy told me he was a rule follower, an upright guy who obeyed the law. Heck, he was a Rotarian, for goodness sake.

Nonetheless, Fiona's eyes were bright with worry. I supposed it was never good to be questioned by the IRS, even if you knew the agent personally and thought you'd dotted all your *I*s and crossed your *T*s.

Might as well cut to the chase, huh? "We have reason to believe several of your workers provided you false documentation to obtain employment here."

"False documentation?" Brett repeated, his forehead

wrinkled in concern. "What do you mean? That my workers aren't who they say they are?"

"It's unlikely." I laid my briefcase on Fiona's desk, unlocked the clasps—*click-click*—and removed the copies of the documentation. I handed the copies to Brett. "Multiple copies of these documents were found in a rental car driven by a man named Salvador Hidalgo. He's a suspected coyote."

"Coyote?" Fiona looked from her husband to me. "What's a coyote?"

"A human smuggler," I clarified. "I'm working with agents from Border Patrol. They've performed several emergency rescues in recent months when smugglers abandoned migrants in the desert without food, water, or shelter. Others were not so lucky. They've found bodies, too. They were able to rescue a toddler who survived when his parents succumbed to the heat, but he'll live his life as an orphan."

"Oh, no!" Fiona wrapped her arms instinctively around her belly as if to protect her child. "That's so sad!"

"It gets worse," I told them. "Three girls who were on their way to the U.S. are missing. The kidnapper contacted their aunt and demanded a ransom. We think Hidalgo had something to do with their disappearance, that the kidnapper is part of his smuggling network." I gestured to the papers in Brett's hand. "There are several people working around the U.S. under those same names and social security numbers. Because that paperwork was found with Hidalgo, we believe he smuggled your workers into the country. Of course, he's claiming that he had no idea the paperwork was in the rental car and that it's not his. Without more concrete evidence and witnesses, the prosecutors won't be able to get a conviction, and Hidalgo will continue killing innocent people. I need to speak with your workers, see if they'd be willing to testify against Hidalgo."

Brett looked down at the paperwork in his hand and thumbed through it. "Julio. Pablo. Miguel. Diego." He looked back up, concern clouding his eyes. "These are some of my best men, Tara. They work their asses off all day in the heat and never complain."

I wasn't surprised. Many undocumented migrants did their best to stay on their employer's good side, to lie low, to behave in a way that would keep them out of trouble, under the radar. The last thing they wanted after risking their lives to come to America was to be deported back to the place they'd taken extreme measures to escape.

I watched him closely. "Did you ever have reason to think they weren't who they said they were?"

He looked me right in the eye, unflinching. "No. Never."

He was telling the truth. I didn't just know it, I *felt* it.

"Will they be deported?" he asked. "Sent back to wherever they came from?"

"Depending on their situation," I said, "and whether they cooperate with the government in its attempt to nail Hidalgo, they might be able to avoid deportation."

"Might." Brett's face clouded as his concern began to border on anger. Clearly he felt protective of the men who worked for him, and I'd become a threat. "You realize these guys have families, don't you? Wives and children who count on them? If they're deported, this will be devastating, for all of them."

I couldn't much blame Brett for his concerns. Hell, I had the same ones. "Look," I said. "I feel for these guys. I really do. That's why I want to help stop unscrupulous smugglers like Hidalgo. Can you imagine what it's like for the people he left to die in the desert? For their families back home? Big Bend is a big place. There could even be bodies that haven't been found yet. Can you imagine not knowing what happened to your loved ones? To just have them disappear?"

He was quiet a moment and I sensed some of his anger resolving, though no doubt the frustration remained.

"I've tried to get information from three other people," I said. "A woman gave me a lead, but nothing's panned out yet. I wasn't able to track one of the men down. He wasn't at his work or his home. The other wouldn't tell me anything. He insisted he was the person named on the documents."

Brett eyed me intently. "You could have arrested him, couldn't you?"

"The real Julio Guzmán has filed an identity theft affidavit. So, yes, I could have arrested the guy who was improperly using his documentation."

"But you didn't." Brett continued eyeing me, assessing me.

"No," I said. "I didn't. I'd figured the guy had been through enough already, and that I could catch more flies with honey than handcuffs."

"That's who you are, isn't it?" A grin tugged at those lips that used to kiss me. "Not quite as tough as you pretend to be, are you?"

I scoffed and pushed back my jacket to reveal the gun at my waist. "Shut your mouth or I'll shoot you."

Brett laughed. "Still the same Tara. Tough but compassionate." Our gazes locked and held for several beats before he let out a long, loud breath. "The guys you're looking for are at a job site. They're putting in landscaping at model homes in a new development in Frisco."

Frisco was the latest north Texas suburb to experience a building boom. Urban sprawl, y'all. With no mountains or oceans standing in the way of development, the Metroplex could easily extend all the way to the Oklahoma border soon.

"What's the address for the housing development?" I asked.

"I'll get it for you." Fiona slipped back into her chair and worked her keyboard. Consulting her computer screen, she read the address aloud.

I inputted it into my GPS and dipped my head, looking from Fiona to Brett. "Thanks, you two. Don't tip them off that I'm coming, okay? The Border Patrol has warned me that sometimes people will disappear if they think they're at risk for being arrested and deported."

Brett let out another sigh, this one shorter and softer. "Okay."

As I turned to go, he said, "Wait! Would it would be better if I come with you? I think the guys will be more comfortable if I'm there to vouch for you."

"That would be great, if you can spare the time," I agreed. Surely the men would be more likely to talk if their boss told them they had nothing to fear from me.

"I've got a meeting with a client here at three o'clock," Brett said, "but I'm free until then." He began walking backward toward his office. "Let me grab my keys and you can follow me."

"Sounds good."

He turned and darted into his office, returning a moment later with a set of jingling keys in hand. He stopped to give Fiona a peck on the cheek before meeting me at the door. She didn't look exactly thrilled that her husband was leaving with his former girlfriend, but she seemed to understand that there were valid reasons for it, ones that would protect their business interests.

With a final scratch under both Napoleon's and Reggie's chins and a "bye boys," I nodded in good-bye to Fiona and turned to exit the building.

Fiona called after us. "It's starting to look nasty out there! Be careful!"

"We will!" Brett called back as we headed out the door.

chapter fifteen

*H*ail, No!

Fiona was right. It was definitely looking nasty outside. The skies were gray and the wind had picked up, the occasional gusts nearly constant now as we fought our way to our cars. Though I squinted, dust carried on the breeze nonetheless found its way into my eyes. I blinked to clear them, the grit scratchy. Nothing like having your retinas sandblasted to put a person in a happy mood. *Ouch!*

Brett had been to the site before and would be familiar with the route, so I let him lead the way. I followed his Navigator out of the lot. Back on the road a few minutes later, I found myself battling Mother Nature as she attempted to blow me off the road and into a ditch. So long as I didn't get hurt, I might not mind if this old G-ride got damaged. Maybe I could talk the new co-director of Criminal Investigations into getting me a new one, maybe a Dodge Charger with a custom candy apple red paint job and shiny rims. But perhaps that would be unprofessional of me to use my personal relationship with my boss for ulterior motives. But if your future husband became your boss, there ought to be some benefits, shouldn't there? Brett seemed to be having trouble, too, his car swerving slightly now and then when a gust of wind hit it.

We'd just reached the suburbs when the storm clouds that had been boiling above north Texas burst wide open. The wind gusts carried buckets of water toward my windshield. *Swoosh-splatter! Swoosh-splatter!* Even on high speed, my wipers weren't up to the task and I squinted so hard my grit-scratched eyeballs threatened to pop. I could barely make anything out.

Brett called my phone. "This is crazy," he said. "There's a diner a half mile up the road. Let's stop there and have lunch while this storm blows over."

"Good idea."

A moment later, I spotted the blurry neon lights of the roadside diner ahead. Brett's brake lights flashed as he slowed to pull into the lot. I turned in after him. I parked as close to the door as I could and ran in, pulling my jacket over my head to shield my hair. Little good it did given that rain was blowing from all directions at once, like an automated car wash. It even seemed to be blowing upward. Not sure how it managed that. Seemed I was destined to get drenched once again.

The wind blew me in the door, slamming it behind me. *Bam!*

"Just one today?" asked the rail-thin redhead at the hostess stand.

The door opened again, blowing Brett into the place, too.

"Two," I replied.

She led us to a corner booth next to the window, where we had a wonderful view of rain pouring out of the clogged gutter overhead. Only a couple of other customers were in the place, both older men drinking coffee and killing time. I guessed they were the drivers of the big rigs parked at the edge of the lot. As hard a time as Brett and I had had keeping our cars on the road, I could only imagine how difficult it would be to try to pilot a tractor-trailer in this mess.

The hostess handed us a couple of plastic-coated menus. "What would you like to drink?"

We both opted for iced tea.

Once she'd gone to get our drinks, Brett eyed me over the table. "It's really good to see you, Tara."

"Good to see you, too."

He cocked his head. "It's also . . . *weird* to see you."

I met his gaze. "Weird to see you, too."

We shared a laugh.

A soft smile played about his lips. "You ever miss me?" he asked softly.

I arched a brow. "You first."

"Honestly?" he said. "Yeah, sometimes. I mean, I love Fiona, but when she's whining about something that needs to be done, I occasionally find myself thinking 'Tara would've just sucked it up and taken care of it herself.'"

"I am pretty self-sufficient, aren't I?"

"You are," he agreed. "But sometimes it's nice to be needed."

And therein was the crux of our problem. I hadn't made him feel needed enough.

"I miss you sometimes, too," I admitted. "When Nick goes full-blown macho shithead over something, I think 'Brett would've just taken this in stride.' But most of the time I love his intensity."

Brett chuckled. "I guess we ended up where we're supposed to be, huh?"

"Yeah. Still good to see you, though."

"You, too." He sat back in the booth and opened his menu.

I opened mine, too, and scanned the options. They had

the usual diner offerings. Burgers. Sandwiches. Chicken with gravy and sides of vegetables. Nothing sounded particularly appealing. But then my eyes spotted a notation at the bottom of the menu. SUBSTITUTE SWEET POTATO FRIES FOR $1 EXTRA.

Oh, hell yeah!

When the waitress came to take our orders, I opted for a grilled sandwich with a side of sweet potato fries.

"Mm-mm." She took my menu. "I love sweet potato fries, too."

Brett and I made small talk while we waited for our food. He had a bid in to do a landscaping project in San Francisco, a challenging endeavor given that the area was on a nearly vertical slope that faced the ocean. "We've got salty air and erosion to contend with," he said, "but there are some plants that do well in that kind of environment. I'm hoping I'll get the gig. It would be nice to go somewhere with a milder climate for a week or two."

I told him about Lu's plans to retire, that Eddie and Nick would be co-directors once she left. He asked whether Nick and I had set a wedding date. I told him things were still in the works, but we were thinking sometime in the fall. He told me about the Lamaze classes he and Fiona were taking, how he'd been practicing the breathing exercises with her, inadvertently hyperventilated, and keeled over in the classroom.

"It was so embarrassing," he said.

I fought a chuckle at the mental image of him passing out at Fiona's feet. "I can imagine."

The waitress returned with our food in her arms and slid my sandwich and sweet potato fries in place in front of me. The diner made the fries waffle style and served them with syrup. Who knew there were so many ways to enjoy these little orange palate pleasers?

"Thanks," I said, reaching for a fry. *Mmm*. These fries were the perfect comfort food for a dreary day. "Want one?" I asked Brett.

"Sure." He reached over and grabbed a couple.

"I said *one*."

"Stingy." He took a quick bite out of both of them. "Wow! These are good."

"Aren't they? I'm hopelessly addicted."

By the time we'd finished our lunch the wind had let up some, but the rain continued to come down. Still, we couldn't spend all day in the diner eating sweet potato fries and hoping the squall would completely blow over. Always a gentleman, Brett insisted on paying for lunch. Rain continued to pummel the earth as he left a tip on the tabletop and paid our bill at the front register. We stepped outside the building to return to our cars. Pulling my blazer back up over my head, and cursing myself for neglecting to check the weather forecast this morning, I bolted back to my car.

Once inside, I wiped the raindrops from my face, started the car, and headed out, once again following Brett. While the rain began to lighten a bit, the shower made the roads slick and it was slow going on the freeways. The white lines separating our lane from the next were barely discernible under the moving water running across the asphalt. As we crept along at fifteen miles per hour—*ping!*—the telltale sound of hail met my ears. *Ping-ping!* Pea-sized bits of ice pelted my car, big enough to cause a noisy racket but not big enough to cause any real damage. *Ping-ping-ping-ping!* We continued on. If neither snow nor rain nor heat nor gloom of night would stop the postal workers from going about their rounds, I wasn't about to let the fact that Dallas had become a midsummer snow cone factory stop me.

It crossed my mind that the landscaping crew wouldn't likely be out in this weather. But given that Texas weather changed on a dime, as well as the fact that Brett said the guys were working at model homes in a new subdivision, I assumed they'd have taken shelter inside one of the houses to wait for the storm to pass.

No such luck.

When we pulled up to the site, not only were there no workers, there were no vehicles, either. The only evidence that Brett's crew had been there were the staked redbud seedlings, the fresh cedar mulch in the flower beds, and the sign out front that read THIS EYE-CATCHING LAWN BROUGHT TO YOU BY ELLINGTON NURSERIES.

After stopping my car, I glanced at my watch. By then it was nearly one o'clock. Maybe the guys hadn't totally given up on their work. Maybe they were merely on a lunch break.

I phoned Brett from my car. "Do you think your guys could be at lunch?"

"I don't know. I'll check with the crew chief and call you back."

While I waited for him to call me back, a photograph and text came in from Agent Castaneda. The text read *An agent found this in a cave in Telephone Canyon*. The pic showed yesterday's date and three names scrawled in the dirt, the short twig that had been used as an improvised writing implement lying beside them. *Nina. Larissa. Yessenia*. Also the word *ayúdanos*. A quick visit to a Spanish-to-English translation Web site told me the word meant "help us."

My heart ricocheted in my chest, not sure whether to sink or be buoyed by this news. One the one hand, the girls had not definitively been located and rescued. They were still in danger, not only from their kidnappers, but from the sweltering west Texas desert heat, either of which could end their young lives. On the other hand, the message meant they'd still been alive yesterday and might not be far from where the message had been found.

My phone chirped now with a call from Brett. "I spoke to the chief. He said he'd checked the forecast and it didn't look like the rain was going to let up all afternoon, so he let the guys go home for the rest of the day. They'll be back here tomorrow morning."

"Dang it!" I needed to speak to these men *now*. Without their testimony, Hidalgo would be set free tomorrow. We had twenty-four hours tops to get some evidence against him or he'd be released. "We're on crunch time," I told Brett. "I'm going to have to visit the guys at their homes."

"I don't have their addresses with me," Brett said. "Want me to call Fiona?"

"I've got their W-2s with me," I said. "Their addresses will be listed on the forms."

I sorted through the paperwork in my briefcase and found the W-2s for the men. Interestingly, all of them showed the same street address, though different unit numbers. They must have rented apartments in the same complex.

We headed back toward town, with me leading the way this time. My GPS instructed me to exit in Garland. I turned down one of the major roads and continued until the voice told me I'd arrived at my destination. Rather than an apartment complex, however, the big blue sign atop the twenty-foot pole told me the place was an extended-stay hotel, the kind with studio-style rooms equipped with kitchenettes and small sofas. Not entirely surprising. It was probably easier and quicker to rent a place here than to secure a lease at a regular apartment building. And since these places came furnished, they'd be perfect for those who'd arrived with nothing to stay in until they got on their feet and amassed the big screen TV set, recliner, and unused exercise equipment that defined a person as an American.

Brett and I parked side by side near the hotel lobby.

I decided to try the unit for Julio Tres first, 226. We climbed the stairs and rapped on the door, which faced the side parking lot. A moment later, a salt-and-pepper-haired woman in her late fifties answered, wearing only a towel and a scowl.

She glanced at Brett before looking me up and down. "I was fixin' to get in the bath. You're a cop, right? You need somethin'?"

Interesting that she'd so quickly pegged me as law enforcement given that the weapons at my waist were hidden by my jacket. In my experience, the people most adept at identifying plainclothes police officers were criminals. I wondered whether this woman might have done time. "I'm looking for Julio. Is he here?"

"He better not be," her words dripped sarcasm, " 'cause I'm the only one paying rent on this place."

"So Julio doesn't live here?"

"I don't know squat about any Julio," she said. "All I can tell you is that I've lived here the past five weeks. *Alone.*"

"Okay," I said. "Sorry to bother you."

Looked like Julio number three had moved on. So should we.

The woman closed the door as we stepped away and headed to unit 243, which was purportedly the home of Diego Robles. I knocked three times but got no answer there. If Diego lived there, he didn't appear to be home.

The third time is supposed to be the charm, right? Brett and I traipsed back downstairs and around to the other side of the building, to Pablo's place, number 105. The door was open, a maid with bushy blond hair vacuuming inside, her body turned away from me, the machine she worked sucking dust at a million decibels. *Krrrrrrr!* The closet doors were open, revealing empty rods. No personal items were visible on the nightstands or coffee table either. But might as well verify that the place was now vacant, right?

"Excuse me!" I called to the housekeeper.

She continued to push the loud vacuum back and forth. *Krrrrr!*

"Ma'am?" I tried again, louder.

Back and forth, back and forth. *Krrr!* Listening to that loud ruckus day after day must have given her a hearing impairment.

Unable to get her attention without shouting loud enough to raise the dead, I stepped inside and walked over to tap the maid on the shoulder. She cried out and jumped back reflexively. I held up my palms to let her know I came in peace.

She flipped a switch to run off the vacuum. "Can I help you?"

"Sorry to interrupt," I said. "I'm an agent for the federal government. I'm looking for Diego Robles. It's my understanding he lives in this unit?"

"He might have," she said. "All I know is this place became vacant as of this morning. I was told to give it a full cleaning so it'll be ready for the next renter."

In other words, I was out of luck.

"Thanks," I said, stepping back out of the unit. I cut a glance a Brett. "We've got one more to try," I said, "but I'm not holding my breath."

We made our way two doors down to 107. Though the door was closed, the curtains had been left open a few inches. A quick peek inside told us this unit was also vacant. Everything was clean and untouched.

"Let's check with the manager." We circled around to the front to consult with the manager on duty, a dark-skinned guy with a friendly demeanor. "Hello, there," he said as we came in the door. "You two looking for a place to stay?"

"Not today, thanks." After introducing myself, I asked about the four men I was seeking.

"Those names sound vaguely familiar," he said. "Let me check the records." He worked his computer mouse and keyboard for a moment. "Looks like Mister Guzmán moved out in February." He went on to tell me that the others had moved out on different dates, but all in early spring.

"Any chance they left a forwarding address?" I asked.

"Sorry," he said, "but we don't ask for that information. We do a walk-through when they leave and work out any damage charges at that time. It's charged to their credit card. There's no need for a forwarding address."

I gritted my teeth in frustration, but managed to say, "Thanks for the information."

The rain had slowed to a mere drizzle as Brett and I stepped outside. We cowered under the covered porte cochere.

I debated my next move. "Any chance the workers provided you with updated addresses?"

"Fiona could tell you," he said. "She handles all the administrative stuff."

I pulled out my cell phone and gave her a call, explaining that I needed to know if the men had updated their addresses.

"I'll take a look," she said. The clicking sound of her keyboard came through the phone. "No," she said a few seconds later. "We still show them all at the address in Garland. Brett pays everyone by direct deposit. Nothing goes into the mail except the W-2s at the end of the year. If they moved since then, they probably didn't think to update their address with us."

I exhaled sharply. "Thanks for checking."

When I ended the call with his wife, Brett asked, "Anything else I can do before I have to head back for my meeting?"

"You can give me the men's phone numbers."

"Of course." He pulled them up on his cell phone and I entered them into my contacts list as he rattled them off.

"I'll see if I can get in touch with them by phone," I said. "If not, I'll swing by the job site in the morning. Any chance you can meet me there?"

He cringed. "Sorry, but I can't. I'm scheduled to present a proposal to the board of directors of a new shopping center in north Arlington tomorrow afternoon and I need the morning to prepare, especially since I've lost time today."

"I understand. Thanks for your help today, Brett. You really went above and beyond."

"Anytime. You take care now."

He stepped forward and gave me a hug, holding on for a long moment. I held him back. We might not have been destined to spend our entire lives together, but neither of us regretted the time we'd shared.

With a final tight squeeze, he released me and we returned to our cars. He gave me a wave through the window as he drove off. I raised a hand, too, wondering when, or if, our paths might cross again.

chapter sixteen

*L*et Them Eat Cake

From my car, I called each of the four numbers Brett had given me. At all four I got only the standard prerecorded message with a computerized voice that referenced the phone number but gave no name. I left a short message for each of the men, identifying myself only as Tara Holloway, a friend of Brett's, and asking them to call me back right away.

I logged into the DMV records to see if any of the men had obtained a driver's license using the names and birthdates of their aliases. Only one driver's license came up under each name, and none of the addresses was local. Looked like the men had used their real names if they'd obtained driver's licenses. Too bad I didn't know what those real names were. Without them, I was at a dead end.

Out of ideas, I returned to the office. Fortunately, the storm had ceased by the time I returned and my clothing had nearly dried. Back at my desk, I phoned Agent Castaneda to give him an update on my end of the investigation.

He sounded hopeful. "Any luck? Got someone willing to testify that Hidalgo smuggled them into the U.S.?"

"Not yet."

"Dammit!" he blurted in frustration.

I felt the same way. "The first Julio should be at the restaurant where he works tomorrow morning. His shift starts at five a.m. I'll check in with him first thing. I doubt Sister Mary Margaret will let me close to Julio number two again, so I don't see any point in going back to Saint Lucia School. Number three works for a nursery, along with three of the others. I tried to catch them at their work site today, but there were heavy rains here and they were gone by the time I arrived. I checked the hotel where they'd been living, but they've all moved out. Their boss doesn't have a current home address for any of them, but I've left each of them a voice mail asking them to call me ASAP. If I don't get what I need from them tonight, I'll head back out to their work site tomorrow morning, see what I can find out."

Castaneda groaned in frustration. "I was hoping you'd have something by now, but I can tell it's not for lack of trying. I appreciate your help, Agent Holloway."

"Glad to do it. I'll be back in touch when there's something new to report."

When we ended the call, I phoned Bethany Flagler. "Any chance the names Amelia Yeo or Gwen Rosenthal sound familiar to you? Maybe Jocelyn Harris or Thomas Hoffmeyer?"

"No," she said. "Should they?"

"Not necessarily," I said. "Just trying to find out if there's a connection I'm missing." I asked her to send me a list of the same information I'd asked Amelia and Gwen for. Addresses and landlords. Doctors. Schools. Anywhere that someone might have both interacted with her personally and have access to her social security number.

"It'll take me a little while to pull all of this information together," she said, "but I'll get it to you as soon as I can."

"Great."

With both of my big cases in a holding pattern, I tackled the next file on the stack. It was a relatively easy one in which a woman who made custom quilts had neglected to report and pay tax on any of her income. She claimed she only performed the services for neighbors and friends, and that the income from her quilts was a gift, not business earnings. Her Web site advertising her services to everyone and anyone said otherwise. I shot her off a letter telling her she had one week to make payment arrangements on her quilting income or we'd begin seizing her assets. Until she responded, I'd be on needles and pins. *Ha.*

A few minutes after five o'clock, Nick stepped to my door. "Just heard from my mother. She and your mom decided they're going to make our wedding cake. They've spent all day in the kitchen baking a bunch of different cakes they want us to sample."

"My mom's still in town?" I'd assumed she'd headed back to Nacogdoches by now.

"She and my mother are having the time of their lives. It's like a girls' slumber party over there."

I rounded up my purse. "Any chance they've made us dinner, too?"

Nick scoffed. "Those two? They probably engaged in a knife fight for the privilege."

Yep, both of our mothers were very old school, priding themselves on their prowess in the kitchen. Nick and I were grateful beneficiaries.

We left the office and walked to our personal vehicles.

I followed Nick to his mother's house, where we found both women in the kitchen. The smells of frying foods filled the air, and a lineup of ten frosted cakes sat on the table. Our own personal bakery.

"Hey there, hon," my mom said, giving me a hug. She stepped back and hesitated a moment, giving me an odd look. "Did you try a different makeup?"

"No," I replied. "Why?"

"Your skin looks a little . . . off."

"Off? What do you mean?"

"You look orange-ish."

Nick stepped closer, bending down and running a thumb over my cheek. "She's right. Your skin looks like a tangerine."

"What?!?" I reached up, grabbed a metal frying pan from the hanging rack, and used it to examine my reflection. As much as I hated to admit it, they had a point. I returned the frying pan to the rack. "I got caught in the rain today. It must've smeared my eye shadow or something." Surely the odd color would wash off once I took a shower.

Nick went to the stove, lifting a lid off a pot. "Is supper ready yet?"

"Whenever you are," Bonnie said. "I set the table in the dining room since the kitchen table is covered with cakes."

The four of us retrieved plates and served up a country dinner with loads of vegetables and sides of warm corn bread. We all poured generous glasses of Bonnie's peach sangria from a glass pitcher to go along with the meal. My mom rounded up a legal pad on which she'd jotted notes and a long list of to-do items. As we ate, we discussed some of the plans she and Bonnie had come up with that day.

"We were thinking we'd look for a caterer who's willing to cook some of our recipes," Mom said. "Everyone's always telling us how good our food tastes."

"They don't lie." I raised my glass of peach sangria in salute. "I love that idea!"

"Sounds good to me, too," Nick agreed. "There's not a professional chef on God's green earth who can out-cook either of you."

Our mothers beamed.

"Now," my mother said, "about the colors."

Nick stopped with his fork halfway to his mouth. "Colors?"

I turned to him. "Couples usually choose a color theme for their wedding."

"Really?" he said. "I never noticed."

"You're a guy," I said. "Of course you didn't notice."

"How about we go with navy blue and silver?" Nick suggested.

I scoffed. "We're not decorating our wedding to look like a Dallas Cowboys pep rally."

Nick slid me a sly smile. "We're not even married yet and you're calling all the shots."

"Not all of them," I replied. "Just this one." Besides, if we were going with team colors, I'd prefer burnt orange and white, the University of Texas Longhorns colors.

"Anyway," Mom said, redirecting the conversation, "Bonnie and I were thinking pale blue and lavender. That way the decorations and flowers will match the color scheme at the house for the reception."

"Sounds great, Mom." I turned to Nick. "What do you think?"

"If it sounds good to you," he said, "it sounds good to me."

Bonnie topped off Nick's sangria. "We thought floral

arrangements with blue hydrangeas in them would be pretty."

Mom nodded. "We could accent them with some purple asters. If you don't like that idea, we could go with calla lilies. Those things come in every color imaginable these days. Or we could mix it up and do some of both, maybe even add some of the roses from the yard."

I enjoyed gardening and had spent untold hours each spring and fall helping my mother in her flower beds. Given my tomboy tendencies, plus the fact that I was a bit of a daddy's girl, gardening had been a special time for the two of us, one of my most cherished mother-daughter memories. "That sounds wonderful," I said. "Let's mix it up."

When we were done with dinner, Bonnie shooed us away from the table. "I'll clear," she said, turning to my mother. "Let them eat cake."

"Then off with our heads?" I teased.

"You can keep your noggin'," Bonnie said with a wink.

My mother led us to the kitchen table, which was covered in cakes frosted with white buttercream icing. She pointed at each cake in turn. "We've got classic white, vanilla, lemon, strawberry, chocolate, Italian cream, hazelnut, red velvet, black forest, and marble. All homemade recipes, of course."

Of course.

"You don't have to pick just one, though," she said. "Bonnie and I are planning on making a five-layer cake, so you can do a combination."

"Five layers?" I asked. "How tall is the cake going to be?"

"With the pedestals?" Bonnie shrugged from her place at the sink. "About four feet or so."

"The cake will be taller than the flower girl!" Still, while the two might be going a little overboard, they were

having a ball. I wasn't about to take this away from them.
And, really, what kind of crazy person would complain
about too much cake? Was there even such a thing as too
much cake?

Mom waved a dismissive hand. "There'll be enough
wedding cake for the guests to have seconds if anyone
wants 'em, and we can let everyone take some cake home
in a doggie bag."

Using a long knife, my mother cut tiny pieces of each
of the cakes for us to sample, arranging them on separate
plates.

Bonnie rounded up a set of dessert forks and handed
them to us. "Everyone try the white first."

We each took a bite.

"Thoughts?" Bonnie asked.

"Not bad," I said.

"But?" she asked, arching a brow.

I hated to sound critical given that they'd slaved in the
kitchen all day, but I knew she wanted me to be honest.
"But not really special, either."

Luckily, she let me off the hook. "I had the same thought,"
she said. "It's too everyday for a special occasion like a
wedding. Okay, now for the vanilla."

We each took a bite.

Mmm. "Now *this* is good," I said. "I've never tasted vanilla quite this way before. What did y'all do?"

Mom grinned. "Bonnie likes French vanilla but you
know I'm partial to Mexican. So we put in a little of both."

It might be a culinary culture clash, but it tasted fantastic. "Let's definitely have a vanilla layer."

His mouth full, Nick nodded in agreement.

We sampled each of the other flavors, finally deciding
on the vanilla, lemon, strawberry, Italian cream, and hazelnut. We'd save the chocolate for the groom's cake, which

Nick suggested be made to look like either a football or a wide-mouthed bass.

"Wonderful!" Mom said, unfazed by the football and fish, crossing *cake* off her list of wedding details. She looked from me to Nick. "Ready to talk invitations?"

"Why not?" Nick said.

Bonnie reached into a tote bag that was sitting on one of the kitchen chairs and pulled out a forest's worth of paper. She had samples of invitations in everything from a basic white with black print to a fancy lavender card with a scalloped edge and silver embossed lettering.

"Whoa," Nick said. "You must have hit every printer in Dallas."

"Just about," Bonnie said. "We wanted to make sure you had plenty to choose from."

Nick and I sorted through them. While I could certainly appreciate elegance, I saw no reason to spend a small fortune on an invitation people would glance at and toss once they'd entered the information in their calendars. Besides, my parents had already splurged on my dress.

Nick pulled out one in a yellowed hue designed to look aged. The edge was professionally frayed. "How about this one?"

I scrunched up my nose. "That looks like something a pirate's treasure map would be printed on."

He chuckled. "That's why I picked it. It feels adventurous."

I picked out another with a line of red hearts across the bottom. "What do you think of this?"

"Looks too much like a valentine," Nick said.

He had a point.

We eventually settled on a white card with a lacy looking watermark. Bonnie and my mother agreed that it was classy but understated.

"You'll need to decide on the wording, too," Bonnie said. She grabbed a computer printout from the countertop. "Here are some suggestions we found online."

Several contained the traditional wording. *Mr. and Mrs. so-and-so invite you to the wedding of their daughter such-and-such to insert-groom's-name-here.* Given that Bonnie was putting so much time and effort into planning the event, I didn't want her excluded.

I pointed to another option. "What do you think of this phrasing?"

Nick read it out loud. "The parents of Nick Pratt and Tara Holloway invite you to a celebration of love." He snorted. "Sounds like we're hosting an orgy, not a wedding."

"An orgy?" Bonnie rolled up the paper and smacked Nick across the shoulder with it. "I raised you better than that!"

He slid her a grin. "You certainly did. It's not your fault Tara has corrupted me."

My mother grabbed the papers out of Bonnie's hand and gave Nick a good-natured smack of her own. "Don't you talk about my daughter that way!"

"Or your future wife." I grabbed the papers from my mom and treated Nick to a third smack.

Nick turned his gaze up to the heavens and raised imploring arms. "Dear Lord. What have I gotten myself into?"

chapter seventeen

$\mathcal{L}$ost Dog

At home Wednesday night, I climbed into bed, my cat Anne curled up next to me. It was after ten o'clock already, but I figured it couldn't hurt to catch another episode of *Amor y Vengaza* before closing my eyes. Besides, maybe one of Brett's workers would call. I hadn't heard a peep from any of them, even though I'd called all four and left a second message asking them to get in touch with me. Were they purposefully avoiding me? Or had they simply not checked their phones? Brett mentioned they had children. Maybe they were busy with dishes and laundry and baths and bedtime stories. I knew how crazy busy it was for my friends who had small children. They could barely come up for air, let alone make a phone call.

This episode of *A y V* was even more engaging than the last. Isidora suspected her new husband wasn't actually at a business dinner as he'd said, so she'd tailed him to an elegant restaurant at a fancy hotel. She'd slipped a bellhop a wad of cash in return for his uniform, tucked her long dark locks up into the hat, and positioned herself in the lobby near the restaurant where she could keep an eye on her husband. Her methods might be crazy, but I had to admire the woman's ingenuity.

When a gorgeous woman with honey-colored hair arrived, Isidora's eyes flared again. *Was this woman a business associate? Or her husband's secret lover?*

Once again, the show ended on a cliffhanger, my questions—and Isidora's—unanswered.

"You're killing me!" I cried at the screen.

The television automatically began the next episode. Who was I to fight technology?

The show opened in the hotel, Isidora's husband and the so-called business associate finished their meal and walked to the hotel's elevators. Instead of parting ways there, they stepped into a car together. The crafty Isidora, still wearing the bellhop's uniform, grabbed a loaded luggage cart when an actual bellhop turned his attention away. She pushed the cart onto the elevator, hiding behind it so that the two wouldn't realize it was she who had entered the car after them. She reached out to the panel of buttons and, taking notice that the one for the tenth floor was lit up, pushed the button for fourteen.

Isidora's husband and the woman exited on the tenth floor. Isidora stayed in place, as if planning to go on up to the fourteenth floor. But we viewers knew better. She was going to follow them. Yep, Isidora was a woman of action. I'd learned that right away.

Just as the doors were about to close, the camera zoomed in on a hand with red-tipped nails pushing them back open. She stuck her head out of the opening, watching with heavily made-up eyes to see which room the two entered. Abandoning the luggage cart in the elevator, she scurried down the hall and put her ear to the door of room 1022. The show ended there, leaving us wondering what, if anything, Isidora might have overheard.

I couldn't very well go to sleep without finding out, could I?

No way!

I watched yet another episode from start to finish, then the next, then the next. Isidora thought she'd heard some moans of passion and left a bottle of champagne in an ice bucket outside the hotel room door, along with two glass flutes she'd laced with poison and a note reading *Compliments of Le Belle Maison Hotel*. Her husband and his mistress—*or was she truly just a business associate?*—barely managed to call for help before succumbing to the poison. The two ended up in the emergency room, fighting for their lives. Of course, Isidora played the shocked and worried wife role as well as any Academy Award winner, sobbing into a tissue at the hospital. When nobody was looking, she sneaked into the room of her husband's business associate and/or lover and turned off the IV drip delivering the antidote into the woman's system.

When I finally checked my clock, it was after two a.m. *¡Ay carramba!* Where had the time gone?

I programmed the DVR to begin recording new episodes of the show so I could watch them once I caught up on the older shows on the app. With a reluctant sigh, I switched the television off and went to sleep, my dreams filled with scenes of *amor* and some of *vengaza*.

When my alarm buzzed at 5:30 Thursday morning, I was tempted to hit snooze, roll over in bed, and go back to sleep. But I wouldn't let myself. I was dead tired after staying up half the night watching the telenovela, but there was too much at stake, most importantly the lives of innocent people taken advantage of by an unscrupulous, heartless coyote. I had mere hours to collect the evidence needed to keep Salvador Hidalgo in jail. The weight of the world, or at least North and South America, was on my shoulders.

While my cats noisily crunched their kitty kibble, I myself crunched my way through a bowl of Fruity Pebbles, washing the colorful flakes down with a steaming mug of coffee flavored with a sweet hazelnut creamer. My RDA of sugar, caffeine, and red dye number three thus fulfilled, I set off to fight for truth, justice, and effective tax administration.

I left my house at the ungodly hour of 6:15. My first destination was El Loro Loco. According to the restaurant's manager, Julio Número Uno should be working the breakfast and lunch shifts today. Thankfully, the sun was out today, and the rain the storm had brought the day before had mostly dried up. The only evidence that a storm had blown through was a few puddles here and there and the humid heat that made you sticky and sweaty, as if soup were coming out of your pores. *Ick.*

I made my way across town in the bumper-to-bumper early morning traffic, making slow progress and wondering what acts of vengeance—or *vengaza*—Isidora Davila would have in store for me when I got home and could watch another episode. The woman might be a psychotic, self-centered, narcissistic psychopath, but she made a damn interesting lead character. And even though I didn't agree with her methods, you had to respect the woman for taking matters into her own hands and never letting anyone get one over on her.

Eddie's car was already in the lot when I arrived a few minutes before seven o'clock. Looked like he'd beat me here. I pulled into the spot next to him and glanced over. He'd reclined his seat and was fast asleep, his mouth hanging open like the squawking parrot's had the other day. Who could blame him for stealing a moment to snooze? Our jobs were demanding enough, but he had two young girls and a good-sized house to take care of on top of that. All I had were my cats and my cozy town house with the postage-stamp-sized patio.

I climbed out of my car and walked over to Eddie's window. From inside his car came the faint buzz of his snore.

"Eddie?" I said softly, not wanting to jar him. When he continued to snooze, I spoke a little louder. "Eddie? Hey, Eddie. Wake up."

He remained in dreamland.

"Good morning, merry sunshine!" I sang, swinging my arms and performing an improvised soft shoe routine.

Zzzzz.

I stopped dancing and raised my voice. "Eddie?" Still nothing. The guy was *out*.

Having failed to rouse him with words, I raise a hand and tapped on Eddie's window. *Tap-tap-tap!*

He woke with a start, shrieked—"Aaah!"—and reflexively threw out his arms, inadvertently hitting the horn. *Honk!*

When he regained his composure, he scrubbed a hand over his face and unrolled his window. "Why the heck did you sneak up on me like that?"

"Sneak up on you?" I raised my palms. "I've been out here calling your name. I even sang to you!"

He shook his head as if to shake himself awake, rolled his window back up, and climbed out of the car. "You owe me big for coming out this early."

"I do," I agreed. "How about I buy you a couple of breakfast tacos to repay you?"

"Make it three and I'll call it even."

"It's a deal."

We entered the restaurant, greeted by the same mechanical parrot from before. *"SQUAWK! Welcome to El Loro Loco!"*

The other day I'd thought the macaw was precocious but cute, but having made little progress on my cases and having enjoyed little sleep the night before, I found his words especially grating this morning. Eddie, who'd never been fond of the bird, yanked out his pocket square and draped it over the bird's head, covering the circular motion sensor on his forehead. "That ought to shut the birdbrain up."

The same older woman was working the hostess stand. She frowned when she looked up and saw the two of us walking toward her. "If you're looking for Julio," she snapped, "he's not here. He called in yesterday and quit." Her pointed expression said she believed I was to blame for his resignation. "All he wanted to do was make a living. Why can't people just live and let live?" She muttered something in Spanish that it was probably just as well I didn't understand.

"I'm very sorry about Julio," I told her. "It was never my intention for him to leave the restaurant."

She answered with an angry wave of her hand, as if willing us to be gone.

I pulled my wallet from my purse. "Can we get three breakfast tacos to go?"

"They're for me," Eddie said, raising his hands in innocence. "I'm only along for the ride."

"Twelve dollars," the woman said, holding out her hand.

I gestured to the chalkboard mounted on the front of the hostess stand. "This says breakfast tacos to go are only two dollars each."

"Not for you," she said. "You give me trouble, you pay double."

"I think that's illegal," I told her with a frown. But I handed her the money anyway. I'd already promised Eddie I'd buy him breakfast and I wasn't going to let him down after he'd risen extra early to help me on my case.

The woman stuffed the cash into her apron pocket, disappeared through the swinging kitchen door, and returned a few seconds later with a paper bag bearing the likeness of the parrot. She shoved the bag at Eddie. "Enjoy."

"Thanks."

He snatched his pocket square back off the robotic parrot's head as we left the restaurant. *"SQUAWK!"* the macaw called after me. *"Rot in hell, Tara!"*

Okay, maybe that's not really what he said. But that's how I heard it.

With a sigh, I slid back into my car and drove to the mobile home park where Julio lived, hoping to catch him there. Eddie trailed along after me. As I pulled up to the unit, I noticed three things. The first was that there was no car in the driveway. The second was the young boy's stuffed dog lying under the porch steps. The third was a white sign with red lettering in the front window: FOR RENT.

Uh-oh.

The curtains on the front windows were open, but the morning sun reflecting off the glass made it impossible to see inside. I climbed out of my car and retrieved the dog from under the steps. Eddie joined me and we ascended the stairs together to rap on the front door. *Knock-knock.*

When no noise came from inside and nobody came to the door, I ventured over to the window. Shielding my eyes with my free hand, I put my face to the glass and peered in. The living room was vacant.

"See anything?" Eddie called from where he waited on the porch.

"The room's empty."

"Aw, shit."

Aw, shit, was right. I continued to the other windows, peering inside them as well. All of the rooms were empty. No people. No furniture. No nothing.

I looked down at the dog in my hand. "Where did your family go?" He was no help whatsoever. He merely stared back at me, his felt tongue hanging out of his mouth in a perpetual pant.

I turned to Eddie and motioned for him to join me. "Let's go talk to the management office. Maybe they'll know something."

We walked down the row of mobile homes until we reached the first one at the entrance, which was designated as the management office. The door contained a metal mail slot for tenants to submit payments after hours. I knocked and a thin middle-aged man in jeans and a polo shirt answered. After identifying myself and Eddie I asked, "I see that the home on lot twenty-eight is for rent. Can you tell me what happened to the family that used to live there?"

"They moved out in the middle of the night Tuesday," he replied. "Slipped a note through the drop box to let me know." He gestured down at the mail slot.

"Do you know why they moved?"

"Not exactly," he said. "They just said they had a family emergency and had to go. Why?"

I explained that the man and woman might have information that could be useful in a criminal investigation.

His eyes narrowed. "They weren't dealing drugs, were they? I don't allow that on my properties."

"No," I said. "Nothing like that. In fact, they were the victims in the crime I'm investigating."

"Oh," he said. "Okay."

"Any chance they left a forwarding address?"

"No," he said. "The note only said they'd had to move out."

"May we see the note?"

He stepped away from the door and returned with the

note, which was printed on wide-ruled notebook paper. It was written in Spanish so I couldn't precisely tell what it said, but the words *familia* and *emergencia* were obvious. There were no numbers on the note, no names of towns or cities or states.

I looked back up at the man. "You can read Spanish?"

"Only a little. One of the other tenants told me what it said."

"Okay if I take a picture of it?"

He lifted a shoulder. "Don't see any problem with that."

"Hold this." I handed the stuffed dog to Eddie and held the note in my left hand while snapping a photo with my right. Nick could translate it word for word for me later. Having lived in Mexico for three years, he was fluent in Spanish.

Eddie and I both gave the man our business cards.

"If they come back or you hear from them," I said, "please ask them to call us."

"All right."

I held out the dog. "I found their son's dog. They might come back for it."

The man looked down at the worn, slightly dirty thing, his nose quirking with minor disgust. He took the dog from me and tossed it in his wastebasket.

Eddie fished the dog out immediately and gave him a disapproving look. "Please also tell them we have the dog and would be glad to return it to them."

He shrugged. "Suit yourself."

Besides being annoyed with him, we thanked the man and returned to our cars.

Eddie handed me the stuffed dog. "What's the plan now?"

"I'm going to check in with four guys at a construction site."

"I'll follow you."

Before I could object, he was already heading to his car. Oh, well. Even though I'd been trying to hide the fact that my coyote investigation involved Brett's business, it couldn't hurt to have a second agent with me this morning, especially since Brett couldn't be there to reassure his men I meant them no harm. If they wouldn't open up to me, maybe they'd relate to a fellow family man like Eddie.

I climbed into my car, placed the dog on the passenger seat, and closed my eyes for a brief moment. Julio and his family had fled to God only knows where. In their quick, late-night departure, his little boy had dropped the stuffed dog that brought him comfort. And it was all my fault.

I opened my eyes and banged my hands on the steering wheel. "Dammit!"

My gut twisted. Sure, I wanted to help nail a human trafficker who'd left people to die horrible deaths in the desert. I also wanted to do whatever I could to help find the kidnapped girls. But I didn't want to scare desperate people, to send them running underground into hiding, to make their lives any harder.

I sat there a long moment, conflicted, before eyeing myself in the rearview mirror. "Are you doing the right thing, Tara?"

Unfortunately, my reflection didn't know the answer any more than I did.

chapter eighteen

$\mathcal{T}$alk Is Cheap.
Lawyers Aren't.

As I left the mobile home park with the stuffed dog riding in my passenger seat, the song "Where, Oh Where Has My Little Dog Gone?" played through my mind. Poor little boy. He was probably singing that song himself. Or a Spanish equivalent of it.

With Eddie trailing along behind me, I headed directly for the job site in Frisco where Brett's men were working. After weaving our way through traffic, we pulled into the new development. Ahead were a lineup of new, green heavy-duty pickups with king cabs and attached flatbed trailers. Lettering on the doors identified the vehicles as part of the Ellington Nurseries fleet. The lettering matched that on the sign at the nursery, including the *I*s dotted with daisies. Those trucks didn't come cheap. Looked like Brett's business was doing well. Good for him. He'd need to earn a pretty penny to send little Spencer or Evan to college. At the rate tuition was increasing, it would probably cost a million dollars by the time the kid was ready to go. I hoped my own Hank or Waylon or Reba or Dolly would land a scholarship.

I pulled to a stop behind the trucks and looked out at the site. The crew wore green uniforms that also bore the logo for Brett's business, as well as matching lightweight hats with flaps along the back designed to keep the sun off the wearer's neck. The group performed various tasks. Two men carried PVC pipes from the trailer to the lawn and began laying them out in a pattern for the lawn sprinkler systems. Another used a shovel to dig holes along the side of the house for the red-tip photinia bushes lined up behind him. A fourth lined a flower bed with decorative stone. I surmised the four must be the men going by Julio Guzmán, Pablo Perez, Miguel Gallegos, and Diego Robles. I wasn't sure who was who, or what their actual names were, but I hoped at least one of them could speak English. Growing up in east Texas, not far from the Louisiana border, I'd opted to take French in high school. In retrospect, Spanish might have been the more useful option. It's not like I got down to New Orleans very often.

I climbed out of my car and stopped at the curb so as not to interfere with their work.

Eddie stepped up beside me and pointed to the sign in the yard. "Ellington Nurseries. Why does that name sound familiar?"

"Because it's Brett's business."

"Brett? You mean that guy you dated before Nick?"

"Yeah."

Eddie chortled. "Well, isn't this interesting. I wonder what Nick would think if he knew you were out here cavorting with your old flame."

I rolled my eyes. "I'm hardly cavorting with my old flame. Brett's not even going to be here today."

"Oh, yeah?" Eddie arched a suspicious bow. "And how, exactly, do you know that?"

Because he'd told me so yesterday when we parted ways

at a hotel. But I couldn't very well say that, could I? I tried to play nonchalant. "Because I spoke with Brett yesterday. It's standard procedure. After all, he's the owner of the business."

"I'll give you that," Eddie said. "How did Nick take it?"

"How did Nick take what?" I asked.

"When you told him you'd spoken with Brett?"

Ummm . . .

My failure to respond in a timely manner told Eddie what I hadn't said in words.

"You haven't told him?" He scoffed. "Not even married yet and already keeping secrets from each other. That's not supposed to start until year three or four."

I replied with a frown. "I don't tell Nick everything I do all day, and he doesn't tell me, either. We share the important stuff. Seeing Brett wasn't a big deal. Besides, why should I tell Nick something that's just going to piss him off?"

Eddie raised his hands in surrender. "Okay, okay. You have your reasons. Just don't expect me to keep your secrets if he asks."

I put my hands on his hips. "But you're my partner!"

"I was *his* partner first. And now I'm his best man."

He had me there. *Ugh.* There was no point discussing the matter further, so I figured we might as well get to work. The crew chief didn't appear to have arrived yet, but we didn't have time to waste. The clock was ticking on Hidalgo's release. I turned to the men. "Hello!" I called. "Are you Julio, Pablo, Miguel, and Diego?"

The men looked our way, looked us over, then looked to each other, exchanging nervous glances. Our plain sedans and conservative clothing probably pegged us as government employees. No doubt they were anxious about our presence here. I did my best to alleviate their concerns.

"Brett told me you would be here," I said. "He and I know each other personally, though I am here on business."

The looks on their faces told me that they didn't quite understand me. The fact that they didn't come closer told me they feared what I might be saying.

"I know Brett," I repeated, hoping that dropping their boss's name would put them a little more at ease.

"Brett," one of the men repeated and nodded. "Brett, *sí*."

I racked my brain. "Brett and I are *amigos*." I supposed it wasn't incorrect to refer to Brett and myself as friends even though we no longer kept in touch, though honestly I'd used the term because it was the only one I knew.

The man nodded again. The others simply continued to stare, the one who'd been digging leaning on his shovel, his grip as tight as the look on his face.

I glanced from one to the other and so on. "I'm investigating Salvador Hidalgo."

At the mention of the man's name, all four men stiffened and began speaking under their breath in Spanish. I raised a palm. "You're not in trouble."

Anxiety tightened their weathered faces. Clearly, they understood the word *trouble*.

I raised the other palm, too. "No trouble."

They exchanged glances again. I was getting nowhere here.

Eddie cut a look my way. "These guys don't speak English?"

"Apparently not."

"And you didn't think to get an interpreter out here?" He gave me a look that told me just how *estúpido* he thought I was.

"I assumed their crew chief would speak English," I

said in my defense, "but he doesn't seem to be here. I guess I could call an interpreter service."

"That'll take time," Eddie pointed out.

Time was something we were running very short on at the moment. We had only a matter of hours before Hidalgo would be released.

I turned to the men. "When will your crew chief arrive?"

They looked from me to each other. Clearly they didn't understand what I was asking them.

I looked to Eddie. "Did you take Spanish in high school?"

"No," he said. "I took Latin."

I threw up my hands. "Why would you study a dead language?"

"Because I'd heard that it would help me do better on standardized tests," he said. "And because a girl I had a huge crush on had signed up for it."

I turned my attention back to the men. "Boss?" I asked, tapping on my watch to indicate time. Apparently my mime skills were no better than my language skills. They stared at me with puzzled faces.

"You need to call Nick," Eddie said. "He knows Spanish from his time in Cancún and he'd want to do whatever he could to help those missing girls."

Eddie was right, of course. That didn't stop me from shooting him a glare, though. I pulled out my phone, took a deep breath to steel myself, and dialed Nick. "Hey," I said when he answered. "Any chance you can come out to a job site and do some translating for me?"

"No problemo," he said. "What's the address?"

I gave him the information. I debated whether to tell him that the men worked for Brett, but decided not to. He'd only fume on the drive up about my failure to inform him earlier of that fact. Better to let him drive up and let me explain in person, when I could bat my eyes and try to look adorable and forgivable.

Eddie and I returned to wait by our cars and the men returned to work, glancing our way occasionally, surely wondering why the heck we were sticking around. Luckily, none of them made any attempt to abscond.

Eddie had been responding to e-mails and I'd just finished watching another episode of *Amor y Vengaza* on my phone when Nick pulled up behind us a half hour later. I stepped to his door and met him on the street. But I was a split second too late. His eyes went past me to the Ellington Nurseries logo on the side of the closest truck. Then his eyes locked on me with a laser-like intensity.

He slammed his door with unnecessary force. *Slam!* "You're interviewing *Brett's* workers?" he snapped. "When were you going to tell me?"

Um . . . never? I tried to sound nonchalant. "When I was looking through the W-2s filed under the aliases, I noticed that several of the men using the fake names worked at Ellington Nurseries." I shrugged. "It was just a funny coincidence. It didn't seem like a big deal."

Nick scoffed. "Nice try. You seeing your old flame might not be a big deal, but you not telling me about it is."

So he was going to play the old *honesty is the best policy* card, huh? I reached out a hand, but he took a step back to get out of my reach. "Come on, Nick. You know I love you."

"Again, not the issue." He arched an accusing brow. "What else aren't you telling me?"

Now he was starting to piss me off. Not because he didn't have a point, but because he was making me feel like the jerk I'd been. "You want to know everything?" I snapped back. "Okay, here goes. Before getting dressed this morning, I sniffed the armpits of this blazer to see if I could get away with wearing it one more time before taking it to the cleaners. Also, the elastic on this underwear is making my nether regions itch."

"Too much information!" Eddie waved his hands in a stopping motion. "*I* never asked to know everything!"

Ignoring Eddie, Nick just stared at me a moment with a look of disappointment and disgust on his face.

In for a penny, in for a pound, right? "I saw Brett yesterday at his office. His wife Fiona was there, big as a barn with their baby boy. They're going to name him Spencer, or maybe Evan. Brett saw my ring and congratulated me on our engagement."

I thought the latter statement would make Nick relax a bit, but it had the opposite effect. "So you didn't tell him about our engagement until he saw the ring?"

I closed my eyes for a moment in exasperation. "Nick, please. Let's be adults."

"I will if you will."

I fought the urge to blow a raspberry at the man I loved. Really, it was only because I loved him that he could irritate me this much, and I knew the same went for him. If only either of us could feel apathetic. But no. "When would I have told him?" I said. "I don't keep in touch with the guy."

He seemed to soften a little at that.

"I'm sorry, okay?" I added. "I won't keep things from you again."

"You better not," he said, an implied threat in his voice.

Or what? I wanted to say. *Sheesh.* This was beyond ridiculous. Two people who cared as much about each other as me and Nick should be above these petty squabbles, shouldn't we?

"Look, can you just help me?" I begged. "Then you can go back to my office and put thumbtacks on my chair if you want."

He grunted and moved past me and Eddie, heading toward the men. With his long legs, Eddie was able to keep pace. I trotted along after them, having to jog to keep up with their strides.

"Hola," Nick said to the men, following it up with his name and the fact that he worked with the IRS.

The men nodded and returned greetings.

Nick turned to me. "What do you want me to ask them?"

"Ask them whether Salvador Hidalgo is the one who provided them with the birth certificates and social security cards they used to get their jobs at Ellington Nurseries."

Nick asked the men the question. Again, they exchanged glances but no information. Nick asked them something else, a question he'd come up with on his own. Three of the men engaged in a two-minute discussion with him while the fourth remained silent. When the men became quiet again, Nick turned to me. "They're afraid you're trying to get them deported. They don't want to talk."

I fought the urge to scream in frustration. While I couldn't blame the men at all, I had to get some concrete evidence for the Border Patrol so they could keep Salvador Hidalgo under lock and key. I racked my brain for any option that might get me the information I needed, while also assuring these men that they were protected. Of course, I wasn't entirely sure that they *were* protected. I didn't know their particular situations. "What if I get them a lawyer who can advise them of their rights?"

Nick turned back to the men and said something about an *abogado.*

The men nodded, which I took as a good sign.

"You get them an attorney," he said, "and if the lawyer

says they're protected, they'll talk. But they can't afford to pay. You're going to have to find one from Legal Aid or something."

The attorneys at Legal Aid bore heavy caseloads and there was no assurance they could get to this matter right away. Fortunately, my best friend, Alicia, was now married to a lawyer. Her husband, Daniel Blowitz, worked for the law firm of Gertz, Gertz, and Schwartz in Dallas. The firm was a rather large one, a full-service firm with attorneys in every legal field from corporate law, to criminal defense, to oil and gas, to immigration. The firm also encouraged their staff to perform pro bono work for low-income clients. The policy was a win-win. People who couldn't afford good lawyers were able to obtain solid legal representation, while the firm was able to tout its charitable work on its Web site and in other public relations materials. *Look at how noble we are! We help the poor and downtrodden!*

I whipped out my phone. "I'll call Daniel. His firm does pro bono work." I hated to bother him while he and Alicia were still on their honeymoon, but it couldn't be helped.

"Good idea," Nick agreed.

I dialed Daniel's number.

When he answered, his voice was gruff with sleep. While he could have chastised me for waking him up so early, he knew I wouldn't have called unless it was extremely urgent. "Hey, Tara," he said. "Everything okay?"

"Not at all." I explained about Hidalgo, the bodies in the desert, the kidnapped girls. I also told him what I needed. "It's urgent. We need affidavits this morning. Can your firm help these guys?"

"It's short notice," he said, his voice fully awake now. "But I'll see if I can round up someone in our immigration department. I'll call you back."

"Great. Thanks."

Nick, Eddie, and I stood around while we waited for Daniel to call back.

Nick cast a glance at the men before looking back at me. "Thought you might be interested to know that the Spanish these guys speak isn't Mexican Spanish. They wouldn't give any specifics until they talk to the lawyer, but chances are they're from somewhere else in Central or South America."

"You can distinguish the accents?" I looked at him with what had to be clear admiration. "You've got mad skills, Nick."

"No shit. From now on, you can call me *jefe*. And that applies to both the office and the bedroom."

Eddie groaned. "You two need to knock this shit off before my burritos come back up."

Lest Eddie lose his breakfast, the two men turned the discussion to last night's baseball game between the Texas Rangers and the Houston Astros, while I watched a few more minutes of an *Amor y Vengaza* episode. I'd become as addicted to the show as I was to sweet potato fries, and that was saying a lot.

A few minutes later, Daniel called back. "Mimi Ibarra is willing to meet with them at ten o'clock."

Thank God! "Thanks, Daniel. You're a lifesaver." *Literally.* We ended the call and I turned to Nick. "Tell them the lawyer can meet with them at ten o'clock."

Nick turned to the men and said something. Their responses were unclear to me. Nick turned a fresh frown on me. "What's pretty boy's phone number?"

"Why?"

"These men want to make sure it's okay with Brett that they take time off to meet with the attorney. They don't want to risk their jobs."

I was tempted to tell Nick that, given the circumstances, there was no way in hell Brett would fire these men for taking time off to see an attorney. But there was no sense in emphasizing to Nick just how well I understood Brett, that I knew intimately how the guy thought and could predict how he would act. There was also no point in offering to call Brett myself. Clearly, Nick didn't want me interacting with the guy. So instead, I rattled off Brett's number, making a show of having to pull it up on my recent calls list so Nick wouldn't realize I still had it memorized. Not that I'd tried to keep the number in my memory banks, mind you. It was simply hanging around in there of its own accord, along with other useless bits of numerical information, like my junior high locker combination *(22-13-8)* and pi carried to eight decimals *(3.14159265)*.

Nick jabbed at his screen, using more force than was necessary. I only hoped he wouldn't break his finger. Or his phone.

He put his phone to his ear. "Hey, Brett. It's Nick." He paused a moment before casting me a heated look that seared me to the core. "Nick Pratt. From the IRS." His jaw flexed. "Tara and I are working this coyote case together. Your men might be willing to talk to us, but first they want to meet with an attorney and see what their rights are. Tara's got someone lined up at Gertz, Gertz, and Schwartz who's agreed to meet with them at ten o'clock this morning. We just wanted to make sure it's okay with you if your men take a couple hours off to meet with the attorney."

Nick was quiet a moment as he listened to Brett's response. "Great. I'll let them know." He ended the call there, turning back to the men and telling them it was a go.

chapter nineteen

*C*omfort Is Yours
in America

Nick agreed to come with me to the law office to act as interpreter. We gave the men the address and Nick told them we'd see them there shortly.

We three agents headed back to the IRS office in our separate cars. I phoned Castaneda on the drive over to give him an update. "We're on our way to the attorney's office now," I told him. "If she gives the guys the go-ahead, they'll speak to us."

"You're living up to your reputation, Agent Holloway," Castaneda said. "You really are a woman who gets things done."

Aw, shucks. He's going to make me blush. "How'd it go at the canyon last night?" I asked. "Did y'all pick up anything with your infrared cameras?"

"Nothing but a gray fox, a couple of bears, and three actual coyotes."

Damn! "So no sign of the kidnapped girls, then?"

"None. Either they're holed up somewhere out of sight, or they're moving by day."

My heart squeezed. *Where are the girls? Are they being*

abused? Have they been abandoned . . . or worse? It was hard to tamp down my fear and frustration, but if I let my emotions get the best of me I'd be of no use to the girls. I had to keep my head on straight and do what I could to help.

Castaneda and I ended our call, and I continued on to the IRS building. Nick left his car in the office parking lot and climbed into mine. Eddie begged off since he was no longer needed as backup and had his own cases to tend to.

I raised a hand in good-bye. "Thanks for your help!"

He lifted his chin in acknowledgment. "Anytime."

As Nick and I drove to the office of Gertz, Gertz, and Schwartz, the song "America" from *West Side Story* played in my head. The song epitomized the immigrant experience, the recent arrivals feeling conflicted about their new home and their motherland. It must be tough, especially if the relocation was made not because of any desire to leave home, but from necessity.

When we rolled to a stop at a light, Nick looked my way. "What's that song you keep humming?"

I told him.

He chuckled, our earlier spat seemingly forgotten. "Funny, I've had the 'Star-Spangled Banner' going through my head."

We engaged in a duet of patriotic songs the rest of the drive, everything from "My Country 'Tis of Thee" to "America the Beautiful." When we sang about the amber waves of grain, Nick added his own refrain, "Grain makes beer!"

"You're a goofball," I told him.

"You're a goofball's fiancée. That's worse."

We arrived shortly after nine. We went into the building and rode the elevator up to the law office. The four men I knew as Julio Guzmán, Pablo Perez, Miguel Gallegos, and Diego Robles were already seated in the reception area, the tight looks on their faces saying they were anxious about their meeting with the immigration attorney. I'd be anxious, too, if I were in their *zapatos*. The meeting with the attorney this morning would determine their fates. Would they have legal grounds for remaining in the United States? Or would they have to self-deport or risk arrest and forced deportation?

I hoped it was the former. Having now met a few of the people behind the headlines and controversy, I couldn't help but feel for them and their families. They'd gone through a lot to get to the United States, while the rest of us simply emerged gooey and screaming from our mothers and happened to land on American soil—figuratively speaking, of course. Though my older brother, Trace, swears he dropped me on my head the first time he held me and that I hadn't been quite right ever since.

To my surprise, Brett walked in shortly after we arrived. Another man was with him, wearing the same green uniform as the workers. Beside me, Nick sat up taller. He also spread his legs a little wider. You know, as if he *had* to. *Men. Sheesh!*

Brett nodded to me and Nick. "Hey."

We "heyed" him back.

He stepped over and stopped in front of me. "My presentation was postponed. I got a call from the board of directors this morning. One of the major investors was served with a multi-million-dollar lawsuit yesterday and things have been put on hold for the time being."

"Oh," I said. "Well, I hope it all gets sorted out."

Brett and his crew chief sat down next to the other four men and exchanged greetings, the crew chief launching in to a whispered discussion with the men in Spanish, occasionally turning to Brett to translate for him.

Although Nick and I wouldn't be permitted to sit in on the men's private discussions with the attorney, we hoped to meet with the men and the lawyer immediately afterward to see what information they could provide about Salvador Hidalgo. I hoped the information would not only give the Border Patrol grounds to keep the coyote in custody, but would also give me grounds for obtaining a search warrant for Hidalgo's bank records.

Promptly at ten o'clock, a Latina attorney opened the door that led back to the private offices and conference room. She stepped through, stopping to speak with the men in Spanish first. When they stood to follow her, she looked my way, "Agent Holloway?"

I stood, too, walking over to her and extending my hand. "That's me."

"Mimi Ibarra." She shook my hand. "Depending on how things go, this may be a while."

"We're prepared to wait as long as necessary." I'd brought some work with me, and if by some miracle I finished that, I had the app on my phone and could watch episodes of the telenovela until they finished. I couldn't get enough *Amor y Vengaza.* "Of course, I hope it won't be too long. Border Patrol needs their testimony to keep a dangerous human smuggler behind bars. He's already been in custody nearly three days."

The attorney nodded, indicating she understood. "I'll try to be as efficient as possible." She turned and led the men through the door. When it closed behind them, I resumed my seat, reaching down to retrieve my briefcase.

While Nick and I looked over spreadsheets and financial records, analyzing evidence in various tax evasion cases, Brett and his crew chief pored over a sketchbook, discussing a landscaping design Brett was working on.

As the minutes ticked by, I eyed my watch repeatedly. *Hurry up!* I silently willed the men and the attorney. *¡Ponte las pilas!*

Just before noon, the door opened again and Ibarra reappeared. I was on my feet in an instant. She motioned with her arm. "Come on back."

Nick stood and began to follow me.

Brett stood, also. "Can I come, too?" he asked. "Those men work for me."

Mimi looked to me to answer the question. "Your call."

Nick emitted an almost inaudible grunt. I knew exactly what it meant. *Sit your ass down, pretty boy, and leave the real work to us law enforcement agents.*

"Sorry, Brett," I said. "Our questions will involve confidential information we aren't permitted to share with anyone not directly involved in the investigation."

He looked disappointed but said, "Understood."

We followed the woman back into the hallway and she led us to a conference room. The men were all seated on the far side of the long table. She took a seat at the end, holding out an arm to indicate that Nick and I should take seats facing the four.

Being that Ibarra billed somewhere in the range of three hundred dollars an hour but was doing this case pro bono, she wasted no time getting down to business, every minute here costing her enough to buy a large latte. "These men are from Honduras. They were riding home from work on a public bus when they witnessed a murder. A gang chased down one of the local prosecutors who'd convicted a drug dealer and shot him dead, right there in the street. The gang members boarded the bus and threatened to kill anyone who reported what they'd seen. These men"—she gestured to the four seated at the table—"worked at one of the textile factories. They were wearing their work badges around their necks when the gang boarded the bus. One of the gang members yanked their badges off and took them. A few days later, members of the gang accosted each of the men outside their homes and beat them. The gang must have tracked the men down by their names on the badges."

I looked over at the men as if truly seeing them for the first time, my eyes searching for evidence of the beatings. Two had significant scars on their faces, one a thick scar that bisected his eyebrow, another that ran all the way from his upper lip to his nose.

Ibarra continued. "They feared the gang would kill them and their families if they stayed in Honduras any longer."

Invisible hands encircled my throat. "That's horrible," I squeaked out.

"Horrible, yes," Ibarra agreed, "and unfortunately all too common right now."

I found myself involuntarily leaning toward her, as one might toward a savior. "Does that give them grounds for amnesty?"

"Not amnesty per se," she said, "but possibly asylum or humanitarian relief. The good news is that refugees from Honduras have been given temporary protected status for another few months, so we've got some time to work on this."

The invisible hand that had been choking me released its stranglehold and my breath released of its own accord. "I'm so glad to hear this."

"Me, too," Nick said.

"Given these circumstances," she said, "I've advised them that speaking to you can only help their cases. Prosecutors can also stay deportation for witnesses who testify in criminal cases here in the U.S."

"So they'll talk now?" I asked. "About Salvador Hidalgo?"

She nodded.

With Nick acting as interpreter, I launched into my questions, writing the men's answers down on my notepad. "What are your actual names?"

As it turned out, Julio Guzmán was Ricardo Montoya, Pablo Perez was Patricio Santos, Miguel Gallegos was Gonzalo Gutierrez, and Diego Robles was Andrés Fonseca. After writing their names down and verifying the spelling, I asked when the shooting occurred and when they had left Honduras.

Gonzalo responded and Nick translated. "In late December two years ago. They fled La Paz with their wives and children on Christmas Eve when they thought there would be less chance the gangs would spot them."

What a way to spend the holiday. Too bad Santa hadn't picked them up and given them a safe flight to the U.S. in his toy-laden, reindeer-led sleigh.

Nick spoke softly. "Ironic that they had to flee from La Paz due to violence."

"Why's that?"

"Because *paz* means 'peace' in Spanish."

Ironic, indeed.

I continued my questions, learning that the men and their families made it through Honduras and Guatemala via a mix of public transportation, walking, and hitching rides with compassionate strangers. It was when they reached the border between Guatemala and Mexico that they first came in contact with a man from Salvador Hidalgo's network.

"What did he tell you?" I asked.

Nick asked the question and relayed their answer. "That he could get them safely to Dallas for one hundred eighty thousand Honduran lempira."

"What's that translate to in U.S. dollars?"

Nick shrugged. "I can translate words, not currencies."

Fortunately, technology filled in where our skills left off. I searched the Internet on my phone, found a currency converter site, and ran a quick computation. "Looks like that many lempira is around eight thousand U.S. dollars."

They indicated that they paid the man they met at the first border a quarter of the amount to get them to Chihuahua, which sits only a hundred and fifty miles from the American border. They paid the remaining amount, around six thousand dollars each, to Hidalgo when they met him in Chihuahua. He was supposed to get them across the border and take them to Dallas. One of the men had a cousin here in the city who had offered to let the men and their families stay at his house until they were able to get on their feet. I could only imagine how crowded the house had been with four married couples and their young children staying there.

I jotted the information down and turned back to the men. "How did Hidalgo's man get you across Mexico?"

Nick asked and provided their response. "By passenger train. He gave them false Mexican papers to use while traveling there, but took the paperwork back when they arrived in Chihuahua. He rode with them on the train, but he sat several rows away and told them if there was any trouble they were not to look to him for help."

In other words, he'd pretend not to know them if the poop hit the fan.

"Ask them what happened once they arrived in Chihuahua. How did Hidalgo get them over the border?"

Nick asked the question, and the men told us that Hidalgo met them at the train station when they arrived. He gave them a car to drive. He was in a separate car. They drove to the northeast for around three hours to a remote area. When the road ended, they left the cars and Hidalgo gave them the paperwork showing that they were U.S. citizens. From there, they traveled on foot for several days and camped at night at sites designated by Hidalgo. They said it was very cold at night and all they had were a few sleeping bags to protect themselves from the elements, no tents or shelter other than a few nights they spent in caves. Hidalgo had a small pup tent he used, though he would pitch it a mile or so from where he left his charges, probably to avoid being rounded up with them if Border Patrol came upon them.

Eventually, Hidalgo led them to a road where a man in a large tanker truck picked the migrants up in the middle of the night. They climbed down through the top hatch and hid inside, only a flashlight to fight the darkness. In the morning, the driver stopped the truck, opened the hatch, and ordered them to get out. They were left on the side of the road just outside Odessa, Texas.

Gonzalo spoke, his voice fast and loud with emotion. Though I wasn't sure what he was saying, it was clear he was angry.

Nick listened and shook his head in sympathy. "He says he told the truck driver that he couldn't leave them there, that they'd paid to be taken to Dallas. The driver said he'd only been paid to transport them as far as Odessa. If they had a problem with that, they could take it up with Salvador Hidalgo."

As if that were actually an option.

With no other alternative, they'd walked into the city, found a bus station, and bought tickets to Dallas with the last of their money. They'd arrived in north Texas with less than a hundred dollars left between them, as well as untreated frostbite. Patricio's wife also had walking pneumonia.

"Were the four of them and their families the only ones who traveled with Hidalgo? Or were there others?"

Patricio responded to that particular question.

"He says there was another couple with a young boy, but they were the only others."

A couple with a young boy? Could this other couple have included Julio Número Uno? I had to know. I reached into my purse and pulled out the stuffed animal. "Any chance you ever saw the young boy with this dog?"

Patricio's eyes brightened with recognition at the sight of the dog and all four nodded their heads. *"Sí, sí."*

This was the first good news I'd heard in days! "Do they know where the boy is now?"

Nick asked the question and turned to me. "They don't know," he said, "but Miguel's wife and the boy's mother became friends on the journey and keep in touch. They said the boy's name was Joaquín and that he called the dog Pepito."

I looked down at the love-worn dog. "We'll try to get you home as soon as we can, Pepito." Was it my imagination, or had he wagged his tail?

Mimi assisted me in preparing the affidavits and, once they'd been printed, I placed each man's affidavit before him. Other than the names and contact information, the affidavits were identical and provided written testimony under penalty of perjury that Salvador Hidalgo had taken money from them in return for smuggling them across the border. The document further noted the details of their arrangement and journey through Big Bend National Park, as well as the fact that Hidalgo had not honored his word to transport them safely all the way to Dallas.

After Mimi translated the document aloud for them, I handed Ricardo a pen. He signed his affidavit and passed the pen down the line so that the others could sign theirs, as well. Patricio handed the pen back to me when he was done. Mimi's legal assistant promptly notarized each of the documents.

"Muchas gracias," I told the men.

Miguel said something to Nick, and Nick turned to me. "They said to thank you for getting them this appointment with the lawyer. They are very relieved to know they will be able to stay in the United States legally. They said their wives will be very happy to hear the news."

I nodded and gave the men a smile, holding out my hand to shake each of theirs. I did the same with Mimi Ibarra and her assistant. "We may have just saved lives," I said.

Mimi glanced over at the men. "I know we did," she replied.

I sent the affidavits via e-mail to Castaneda, following up with a text to let him know they were on their way.

He replied a moment later. *Got them. On way to court-house.*

With any luck, the judge would keep Hidalgo in jail on human trafficking and kidnaping charges.

As we walked back into the reception area, Brett and his crew chief stood. While Gonzalo explained things to the crew chief and he, in turn, translated for Brett, Nick and I headed for the door.

"Tara!" Brett called after me. "Wait a second."

Nick and I stopped and turned around. Brett walked over and thanked me, too. He'd retain his best workers, and they'd keep their jobs. It was a win-win for everyone at Ellington Nurseries. "All's well that ends well, right?"

Unfortunately, while the situation might be over for Brett and his men, it wasn't over for federal law enforcement and wouldn't be until Hidalgo's minions were tracked down and the kidnapped girls found. But no sense pooping on their party. I responded with a simple "yep" and a smile.

chapter twenty

$\mathcal{M}$aking Up Is Hard to Do

Nick was quiet as we rode the elevator down to the parking garage to retrieve my car.

I looked over at him. "You still mad at me?" Or should I say, *mad at me again?*

"Yes. And I've got every right to be."

"Let me make it up to you," I implored him.

He scowled at me. "How?"

"I'll buy you lunch. Including a huge platter of sweet potato fries."

"You're the one who's addicted to the things."

"True." Still, who didn't like them? Only crazy people with malfunctioning taste buds, that's who. "I'm trying here, Nick. Put yourself in my place. I said I was sorry. Please?"

He looked at me, and I tried my hardest to look pathetic and penitent. I saw his resolve melting a little. He heaved a sigh. "Lunch isn't going to get you completely off the hook," he said. "But it's a start. I'm also going to expect some really raunchy makeup sex."

"Duly noted." *And anxiously anticipated.*

After rounding up my car, I drove to a café at the edge

of downtown and a few minutes later we were seated at a table, perusing the menus. As I scanned the entrées, my phone pinged with an incoming text from my mother. *What do you and Nick want to do for your send-off? Traditional rice? Flower petals? Some people use bubbles but they might leave spots on your dress. How about mini beach balls, ribbons, bells for the crowd to ring, flags, streamers, or confetti poppers?*

Clearly, she'd been playing around on Pinterest, looking for wedding ideas.

I broached the subject with Nick.

"This is Texas," he said. "We should give everyone a shotgun and let them fire it in the air."

"In other words," I said, frowning at him. "You don't give a rat's ass."

"Exactly. Who cares whether we get pelted with rice or flower petals? All I really care about is making you mine." A naughty grin tugged at his lips. "And then consummating our marriage. I hear it takes twenty or thirty times to make sure it sticks."

His words warmed my heart. Something a little lower warmed, too. "So you're not mad at me anymore?"

"Hell, yeah, I'm still mad at you," he said. "But it's not the first time you've pissed me off and I sincerely doubt it's going to be the last."

He knew me well. "I'll admit I was wrong not to tell you about going out to Brett's place," I said, "but you've got to admit you're overreacting. There's no reason for you to be jealous or worried. Nothing is going to happen between me and him."

"I know that," he replied, setting down his menu. "It's what's happened between you two in the past that gets me riled up. I don't like to think about it."

"Then don't." Really, it was that easy, wasn't it? "Besides, it's not like you never had girlfriends before you met me."

Okay, I was being a total hypocrite here. I once trailed Nick to the home of his former fiancée, Natalie, whom he'd taken on a date again after she'd popped up as a match for him on a dating site. Of course, Nick and I had not been dating at the time. I'd been struggling to decide whether to stay with Brett or take a chance with Nick. Seeing Nick with the woman he'd once been engaged to had given me an incredibly icky feeling, even though he'd been the one to realize they weren't right for each other and had ended things with her. Could I really blame him for being so angry with me? I had no right, really.

Fortunately, the waiter arrived to take our order. When he left, Nick changed the subject back to our wedding send-off. Though I knew he hadn't quite forgiven me yet, I was glad not to be talking about my dishonesty any longer.

"Confetti poppers could be fun," he said. "Let's go with that."

"Works for me." I sent a return text to my mother. *Confetti poppers.*

One more wedding detail taken care of. *Hooray!*

As we waited for our food, Nick sat back in the booth, a distant expression on his face as he gazed off into nowhere, lost in his own mind.

I nudged his foot with mine. "You okay, *jefe?*"

He snapped back to reality. "Yeah," he said solemnly. "Just thinking about those guys. I can relate to them, you know? When I was in Mexico, the people were friendly to me, and the food was great and the beaches were beautiful, but something was missing. I mean, it wasn't my choice to be there. It was . . ." He drifted off, searching for the right word. "I don't know. Lonely, I guess. But that doesn't quite say it all. I guess . . . it just never felt . . . like *home*." He was quiet a long moment. "I hope those men and their families can find their way home again, wherever that might be."

"Me, too." Maybe the U.S. would begin to feel that way to them if they were allowed to stay.

We switched to lighter topics—the silly antics of his adorable Australian shepherd mix Daffodil, a movie we planned to see soon, whether we should try scuba diving on our honeymoon—until our food arrived.

After I'd eaten half my weight in sweet potato fries, Nick and I left the restaurant. I found my ring finger feeling itchy and realized my engagement ring seemed a little tight. Had all these sweet potato fries caused me to put on a little weight? It was likely. I'd noticed the waistband on my pants had felt a little snug this morning, too. Still, I chose to believe I'd simply ingested too much salt and was retaining water. Why blame myself when I could blame an innocent seasoning?

We returned to the IRS office. While I planned to use the affidavits from Brett's men to request a court order for Hidalgo's bank records, now that he'd be kept in jail I'd bought myself a little time. I was scheduled to meet with Thomas Hoffmeyer at four o'clock, so I figured I'd spend the afternoon on the prize scam investigation and seek the bank records in the morning.

"Where are you off to now?" Nick asked me.

"Tanning salon," I told him. "A woman there had a false 1099 filed on her."

"You getting any closer to figuring out who did it?"

"Who knows? I'm not seeing any common threads so far. There were two victims from the same business," I said, referencing Amelia and Gwen from MetalMasters. "That made me think that there could be a workplace connection. But the two had gone to school together and are friends outside of work, too. The link could be from their personal lives."

"They don't have any suspicions?" he said. "Seems like they'd know if someone was angry enough with them to pull a stunt like filing a false tax report in their names."

"You'd think so," I agreed. "But they said they get along with pretty much everyone."

"I'm sure you'll figure it out," he said.

"I hope so." So far, none of the leads seemed to be panning out.

We parted and I went down the hall to round up Eddie again, stopping to lean against his doorjamb. "I need my partner again."

"Where to now?" he asked.

"Tanning salon," I said. "One of the women there was a victim of the prize award scam."

"Tanning salon?" He arched a brow. "So there will be women parading around in skimpy bikinis?"

I shrugged. "Probably."

Josh called out from his office nearby. "I'll go if Eddie doesn't want to!"

Eddie stood up from his desk. "I got it covered, buddy!" he called back.

"Darn," we heard Josh mutter.

"I hope this lead pans out," Eddie said as we headed down the hall. "I'm tired of you dragging me all over town."

"Enjoy it while you can," I reminded him. "Once you're the co-director, you'll be spending a lot more time sitting behind a desk."

"Don't remind me," he said. "I'll probably get hemorrhoids and a bad back. You think I could get Uncle Sam to pay for one of those fancy massaging chairs?"

"Not a chance."

chapter twenty-one

Sunny Side Up

A woman with toasty brown skin was exiting as Eddie and I approached the door of Eternal Summer Salon. I couldn't understand why people would go to a tanning salon. I mean, sunshine was both free and readily available here in Texas. You could soak up as much as you wanted and then some at absolutely no charge. Besides, according to Doctor Ajay, tanning beds might as well be called Melanoma Machines given the high incidence of skin cancer among those who used them. Recognizing the dangers of the equipment, and the resulting drain on the health-care system, Congress had included a provision in the Affordable Care Act imposing a 10-percent excise tax on indoor tanning services. It was like the taxes imposed on alcohol and tobacco sales, but instead of a sin tax it was a sun tax.

As Eddie opened the door for me, he said, "I feel sorry for you poor, pasty-faced white folks. Having to pay for pigment when us black folks get it naturally for free."

"Enjoy your black privilege," I told him.

Eddie glanced around as we stepped inside. All we

could see were closed doors with numbers on them. "I'm not seeing any bikinis."

"Keep looking," I told him. "Maybe you'll get lucky."

We approached the counter. The twentyish girl working the desk looked up. "Hi, there," she said. "You two have sessions scheduled?"

Eddie replied with a snort but, really, who could blame him?

"No," I said. "I'm not here to tan."

The girl squinted at me, cocking her head as her gaze roamed my face and neck. "Looks like you had a bad experience with self-tanning cream."

Huh? "What are you talking about?"

She gestured to my face. "You look orange. That's from tanning cream, right?"

First my mother and Nick, and now this girl. What was going on? I pulled my pressed powder compact from my purse and took a look in the mirror. *Holy crap, this girl is right!* My face had an odd orange glow to it, much more pronounced than before, the tone visible even through my makeup. I'd become a human traffic cone. A five-feet-two-inch Creamsicle. A woman with the complexion of canned peaches. What the heck was going on? The only other time I'd looked like this was when Alicia and I had slathered our cheeks with orange face paint before attending football games back in college.

Was I getting sick? Had I been exposed to something toxic without realizing it? My mind went to Isidora Davila and the poison she'd used to lace the champagne flutes. Could someone have done something similar to me? If so, who? And when? And how? And why?

Though I wanted the answers to those questions, I knew I wouldn't find them here in the tanning salon. Better to get the information I came for, and worry about my odd skin tone later. I could run by the doc-in-a-box and have Ajay take a look.

I returned my attention to the receptionist. "Actually, I'm here to see Jocelyn Harris. Is she in?"

"Yeah," the girl said. "She works in the back. She handles billing. I'll see if she's busy. What are your names?"

"Tara Holloway and Eddie Bardin," I told her. "We're with the IRS."

"Okay."

The girl stepped down a short hallway behind her counter and knocked on a door. When a voice inside called "Come in!," the girl opened the door and stuck her head inside. "There's two people from the IRS here for you. Miss Holloway and Mister Bardin."

The disembodied voice spoke again. "Send them back."

The girl motioned for us to come around the counter and down the hall. I thanked her at the door and stepped inside Jocelyn's office, closing the door behind us.

Jocelyn was a slightly chubby woman in her early thirties, with reddish hair and fair skin that told me she didn't partake in the services offered there. She had more of an eternally overcast kind of complexion. She stood and stretched a hand across her desk to shake first mine, then Eddie's. "I'm assuming you're here about the 1099? The one for the supposed prize?"

"You got it." I dropped into a chair when she held out a hand to indicate we should take a seat. Eddie plopped down into the one next to me. "We'd really like to get to the bottom of this as soon as possible," I said. "These types of fraudulent filings don't just hurt innocent people like you, they cause all kinds of problems for the IRS. Our staff spends a lot of time trying to figure out whether the reports are truly inaccurate and getting accounts corrected. It's a nightmare."

"I'd imagine," she said. "We once had a girl here who was supposed to set up our payroll system and she got everything out of whack. She transposed social security numbers and spelled everyone's name wrong. She entered my salary in the file for one of the part-timers, and coded the system to pay me minimum wage." She groaned. "There's nothing worse than expecting your paycheck and getting a pittance instead."

I could think of many worse things, such as feeling forced to flee your home in the middle of the night and losing the stuffed dog that brought you comfort, but there was no point belaboring that fact when it was clear she was simply exaggerating to make her point.

"Did you fire the employee?" Eddie asked.

"Couldn't," she said. "She didn't work for us. She worked for an outside company we'd signed up with to process our payroll. Besides, by the time we realized the errors she'd made, it was two weeks later and she had already moved on to another client."

I followed up with another question. "Did you complain to her boss?"

"No, I didn't have it in me. I didn't want her to lose her job. She was one of the nicest people I've ever met. Complimented everyone on their hair or outfits, always had a smile for us. Besides, we don't have a large staff. It only took a few minutes to correct her errors."

Hmm. "Any chance she could be the one who issued the incorrect 1099 to you?"

Jocelyn issued a soft sigh. "As much as I hate to say it, I doubt she'd be able to get a 1099 filed correctly."

"Point taken."

While the girl would have had access to the social security numbers for the staff of Eternal Summer Salon, that fact alone wasn't enough to make her a suspect. People didn't do things without a motive, and there didn't appear to be any reason for her to file a fraudulent report against Jocelyn. After all, she hadn't even known Jocelyn was unhappy with her work.

"Any other ideas who might have issued you the 1099?" I asked. "Any bad breakups with a vindictive boyfriend? Nasty neighbors? Maybe a family member you don't get along with?"

"Nothing out of the ordinary," she replied.

Gee. This visit has been a waste of time, hasn't it?

I decided to be honest. "We can't seem to find a connection between all the victims. Without that, we'll never be able to determine who the culprit is. Are you sure you can't think of anyone? Someone you cut off in traffic? An old high school classmate who had it in for you? A customer who got a sunburn on their butt? Anything might help."

She shook her head. "Sorry. Nobody comes to mind at all."

Either she and the other female victims weren't being honest with me, or they didn't realize they'd given the culprit reason to be unhappy with them. "Do the names Bethany Flagler, Amelia Yeo, Gwen Rosenthal, or Thomas Hoffmeyer mean anything to you?"

"No. Should they?"

"Not necessarily."

I jotted down a note that Jocelyn didn't recognize any of the other victim's names. "What about the name Robin Beck?" Might as well find out if Jocelyn knew Bethany's former roommate.

While no flicker of recognition had crossed over her

face when I'd mentioned the other names, this time Jocelyn's face lit up. "That name I know."

"You do?" I sat bolt upright. Had I found the connection? Lord, I hoped so! I wanted to get this case over and done with so I could move on to the other case files loading down my desk.

She raised her index finger, indicating for me to hold on. My right leg began to bounce of its own accord. Patience was not one of my virtues.

She turned to her computer, keyed in some information, and slid her mouse to and fro, clicking it a couple of times. When she finished, she motioned for me and Eddie to come around her desk. When we did, she pointed at the screen. "Two months ago, Robin Beck signed a contract for a year of tanning sessions. She bought the Golden Goddess Package for sixty-nine dollars and ninety-nine cents a month. She paid the first month in cash when she signed up, but she gave us a debit card number to use for the remaining months. As you can see here"—she tapped the screen—"the card was declined the first time we tried to use it."

"Have you tried to collect from her?" I asked.

"We have," Jocelyn said. "The first thing we do when there's a situation like this is we send a courtesy e-mail asking them to update their payment information. If they don't respond in ten days, I follow up with a phone call. I had to call her. That's why I remember her name."

"So you talked to her?"

She glanced at the screen and shook her head. "No. I always make a note in the file when I call a client. You know, to have a record of my attempts to contact them? That way if they say they never got my call I can show them a detailed log." She pointed at the screen again. "My notes here say that I left her three voice mails over the course of a month but that she never returned my calls."

"What's your next step in a situation like that?"

"We turn the matter over to a collection agency and report the default to the credit bureaus."

"And you did that in Robin's case, too, I assume?"

Jocelyn nodded. "Yes. We followed our standard procedure."

Assuming the Robin Beck who'd signed the contract with Eternal Summer was the same Robin Beck who'd been Bethany Flagler's roommate, the information Jocelyn had given me told me two things. One, Robin was still in the north Texas area. And, two, Robin might have a motive to retaliate against Jocelyn. Even so, I wasn't yet convinced she was the culprit. After all, neither Amelia Yeo nor Gwen Rosenthal knew Robin. Nonetheless, it was a decent lead. Maybe Amelia and Gwen had crossed paths with Robin without knowing it, somehow. Bethany had mentioned that Robin often worked retail jobs. Maybe they'd shopped somewhere Robin worked.

"Can I get Robin's phone number from you?" I asked Jocelyn. "Her address, too."

"Sure. It's all here." She gestured to the screen.

I bent over to take a screenshot with my phone and also wrote the information down in my notes. When I finished, I stood up and thanked her for her time. "I'll let you know if there are any developments."

"Great."

Eddie and I exited her office, closing the door softly behind us. As we passed the front desk, I noticed the receptionist was reading a copy of *Soap Opera Digest*. Isidora Davila graced the cover, the tagline reading *American Viewers Obsessed with Crossover Hit!* I could vouch for that. I was obsessed with the show, too.

Eddie exhaled sharply. "This was disappointing. I didn't see a single woman in a bikini."

"Sorry, buddy," I said. "Better luck next time."

A door creaked as it opened behind us. We turned back to see a man wearing tiny goggles and the skimpiest bathing suit possible. Though he had hair on his head, his body was hairless, waxed within an inch of its life. "I need some help in here," he called to the receptionist. "I can't get the bed to turn on."

Eddie turned back around, blinking as if to erase the image. "I guess I should be careful what I wish for, huh?"

"That's karma," I said as I pushed the door open. "It's coming back to bite you on the ass for giving me crap about Brett and Nick."

When we left the salon, a woman on her way in ran her gaze over me and gave me an odd look. At the car, I checked myself in the rearview mirror once again. Yep, my skin was orange. No doubt about it.

I hooked a finger in the top of my blouse and looked down it. While my bra covered my boobs, the part of my chest I could see looked orange, too, as did my belly. I reached down, lifted the hem of my pants, and pulled down my sock. Yep, orange ankles. I was the skin tone of Velveeta.

Eddie eyed me. "What are you doing?"

"Checking to see if the color has spread. It seems to be everywhere."

"If I were you," he said, "I'd see a doctor. That's not normal."

"You think this is some kind of reaction to the wasps? Or the pepper spray?"

"Hell if I know," he said.

What could the problem be? Were my kidneys giving out? Was my pancreas on the fritz? Did I have too many red blood cells or something like that? I felt absolutely fine and had experienced no other symptoms. I wasn't unusually thirsty. I hadn't been running a fever. My body was free of aches and pains. All systems seemed to be functioning normally.

After dropping Eddie back at the office, I aimed my car for the medical clinic. I might not be able to get to the bottom of the 1099 scheme just yet, but maybe I could at least find out what was causing me to turn orange.

Twenty minutes later, I sat on the paper-covered examination table, waiting to see the doctor. The door opened and Ajay stepped in. After placing his laptop computer on the counter, he walked over in front of me. Today, his T-shirt bore an image of Betty and Veronica from the Archie comics sitting back to back in tight tops. Sexist, sure. But I was more concerned at the moment with finding out what was wrong with me than giving the doc a lecture on feminism.

Ajay took one look at my face and exclaimed, "What the hell is going on with you?"

I scoffed. "You're the doctor. Aren't *you* supposed to tell *me* that?"

He cupped my chin and turned my face from one side to the other, leaning in to look at my skin. He reached down and lifted my hand, inspecting the skin there, too, going so far as to scratch at it to see if the color came off. "I'm assuming your skin is evenly discolored all over. Is that correct?"

"Yes." I hadn't noticed any blotches anywhere when I'd taken my shower this morning.

"Does your skin feel tender or itchy?"

"Only where the wasps stung me. The rest feels okay."

"Have you been having any unusual symptoms? Blood in your urine or anything like that?"

Eek! "No." *Thank God.*

He listened to my heart, looking in my eyes with a pen-light, and took my blood pressure. "All of your vitals are good. Have you been any more tired than usual?"

"No." My job was exhausting, but I always managed to power through.

"Nausea? Intestinal pain? Cramps?"

"No, no, and no."

"Any blurred vision? Trouble hearing?"

"Nope. None."

"Sore throat? Itchy eyes? Sneezing? Congestion?"

I shook my head.

"What about topical products?" he asked. "Are you us-ing a new skin lotion or powder or shower gel?"

"Nope."

He cocked his head and narrowed his eyes at me. "You haven't been using LuvLub again, have you?"

A hot blush rushed to my cheeks. I'd once had an al-lergic reaction to a sexual enhancement product and Ajay had never let me hear the end of it. "Absolutely not." Last I'd heard, the FDA had taken the stuff off the market.

His face grew pensive as he seemed to be contemplat-ing my dilemma. "Skin conditions can result from bacteria or fungus. Any chance you've been exposed to an unsani-tary environment? Have you gone swimming recently or spent time in a sauna or steam room? Anything like that?"

I was getting tired of all the questions, but I had to give Ajay credit. He was thorough. "I threw myself into a pond when I was trying to get away from the wasps."

"Was the water clean? Clear?"

"Looked clean enough to me. Besides, it was on the grounds of a Catholic school and the Virgin Mary was keeping watch over it. Maybe it was filled with holy water."

He scoffed. "Yeah, and people bathe in the Ganges River to purify themselves, but the water is filled with the bodies and ashes of the dead. Raw sewage, too. You might wash away your sins, but you've got a good chance of catching dysentery, cholera, typhoid fever, or hepatitis."

Yikes. "You think I've got one of those diseases?"

"Probably not," he said. "You'd likely be having other symptoms. But I'm not ruling anything out yet. Anyplace else you've been?"

"I also went to a tanning salon. But I only went inside to speak with the manager, and that was right before I came here. I didn't use any of the tanning beds and I was already orange when I went in the place."

"It could be jaundice," he said. "That would be indicative of liver or gall bladder problems. Would you say you drink alcohol to excess?"

"No." I had a drink every now and then, but no more than anyone else I knew.

He cocked his head. "You being honest with me?"

"I am."

"Okay, then. What about medications?" he asked. "Have you been on steroids or penicillin? Maybe taken a lot of acetaminophen lately?"

"No."

"What about birth control pills. Have you switched prescriptions lately?"

"Nope."

He ran his gaze over me once more before giving me a shrug. "That's all I've got. We'll have to see what your body fluids tell us." He retrieved a clear plastic cup from the cabinet and handed it to me. "Take this to the bathroom and fill it. I'll have the nurse draw some blood, too."

"Lovely."

He reached into his pocket and pulled out a purple lollipop. "Here you go."

I took the sucker from him. "Grape. Yum!"

I did as I'd been told, leaving the urine sample with the nurse outside, then sitting down to let her draw blood from my arm. I watched as the vial filled. My blood looked normal. Deep red, not orange. That had to be a good sign, right?

"It'll be tomorrow before we have your results," the nurse said. "We'll give you a call."

"Thanks."

With that, I returned to my car, wondering whether my days on earth were numbered. Would I survive until my wedding? And if I did, would I look like a circus peanut in a bridal gown?

chapter twenty-two

$\mathcal{M}$issing Connections

By the time I left the medical clinic, it was late afternoon.
I tried Robin Beck's cell number, but all I got was her voice
mail. I didn't bother leaving a message. If she hadn't returned a call from the tanning salon, she sure as heck
wouldn't return one from the IRS. I'd try her back later.

I slid my cell phone into the car's cup holder. I had one
more stop planned, at Thomas Hoffmeyer's place. Before
I could head out, my cell phone rang. The caller ID indicated it was Agent Castaneda calling.

"How'd it go in court?" I asked.

"It was a mixed bag. The judge seemed convinced by
the affidavits, especially since the men you tracked down
were using the aliases found on the documents in Hidalgo's rental car. He also seemed convinced Hidalgo could
be a flight risk. But Hidalgo's attorneys argued that there
was nothing definitive linking him to anyone named Zaragoza or to any kidnappings or deaths. The judge compro-
mised. He didn't deny Hidalgo bail, but he put conditions
on it. He'd have to turn over his passport and remain in
the U.S. And he set the bail high."

"How high?"

"A million dollars."

In the state of Texas, a typical bail bond premium cost 10 percent of the amount of the bail. In other words, someone would have to pay one hundred thousand dollars to spring Hidalgo from jail. Unless he had some rich friends or family, that wasn't likely to happen. Heck, you could buy a house for that kind of money. Few people could spare such a large sum.

"Looks like he's staying put, then," I said. *Good*. Now I could enjoy my time in Vegas without worrying whether he was leading more people to their deaths, like a heartless pied piper.

"I'd say so," Castaneda replied. "With Hidalgo in jail, we may be able to negotiate with him, maybe offer a reduced sentence if he tells us where the kidnapped girls are. Of course, he may refuse to talk at all. That's what he's done in the past."

I thanked him for the update. While the girls were still out there somewhere, at least it seemed like law enforcement might be getting closer to finding them.

I drove out to Colleyville, a suburb that sat directly west of the Dallas–Fort Worth airport, and stopped at a condominium complex. The place was surrounded by an eight-foot-high wall of terra-cotta-colored stucco. Fast-growing ivy had made good headway crawling up the wall, obscuring most of the name, only the word *Villas* fully visible. I pulled up to the tall iron entrance gate and punched in the number for the Hoffmeyers' unit at the security keypad. The sound of a phone ringing came over the speaker. After a couple of rings, a female voice answered. "Hello?"

"Hi, there," I called at the speaker. "It's Tara Holloway from the IRS. Mr. Hoffmeyer is expecting me."

"I'll open the gate for you."

A few seconds later, the gate slid open and I drove through. While the connected two-story units featured garages, a few vehicles were parked in driveways or along the narrow streets. All were high-end, late-model vehicles, ranging from a black Cadillac to a white Lexus. The immaculate Mediterranean-style buildings and well-tended grounds whispered luxury. Though the villas were connected and thus shared walls, they were as big or bigger than the average single-family dwelling. This looked like the type of place busy, six-figure-salary professionals would call home, where wealthy people might move when they retired and didn't want the hassle of keeping up a yard they no longer used.

I circled the interior road a couple of times before spotting the unit I was looking for tucked away between two narrow pine trees. I parked on the street, admiring the teal-toned Mercedes E300 sedan in the driveway. *Nice ride.* Thomas Hoffmeyer had clearly done well for himself. I went to the door and rang the bell. *Ding-dong!*

Yip-yip-yip! Scratch-scratch. *Yip-yip-yip!*

A male voice came from inside. "Hush, Fritz!" The door opened a moment later to reveal a white-haired man who appeared to be in his mid-sixties in khaki shorts and a striped golf shirt. He had a slight paunch on his belly and a squirming dachshund in his arms. The dog's reddish fur was only a few shades darker than my odd skin tone. The man's golf clubs leaned against the wall just inside the door as if waiting for him. Behind the man stood a woman who also appeared to be in her mid-sixties, but who'd taken pains to preserve her appearance. Her perfect blond dye job offered not the slightest hint of gray at the roots, her stylish sheath dress showing off a body that was as well-maintained as the outdoor landscaping. She squinted at me, looking confused and concerned, but at least she had the courtesy not to ask about my ginger skin tone.

"Hello," I said. "I'm Special Agent Tara Holloway with the IRS. Are you Thomas Hoffmeyer?"

"I am." The dog squirmed even more and the man tightened his grip.

Given that his arms were full of cute little dog, I didn't bother trying to exchange handshakes with Hoffmeyer. But when his wife introduced herself, I held out my hand. She looked down at it, noted the odd color there, too, and hesitated. *Ugh.* Now I knew how those poor lepers felt.

Rather than worry the woman that I was carrying some type of contagious disease, I lied. Probably not the nicest thing to do, but I needed these people to focus on the matter at hand, not on my skin. Fortunately, I had a convenient excuse at the ready. "I realize my skin looks funny," I said. "The self-tanning cream I used turned me this strange color."

"Oh!" Her features relaxed in relief. "I was wondering, but didn't want to be rude and ask. Come on in."

I stepped into their condominium and she closed the door behind me. Now that the dog's escape plan had been foiled, he quieted, defeated. Hoffmeyer bent down and released him onto the tile floor. The dog's toenails clacked as if he were performing a canine tap dance as he skipped over to sniff the hem of my pants. No doubt he smelled Anne and Henry. I couldn't seem to make it out of my town house without their fur on me somewhere.

I knelt down and stroked his long back, my hand appearing even more orange when up against his fur. "Hello, there, Fritz."

His tail whipped back and forth so fast it was an auburn blur.

"Take a seat," Hoffmeyer ordered, gesturing to a nearby easy chair. Clearly, he was used to bossing other people around. "Let's get to the bottom of things. I've got nine holes to get in before sunset."

As I dropped into the chair, Hoffmeyer plopped down on the sofa. He jerked his head to indicate his wife should join him. While she settled in, I took a quick glance around the room. Frozen on the screen of their television set was the face of Isidora Davila, her eyes narrowed and lips pressed into a thin line as she plotted her next act of vengeance against her husband, whom she was staring down. Apparently, he'd dared to use his catchphrase on her, his words immortalized in the subtitles below. *Isidora, put in your batteries!*

I must've caught the Hoffmeyers in the middle of watching the episode, and they'd paused it to resume watching once I'd left. I turned back to the couple. "You watch *Amor y Vengaza,* too?"

"Not *me,*" Hoffmeyer snapped, derision dripping from his words. He hiked a thumb at his wife. "That's all her."

Mrs. Hoffmeyer offered a sheepish smile. "It's a silly show, but I'm hooked on it."

"Me, too," I replied. "Seems like no matter where I go, everyone's watching it." I pulled out a pad of paper and pen to take notes and turned my attention to Mr. Hoffmeyer. "I've got some questions for you."

"Questions?" He scoffed. "I was hoping you'd have answers."

I fought the urge to scoff right back at him. "Questions lead to answers. That's how an investigation works." *You old blowhard.* "The key to solving this case is figuring out what the link is between you and the other victims, what you all have in common."

He raised an arrogant, argumentative brow. "What if

there's not a link? What if whoever did this just picked our names haphazardly? It could just be some hacker playing games."

I had no choice but to admit he might have a point. "The culprit may have done just that. Picked victims willy-nilly with no real reason behind it. Nonetheless I believe it's likely, even probable, that the culprit obtained your names, social security numbers, and home addresses from the same source. I'm trying to figure out what the common source might be. It could be a financial institution, a doctor's office, a school." I reached down to scratch Fritz, who'd flopped onto his side and was now lying at my feet. "Even a veterinary office. Anywhere you provided those pieces of information."

"That covers a lot of ground," he said. "I have multiple investment accounts. We own quite a bit of real estate."

"Tom sees several doctors, too," Mrs. Hoffmeyer added. "He's got an ophthalmologist for his cataracts, a cardiac specialist for his high blood pressure, a rheumatologist for his arthritis, a proctologist for his—"

"She doesn't need to know all that!" Hoffmeyer barked. "She just needs their names and phone numbers."

His wife shrunk back on the couch, speaking much quieter now. "I was only trying to help."

It irked me to see the woman cowed by her overbearing husband, but I was here to get information about a pending tax fraud case, not to serve as a marriage counselor. Besides, what did I know about marital relationships? I'd only recently become engaged. I knew being married would require some sacrifices and compromises. I only hoped this woman was content with the ones she'd made.

I took notes as Hoffmeyer rattled off the names of his doctors, dentist, and periodontist. "Do you attend church?" I asked, looking up.

"Of course," he said. "First Baptist, here in Colleyville."

Good thing he'd clarified because there had to be a dozen or more First Baptist Churches in the Metroplex. *Everyone wants to be number one.*

I noted the name and location of the church. "You mentioned that you golf. Are you a member of a country club?"

"Timarron," he replied, referencing a country club in the adjacent city of Southlake.

"Who's Fritz's vet?" I asked.

Hoffmeyer looked to his wife. Obviously, she was the one who took primary care of the cute little dog. She provided the veterinarian's name and I jotted it down.

"Have you attended any schools recently?"

"Are you kidding me?" Hoffmeyer scoffed again. "I haven't set foot in a classroom in forty years."

"Just making sure I've covered all the bases," I said in my defense. I'd hazard a guess that when he'd been a student all those years ago, he'd been the class bully, doling out a fair share of wedgies and wet willies. "Are you a member of a gym?"

"No. Those places are for brainless muscle-heads."

All righty, then. "You mentioned that you have multiple investment accounts and own real estate. Can you tell me which financial institutions you've dealt with?"

He ran through a litany of banks, brokerage houses, mortgage companies, and title companies, his memory surprisingly thorough.

"I understand you're retired now," I said, "but at the time the 1099 was filed two years ago you were working as the controller for Snippy's Barber Shops Incorporated. Correct?"

According to my research, Snippy's was a relatively new franchisor that provided opportunities for those wanting to open an independent hair salon under a recognized name. While there were only a couple of Snippy's franchises in the Dallas–Fort Worth Metroplex, the stores were much more common in smaller towns and had quite a toehold in Oklahoma, Arkansas, and Missouri. The company's revenues had skyrocketed in recent years as more and more people signed up to become franchisees.

"That's correct," Hoffmeyer replied. "I was in charge of the entire accounting department. Had a staff of six working under me at the time I left."

"And how was your relationship with those six?" If he was half as abrasive with them as he'd been with me, he'd likely had a lot of unhappy people answering to him.

He snorted now, apparently tired of scoffing. "If you're asking whether my workers liked me, the answer is no. When it comes to my work, I can be a real hard-ass."

He could be a real hard-ass about everything, it seemed, though I didn't bother to correct him. "It seems likely that whoever filed the fraudulent 1099s is a financial type who knows something about tax forms. Was there anybody at Snippy's you had trouble with? Someone you fired, maybe, or who you gave a poor performance report?"

He offered a patronizing smile. "Managing people isn't for sissies, Miss Holloway. If I didn't upset at least one person every day I wasn't doing my job. We had a lot of numbers coming in from a lot of franchises and it was critical things be accounted for accurately. I didn't tolerate mistakes. Sure, I issued some bad reviews, but they were deserved."

"I need you to be more specific," I said. "Name names."

"We had an entry-level girl a few years ago," he said. "Hired her to help out when we were making a big push at conventions and getting a lot of interest from potential franchisees. She was supposed to run credit checks, verify assets, and work up the numbers so that I could make a decision on whether to approve an applicant. She wasn't bad at what she did, she was just too damn slow, couldn't handle the volume. We needed someone who could handle the backlog, so I let her go."

He seemed to be just as demanding a boss as Isidora's husband, ordering everyone to put in their batteries. *How do you say that in Spanish?* I racked my brain. Oh, yeah. *¡Ponte las pilas!*

I was tempted to remind him of the old adage that you could have a job done fast or you could have it done right, but not both. There was no sense in antagonizing the guy, though. He'd probably just complain to Congress again and I'd be the one ending up with a bad performance report. "Did she take it badly when you terminated her?"

He shrugged. "She cried a little at first, but then she said it was probably for the best because she didn't like working for an asshole anyway. That rude little twit got twenty weeks of unemployment insurance out of us."

"Did she handle tax matters for the company?" I asked.

"No," he said, "just the franchisee applications and occasional internal stuff."

It wasn't clear to me whether she was a good lead or not, but good or bad at least she gave me something to go on. "What was her name?"

He raised his hands. "I don't remember. Laura. Lauren. Laurel. Something like that."

Hoffmeyer might not remember her name, but I'm sure she remembered his. "Did she have access to employee social security numbers?"

"Maybe," he said. "Before we contracted our payroll out of house, the staff took turns handling payroll duty. We had them on a four-week rotation."

Hmm. If Laura/Lauren/Laurel handled payroll, that

could explain how she might have Hoffmeyer's social security number. But it didn't explain how she'd have Bethany's or Amelia's or Gwen's.

"Any others?"

"A couple guys quit on me, but they found jobs with better pay so they didn't seem to be too bitter when they left."

"What about a franchisee or potential franchisee?" I asked. "Did you have any problems with any of them?"

Mrs. Hoffmeyer perked up, sitting straight up on the couch and pointing a finger at me. "You might be on to something there." She turned to her husband. "Who was that guy you told me about? You remember the one. The barber from Longview." She looked back to me now. "He'd been operating out of a converted barn and got angry when Tom told him the place wasn't up to Snippy's standards and he'd have to move to a different location."

"That's right. I'd forgotten about him." Mr. Hoffmeyer looked up in thought. "His name was Phillip Gentry. I remember that because he sent me a dozen angry e-mails."

I jotted down a note. *Phillip Gentry. Longview. Barber. Barn.* It was a long shot, though, and I knew it. A disgruntled franchisee might have reason to get back at Hoffmeyer, but would he have the means to obtain Hoffmeyer's social security number? It seemed doubtful. Then again, he could've convinced someone on the inside to give it to him, maybe even Laura/Lauren/Laurel. Anything was possible. But if Gentry was the guilty party, what was his connection to Bethany, Amelia, and Gwen?

"We've covered your work and business contacts," I said, "but what about personal ones? Is there anyone you know personally who might have some reason to want to cause you trouble?"

Hoffmeyer sneered. "There were a couple young punks

who used to live next door. They were around all the time, didn't seem to go to school or have jobs. At least not regular ones, anyway. Their parents owned the unit and they thought that gave them carte blanche to do whatever they wanted. They played their music loud and left soda cans and beer bottles all over their patio. Their friends ran in and out at all hours of the night and day, slamming their doors and honking their horns."

Mrs. Hoffmeyer reached over and picked Fritz up from the floor, settling him on her lap. "All their commotion drove this little guy crazy."

"I can imagine." Given how much the dog had yipped and yapped when I'd arrived, it was clear he took his watchdog duties very seriously.

"This development has rules," Hoffmeyer said. "Most of the people who live here are retirees and we like things clean and quiet. Several of us asked the boys repeatedly to clean up their patio and keep the noise down, but they wouldn't do it. In fact, they had the nerve to tell my wife that what they did in their condo was none of anyone else's business. They even contacted the president of our homeowners' association and complained that they were being harassed by the other residents. Of all the nerve!"

Mrs. Hoffmeyer interjected. "Of course, the HOA saw right through them and gave them the boot. We came out the morning after they left and found an empty soda can on our porch. Our door and stoop were covered in sticky brown liquid, so it looked like the boys had shaken the can up and intentionally sprayed our door before they left."

Hoffmeyer rolled his eyes. "Typical juvenile behavior."

"Do you know their names?" I asked.

"I can't remember," Hoffmeyer said. "Not sure I ever knew them."

"Same for me," Mrs. Hoffmeyer said. "The HOA should have that information in their records, though."

I mulled the information over for a moment. While it was possible the young men were behind the 1099 scam, in my experience slackers like them were too lazy to even hold a grudge. They'd take some type of petty revenge, like the soda incident, and move on to annoy someone else. Still, there were exceptions to every rule. Maybe the Hoffmeyers had said something in particular to set one or both of the boys off more than usual. But would the boys be financially sophisticated enough to know how to use a tax form as a means of revenge? And how would they have obtained Thomas Hoffmeyer's social security number?

"I'll check with the HOA," I told the couple. "One last question before I go. Do you happen to know Bethany Flagler, Amelia Yeo, or Gwen Rosenthal?"

"None of those names mean anything to me," Hoffmeyer said. "But unless somebody can make me money or a dirty martini, I don't bother committing their names to memory. I mean, what's the point?"

Uh, gee, common courtesy? Basic manners? Human connection?

"What about Robin Beck?" I asked. *Please say yes,* I thought. *I want to get this case over with.*

But alas, he did not say yes. Instead, he said, "That name doesn't mean anything to me, either."

Having obtained all the information that appeared relevant at this point, I slid my notepad back into my briefcase and stood. "If you think of anyone else who could be a suspect, let me know. My phone number and e-mail address are listed here." I held out a business card.

Hoffmeyer took the card from my hand. "I'll expect updates from you."

"If and when I learn something, I'll let you know. In the meantime, I'd appreciate it if you'd inform the senator's office I've been by to see you."

Hoffmeyer cut me a snide grin. "Let's say I let them know once you've found the con artist who screwed me over and put him behind bars."

Let's say I put my foot in your ass.

Hoffmeyer followed me to the door. I thought he was finally showing some manners, but when he grabbed his golf clubs and squeezed out past me, I realized the only thing he was showing was how big a self-centered jerk he could be.

I stopped at the threshold. Mrs. Hoffmeyer stopped next to me, both Fritz and the television remote cuddled against her chest. The two of us watched as her husband squeezed the key fob in his hand to pop open the trunk of his Mercedes. He laid his golf clubs in the back, circled around to the door, and backed out of the driveway at warp speed. He hadn't even bothered to tell his wife or me good-bye.

From next to me, Mrs. Hoffmeyer growled. "My plan is to long outlive that bastard."

I cast her a glance, saw the determined gleam in her eyes, and wished her longevity. "May you enjoy many years of blissful solitude, ma'am."

She replied with a chortle. "Take care, Miss Holloway. Thanks for your help."

"Bye now." I gave the adorable little Fritz a final pat on the head.

Mrs. Hoffmeyer wasted no time getting back to the show, aiming the remote control at the TV and punching the play button. As the door swung closed, I heard Isidora call out in Spanish, almost as if she were speaking to me. "¡Adios!"

chapter twenty-three

$\mathcal{C}$upcakes and Chaos Theory

I placed a quick call to Lu. "You can tell Senator Perkins that I've met with Mr. Hoffmeyer."

"How'd it go?" she asked.

"He was an ass of epic proportions. Probably anyone who's ever interacted with the guy would have reason to wish him harm."

She grunted. "Well, at least you've had some success in the coyote case."

"I won't consider it a success until the missing girls are safe and sound at their aunt's house."

"We'll call it *progress,* then," Lu said.

We signed off. As long as I was in the general area, I decided to drive a few more miles up the freeway to Grapevine. I had a major cupcake craving, and I knew just the place that could give me a fix.

Not long ago, Lu had tasked me with pursuing abusive tax preparers who perpetrated fraud on a wide scale, claiming all sorts of bogus deductions and credits for their clients, pulling the numbers they put on the returns out of the air, or perhaps out of a certain orifice located below and behind the belly button. Many of them used gimmicks to catch the attention of potential clients and lure them in. One called herself the Deduction Diva and ran her business out of a space decorated more like a brothel than a tax office. Another operated his tax business under the name Refund-a-Rama and dressed as Elvis, complete with a pompadour wig and a white, bell-bottom jumpsuit. It might be one for the money, two for the show, but it was zero taxes paid to the IRS and six months in the slammer for the king of rock 'n' roll.

One of these suspected abusive preparers had been the Tax Wizard, a former IRS employee. As it turned out, though the returns the Wizard had filed contained pure hogwash, his motives were not as sinister as we'd originally thought. He was simply an aging man whose mental faculties had begun to diminish. Needless to say, we let him go without punishment, though he was given strict orders to stop preparing tax returns and retire, maybe take up a hobby. Model trains, perhaps.

The Tax Wizard had been operating out of the front room of a space in which a woman known as Madam Magnolia performed psychic readings in a dark, incense-scented chamber. At first, I'd thought Madam Magnolia's business produced as much hogwash as the Tax Wizard's. But then she'd enticed me to join her for a session and, to my surprise, she made some amazingly accurate predictions and given me information that led me to an elusive target. It wasn't clear to me whether she could actually see into the future or just tossed out ideas, hoping something would pan out. At worst, though, I decided she was entertaining and harmless. Or as harmless as she could be given that her chamber sat right next to a bakery that made the most delicious cupcakes on the planet. If I were her, I'd weigh three thousand pounds by now.

Luck was with me as I drove up Main Street in the historic district of Grapevine. A minivan pulled away from the curb in front of the bakery and I slipped into the spot they'd vacated. As I climbed out of my car, I glanced next door. Madam Magnolia's place hadn't changed since the last time I was there. Purple curtains trimmed with gold fringe hung in the windows, the psychic's name spelled out in gold lettering across the glass of the front door.

As I entered the cupcake shop, the bells on the door jingled. An older woman with white hair peeked out from the back room, from which wafted the delicious scent of warm vanilla cupcakes, nutmeg, and cinnamon. *Heaven must smell like this.*

"I'll be right with you!" the woman called.

"No rush!" I called back. After all, I needed a little time to decide between the chocolate coconut, the strawberry ganache, or the butter pecan. *Decisions, decisions . . .*

Wait!

At the end of the row sat a new featured flavor. Sweet potato with brown sugar cream cheese frosting. *Oh, hell, yeah!*

The woman stepped out, wiping her hands on her apron. "What can I get you?"

"I'll take a dozen of the sweet potato cupcakes."

She reached for a box. "These sure have been popular. I never thought I'd see a cupcake that could outsell our classic chocolate, but these have been giving the old stand-bys a run for their money."

She filled the box, squeezing in a bonus strawberry ganache to make it a baker's dozen. I swiped my debit card through the machine, entered my pin, and took the box. "Thanks so much."

"Enjoy."

Oh, I'd enjoy them all right. And on that topic, why not

start enjoying them right away? On my way to the door, I lifted a corner of the box, fished out a cupcake, and took a huge bite, frosting tipping the end of my nose. As I stepped out onto the sidewalk, I came face-to-face with Madam Magnolia. She was dressed, as usual, in bangles and beads and baubles, a bohemian skirt blowing in the breeze around her legs.

She tilted her dark head, narrowed her green eyes, and gave me a knowing look. "Congratulations, Tara."

"On what?" I asked, wiping the frosting from my nose with the back of my hand. Which didn't solve the problem. Now I had frosting on the back of my hand.

"On what?" Madam Magnolia struck a long match and lit an incense stick before placing it in a vented burner on a pedestal just outside her door. "Your engagement, of course."

Wow. She'd known I was engaged? *Amazing.* I mean, we hadn't put an announcement in the newspaper, and neither Nick nor I put anything personal on Facebook or other social media sites. Federal agents had to lie low. And it's not like Madam Magnolia ran in the same circles as us. "How did you know?"

She gestured to my left hand. "By the ring on your finger."

"Oh!" *Duh.* "How have you been?" I asked. The woman might be a bit offbeat—okay, *a lot* offbeat—but she was undeniably likable and you felt like she had your best interests at heart, even when she was charging you for advice and information.

"I've been good," she said, tossing a lock of her dark hair over her shoulder. "But you need to be careful. Very careful. On the day of your wedding, Mercury will be in retrograde. And you know what that means."

Did it mean this woman was full of hooey? "Could you be more specific?"

"Things will not go as planned."

I laughed at that. With my mother and Bonnie in charge and nailing down every detail, things would go *exactly* as planned. But that fact aside, I felt the need to point out a flaw in Madam Magnolia's prediction. "We haven't even set a wedding date yet. How can you know that Mercury will be in retrograde then?"

She gave me a long-suffering smile. "Because I'm a seer, hon."

Despite the fact that events in the past had played out much as she'd predicted, I harbored serious doubts about her, or anyone's, true ability to see into the future. Still, it couldn't hurt to get more information, just in case, right? That way I could prepare myself. "When you say things won't go as planned, what exactly do you mean?"

She lifted a shoulder. "I can't say. I haven't had a clear vision, only a general sense of . . ." She waved her arms around as if she could make the word appear in the air. She finally completed her sentence with "chaos."

"Chaos?" *Great.* "You're a real party pooper, you know that?"

She raised the shoulder again. "I call it like I see it. I also see bad things in your near future if you don't give me one of those cupcakes." Her eyes flickered down to the box and back to my face.

I had to laugh at that. "That's what this is all about, isn't it? You want a cupcake."

She said nothing, just held out a hand bearing a colorful ring on each finger and four noisy bracelets around the wrist. I finagled another cupcake out of the box and handed it to her.

She grinned. "You're safe now. At least for the near future. But on your wedding day, watch out."

She might be on to something. Then again, she might be full of shit. Still, she'd had visions of where one of our targets had been hiding out, even given us the name of the campground where he'd taken his RV. And she'd purportedly visualized Nick and Brazos Rivers, a country-western star, engaged in a brawl, a premonition which also turned out to be true. While it was tempting to discount her entirely, it might not be wise to do so. The fact that she'd made me feel uneasy, though, sort of pissed me off. What was she trying to do, ruin my wedding? It should be one of the happiest days of my life, not one I looked forward to with apprehension.

Before I could decide what to say to her, she spoke again, "Put me on your guest list. Maybe I can help out. Besides, it's going to be crazy. I don't want to miss that."

Is that what this was all about? She wanted to come to the wedding? Was all this woo-woo stuff simply her way of finagling an invitation? "I'll put you on the list," I said. "But it's going to be in east Texas. Hope you don't mind a three-hour drive."

She waved a dismissive hand. "It'll be fun. I'll take the party bus. I can do readings on the way. Your guests will enjoy that."

"Party bus? What party bus?"

Her lips curved up in a knowing smile. "Talk to your mother."

I knew it was a long shot, and I still wasn't sure about Madam Magnolia's abilities, but it couldn't hurt to see whether she had any premonitions or visions about the current cases I was working on. "Can I ask you something?"

"About an investigation?"

Weird that she knew what I'd planned to ask about, huh?
"Yeah."

"You can," she said, "but those services will cost you."

"How about you waive your fee and we'll consider it your wedding gift?"

She lifted her chin in acknowledgment. "You're a shrewd negotiator."

"That's what they tell me." Or at least it's what *I* told myself. Hey, sometimes you have to pat your own back, too. "I'm trying to figure out who issued reports of bogus prize winnings to several people in the Dallas area. I've got a current suspect, but I'm not sure she's the right one."

Madam Magnolia placed her cupcake on the windowsill, reached out with her left hand, and placed her palm on my forehead. Closing her eyes, she raised the other hand toward the heavens. She said nothing for a moment, though after a few seconds her mouth slowly spread in a wide, toothy smile.

"What do you see?" I asked.

She opened her eyes. "Nothing. Nothing at all."

"Then why are you smiling?"

"I don't know." She shrugged. "That's for you to find out."

Some wedding gift, huh? I'd been gypped.

chapter twenty-four

The Wheels on the Bus Go Round and Round

On my drive back to my place, I contemplated Madam Magnolia's spiritually inspired smile, wondering what it meant. Like my fortune cookie had said, *a smile can hide a thousand feelings*. Looked like it could also hide a psychic's inability to give detailed information. Or, more likely, she was thinking how she'd gotten away with not having to bring a gift to our wedding while still getting to have fun on the party bus and enjoy the buffet dinner and open bar.

I swung by the address Robin Beck had given to the staff of Eternal Summer when she'd signed her contract. It was an apartment complex in Irving, a building that was neither old nor new, neither fancy nor rundown. Just a typical run-of-the-mill complex, one of many that sat behind the strip centers flanking Interstate 30.

Spotting a sign on Building D, I parked between two pickups and climbed the stairs to the third floor, stopping before the door bearing black metal letters identifying it as apartment 323. The sounds of a sitcom rerun came from inside, the typical program run in the six o'clock time slot by stations without a newscast.

Rap-rap-rap.

A few seconds later, the door opened a few inches, and a young woman with dark hair and eyes peered out.

"Hi," I told her. "I'm looking for Robin Beck."

The eyes narrowed and the mouth pursed. "Well, she's not here, that's for sure!"

With that, she slammed the door.

I knocked again, but she didn't open the door. If I had to hazard a guess, I'd say Robin had bled this roommate dry, too. "Ma'am?" I called. "I'm with law enforcement."

She jerked the door open, apparently having remained standing behind it, probably watching me through the peephole. "Why aren't you wearing a uniform? Are you a detective or something?"

"Yes." No sense going through the whole rigmarole. Even after I explained that I was a criminal investigator for the IRS, many people didn't get it. They thought only FBI, CIA, DEA, and ATF had agents with guns. Might as well keep things simple. "I'm trying to track down Robin Beck. I believe she has some information on a case I'm working. A moment ago, you said Robin's not here. Did you only mean she's not here at the moment?"

"No. I meant that she doesn't live here anymore. I kicked her out."

"May I ask why?"

"'Cause she was just using me. She asked to move in for a few weeks when she and her boyfriend broke up. I thought it wouldn't be any big deal. But then she ate all my groceries and used all of my laundry detergent and watched a bunch of movies on pay per view and never chipped in for anything. She kept telling me she'd pay me back when she got her next paycheck, but next thing I knew she'd be coming home with new clothes and stuff. She only cared about herself."

"When did you kick her out?"

"Last week."

Dang! If only I'd had this case then. Maybe I could've caught up with Robin here.

"Any idea where she's living now?"

"No, and I don't give a—" She caught herself. "Robin can be living in her car for all I care."

"What kind of car is she driving now?"

The girl shrugged. "Some piece of sh—" She caught herself again.

"Shit?" I said, letting her know she didn't need to use a filter. I was more interested in getting information than whether this girl had a potty mouth. Besides, I'd been known to use a choice word or two on occasion. I considered curse words part of my repertoire of expression.

"Yeah," the girl said.

"What make is it? A Ford? Toyota? Dodge?"

"I have no idea. Just a little boxy beat-up thing. It was silver. Does that help?"

Little, but I'd take it. "Yes. That helps. Any chance you know the license plate?"

"No," she said. "I didn't really pay attention to it."

Even if the girl knew the plate number, it wasn't likely to help. Robin didn't exactly seem to keep her records up to date.

"How did you two know each other?" I asked.

"From work."

Aha! Maybe I could corner Robin there. "Where do y'all work?"

"At Irving Mall," she said. "I mean, at least I do. Robin got fired for stealing merchandise from the store. I don't know where she's working now."

"Did the store manager have her arrested?"

"No. Robin started bawling and offered to pay for the

stuff and was making such a scene the manager just wanted her to go. It was scaring off the customers."

I had my doubts whether Robin's tears were real. She'd probably just manipulated her boss to avoid another arrest and conviction. "What store do you work at?"

She mentioned the name of a trendy women's clothing store that was popular with both the twenty-something nightclub crowd and older women who wanted to show off a recent tummy tuck or weight loss by wearing something skimpy. She also gave me the manager's name.

"Does Robin have family in the area? Maybe another friend she'd move in with?"

"Nobody I can think of," the girl said. "She sort of gloms on to one person at a time and then moves on. At least that's the impression I got. She's from Houston, but I think she got too many people down there mad at her so she moved up here to start over. I guess she could have gone back to Houston. I don't really know."

Having gotten as much information as I could from the young woman, I pulled out one of my business cards and handed it to her. "If you happen to hear from Robin, see if you can find out where she's living or working now and give me a call. But don't let her know I'm looking for her, okay?"

"All right."

"Thanks."

Feeling defeated, I tromped down the two flights of stairs and returned to my car. I promptly looked up the phone number for the store and asked whether the manager was in. I got lucky. She was working the evening shift tonight and hadn't left yet.

I identified myself and told her I was with law enforcement and trying to track down Robin Beck. "I understand she was fired for stealing merchandise."

"That's right. I caught her stuffing a dress into her purse."

Must've been a tiny dress. "Did she provide you with an address to mail her final paycheck to?"

"No," the woman said. "I didn't ask her for one, either. If she wants that check, she'll have to come by and get it. Given what she did, that would take a lot of nerve."

Robin didn't seem to be low on nerve. Common sense, maybe.

"If she comes by, would you mind telling her you'll have to mail her last paycheck? If you can get a current address for her it sure would help me out."

"No problem."

"I appreciate your help." I gave the woman my cell phone number and e-mail address.

On my way home, I picked up a couple of bean burritos at a drive-through and ate them on the couch at my town house while looking over the information Bethany, Amelia, and Gwen had e-mailed to me today. I leaned into the computer on my lap, hoping to see some information repeated, some common source that would tell me where the person who filed the fraudulent 1099s had obtained their social security numbers. While I saw no connection, I did see a dollop of salsa that had dripped from my burrito onto the screen. Fortunately, a quick swipe with a napkin took care of that problem.

When switching back and forth between the three e-mails proved too cumbersome, I stuffed the last of the burrito into my mouth, plugged my laptop into my printer, and printed out the communications. I laid them side by side on my coffee table, where Anne hopped up to help me. I scooped her onto my lap. "Sit here, girl. Mommy's working."

While both Bethany and Gwen had memberships at the same gym chain, they'd signed up and worked out at different locations. While Bethany, like Hoffmeyer, attended a Baptist church, it wasn't the same congregation. Amelia and Hoffmeyer had checking accounts at the same large national bank, but banked regularly at different branches given that they lived miles apart. Gwen and Amelia were patients of the same dental practice, not surprising since they lived within two miles of each other, but the four victims had no other doctors in common. Nobody had bought vehicles at the same dealership, nor did anyone have a landlord, realtor, or mortgage company in common. In other words, there was no clear link between all of these victims and the last half hour I'd spent going over the information had been a total waste of my time.

My only remaining leads were Laura/Lauren/Laurel and Phillip Gentry. The barnyard barber seemed like the longer shot, so I decided to start with the young woman who'd worked in Snippy's accounting department. It didn't take long for me to identify her. Laurie Murphy was the only person with a name similar to Laura, Lauren, or Laurel who'd received a W-2 from Snippy's two years ago.

To learn a little more about her, I pulled up her Facebook page. According to her data, she'd been working at the Small Business Administration since leaving Snippy's. So she was now a fed, like me. *Interesting.* Unfortunately, the SBA's district office was located in Fort Worth, also known as Cowtown given that it had been a major hub on the cattle trails back in the day. Fort Worth sat thirty miles, and approximately nine million construction zones, to the west of Dallas. Going to see Laurie would take a good chunk of a workday, and I wasn't sure I had that much time to spare. Between the Hidalgo case I was working for Border Patrol and this investigation, I'd hardly had time to glance at my other files.

A quick look over her Facebook friends list told me that

Bethany Flagler, Amelia Yeo, Gwen Rosenthal, and Robin
Beck were not among them. When I checked her work and
education entries, I saw no overlap among her workplaces
and schools and those of the other victims. I did note, however, that she had not included Snippy's Barber Shops
among her places of employment. Couldn't much blame
her, though. It didn't sound as if her time there had been a
positive experience.

While I wasn't sure if driving to Fort Worth to visit
Laurie Murphy would be an efficient use of my time, I
knew for certain that driving four times as far out to
Longview definitely was not. Phillip Gentry would get a
phone call, not a visit.

It took a few minutes of digging online to determine
that Gentry owned a barber shop/beauty salon called the
Cutting Corral. A cute photo on his Web site showed a
young boy sitting on a saddle while Gentry, who appeared
to be in his mid-fifties, gave the kid a traditional buzz cut.
Another showed Gentry using what appeared to be the
same clippers to trim a gray horse's whiskers. The site indicated the shop's hours were from ten a.m. "'til the cows
come home."

I wasn't sure exactly what time cows came home. I supposed it depended on their curfew. But it couldn't hurt to
give the number a try and see if Gentry was still around.

I got lucky. When I dialed his number, a man's voice
came over the wire. "May I speak to Phillip Gentry, please?"

"You got 'im, ma'am."

I identified myself and told him I was calling to discuss
his relationship with Snippy's and Thomas Hoffmeyer.

"There is no relationship," he said. "I applied for a franchise a while back but they turned me down. End of story."

Was it truly the end of the story? Or was he only giving me the condensed version of the tale? "Mr. Hoffmeyer told me you sent him several e-mails expressing your disappointment."

"Ah, hell. That's all water under the bridge. I got my nose out of joint when they turned me down, sure. They said I'd have to move locations, rent a space in town. I saw no good reason why I should pay someone else rent on a space when I had a perfectly good, paid-up barn to operate out of. But I'm not holding a grudge, if that's what you're thinking. In fact, things worked out for the best. I've got a new guy working for me now. Goes by Jax. Fresh out of barber school. He's covered in tattoos and leather, wears his hair in a Mohawk. Drives a motorcycle with a sidecar, too. The teenagers love 'im. Got lines out the door, everybody wanting the sides of their head shaved. It's like the eighties all over again. He'd never come to work for me if my shop was in some suburban strip mall. He's said as much."

While Phillip might have convinced me he harbored no ill will now against Thomas Hoffmeyer, he hadn't quite convinced me that he hadn't been angry enough two years ago to give the guy a little hell. Even so, while Phillip had motive to want to get back at Hoffmeyer for rejecting his franchise application, he didn't seem to have the means to accomplish vengeance via a fake 1099. In other words, I still didn't see how he'd have obtained Hoffmeyer's social security number. What's more, it seemed unlikely a middle-aged barber out in east Texas would have crossed paths with Bethany, Amelia, Gwen, and Jocelyn, four young women working in the big city of Dallas. Yep, barring any fresh revelations, I was going to cross Mr. Gentry off my list of potential suspects.

"Thanks for taking my call, Mr. Gentry."

"We good, then?" he asked.

"Yeah," I said. "We're good."

Frustrated, I tossed my phone on the couch and went to the kitchen to pour myself a glass of wine. Returning to the living room, I plopped back down in front of my TV, hoping to take my mind off my work for a little while. You can probably guess what I was watching. Yep, another episode of *Amor y Vengaza*.

In this episode, Isidora caught her flirtatious barista turning his charms on another customer, one less beautiful and several years older than her, one who also worked in Isidora's husband's business. The barista, however, was unaware of Isidora lurking in the shadows, spying on him as he prepared a drink for the woman and fed her the same line he'd given Isidora. *"Just the way it should be. Hot, steamy, and only for you."*

Isidora's dark eyes flashed with betrayal and fury. She escaped, unseen, onto the sidewalk, where she dropped to a bench and whipped out her journal and fancy pen to immortalize her feelings in purple prose. *Has he only been playing with me? Treating my heart as a toy for his entertainment? Were his compliments and flattery only offered in the hopes of receiving bigger tips? It's clear. My young lover has made a fool of me! I'll show him.*

And show him she did.

She flounced back to her husband's office, told him she needed something to do and wanted to run her own business. He tossed her a generous allowance, clearly designed more to shut her up than because he thought she could run a successful enterprise. But to hell with her husband. Isidora's sights were set on a certain unfaithful barista and her scheme for *vengaza*.

Isidora contacted the coffee shop's owner and made him an offer he couldn't refuse. After buying the place, she promptly slipped inside the coffeehouse through the back door and issued the barista an unsigned notice via e-mail that his hourly pay had been reduced to the legal minimum due to his inappropriate behavior on the job. If he wished to discuss said behavior, he could come to the back office to discuss the matter with his as-yet-unidentified new boss personally.

The episode ended with her door down the back hall of the coffee shop being flung open by the enraged young man, whose shirt was, for inexplicable reasons, halfway unbuttoned, exposing his muscled, freshly waxed chest. *"Isidora?"* he cried, his expression incredulous. *"You are my new boss?"*

A smile spread across her face. *"Indeed I am."*

"But what we had was so special! Why do you treat me so poorly? Do you love me no longer?"

The episode ended there, leaving viewers to wonder whether things were over between Isidora and the latte-slinging Lothario. I was just about to start the next episode when my cell phone rang. The caller ID indicated it was my mother calling. As much as I hate to admit it, I was tempted to ignore her call and return it later. *What is Isidora going to say to her deceitful lover?* I couldn't wait to find out!

But I couldn't in good conscience turn my back on my mom, especially when she was no doubt calling about the wedding plans. What kind of person would that make me? Not much better than that conniving coffee Casanova or the violent and vengeful Isidora. *Okay, now I'm the one being dramatic.*

I jabbed the button to take the call. "Hi, Mom."

"Hey, hon. Just wanted to let you know that, once we've got a date, I plan to reserve a block of rooms for the wedding guests at the Holiday Inn. That's about as fancy as it gets out here."

My hometown wasn't large, and the mid-priced chains were all that was offered in the way of accommodations. Still, I didn't run with snobs. The hotel would be fine. "Sounds good, Mom. Thanks."

"Bonnie and I have been discussing the welcome baskets. We want to make sure the out-of-town guests are comfortable and have a few treats. We're thinking we'd put a bottle of wine and a personalized corkscrew in each basket."

"Personalized corkscrews?"

"That's right," she replied. "We found some online. We can have your and Nick's names put on them along with the date of your wedding. We thought it would make a nice souvenir."

"It will. Great idea." I should've known my mother would come up with something inventive and useful. I'd been smart to turn the planning over to her. Lazy, too, but mostly smart.

"Okeydoke," she replied. "So my next question is, should the wine be red or white?"

My creamy cat Anne hopped up on the couch next to me, her light-colored fur providing my answer. "Let's go with white."

"Imported or domestic?"

Again, my domestic short-haired cat provided the answer. "Domestic," I said, scratching my kitty under the chin. She responded with a vibrating purr of appreciation.

"What kind of white wine?" Mom asked. "Sauvignon blanc? Chardonnay? Riesling? Pinot grigio?"

"Chardonnay." That seemed to be the most popular among the choices.

"Perfect," she said. I got the impression she was making notes as we spoke, crossing items off a list. "My next question is, what else should we put in the basket? Bonnie and I were thinking nuts, pretzels, and a piece of fresh fruit. Maybe an orange or an apple. Or, if you don't like that idea, we could go with cheese and crackers. Or cookies, maybe?"

"I'm fine with the fruit and nuts. Let's go with that." As long as the guests didn't starve, I didn't think they'd care much one way or another. Most of the people we knew weren't difficult to please.

"Got it. Now for the baskets themselves. Should they be an actual basket? Bonnie thought a tin planter would be a cute alternative. We could add a cut flower in a vase or maybe one of those little succulent plants? A flowering portulaca would be nice. That way they could take it home as a keepsake."

They sure had put a lot of thought into this, hadn't they? Far more than I ever would have, given the limitations in my time and creativity. "The tins sound wonderful."

"Good. I liked that idea, too. We've been debating whether to add something for the bath. Maybe some lavender lotion or bath oil?"

"Lavender lotion would be great."

"Or would you prefer a different scent? Maybe jasmine or vanilla?"

"Lavender is fine."

"Are you sure?"

The only thing I was sure of was that all of these details were making me think that Ajay and Christina had the right idea running off to Vegas and keeping things simple. "I'm sure, Mom. Lavender is perfect."

"All righty. By the way, I took Jesse shopping for flower girl dresses. We found a pretty little purple one that will match your wedding colors. But you know Jesse."

Of course I knew my little niece. She was a three-and-a-half-foot-tall, much younger version of me, full of piss and vinegar and sugar and spice and puppy dog tails. Hey, puppy dog tails weren't just for boys anymore. *Hooray for gender equality!*

"And?" I asked.

"And she doesn't want to wear fancy shoes. She's insisting on wearing her pink cowgirl boots with her dress."

I couldn't help but laugh. "I wouldn't want her in anything else." Heck, I couldn't remember the last time I'd seen her in anything else. She even slept in the boots on occasion.

"I've been looking at mother-of-the-bride dresses online. Some of them sure are dowdy. But I found a few pretty ones, too. I'll send you the links. Let me know what you think."

"Okay," I agreed. "Hey, by any chance have you and Bonnie planned to rent a party bus to take people from Dallas to Nacogdoches?"

"No," she said, "but that's a wonderful idea! It sure would make things easier for the guests. We could stock the bus with Bonnie's peach sangria, maybe play some movies or games on the ride out, and make it a real fun time for everyone. I'll look into it."

I wasn't sure what to make of this. Had Madam Magnolia actually predicted the future, or had she just manipulated it? *Hmm* . . . My mind went round and round, much like the wheels on a bus.

We made small talk for a couple more minutes, then I begged off. "Gotta go. But thanks for everything, Mom," I said with complete sincerity. "I don't know how I'll ever repay you for all the effort you're putting into the wedding plans."

"Just give me a couple of cute grandchildren I can dote on and we'll call it even."

Jeez. I wasn't even down the aisle yet and already my

mother was talking babies. I only hoped I could be half the mother to my own kids that my mom had been to me.

We ended the call with mutual declarations of "Love you!"

As much as I wanted to return to *Amor y Vengaza* and see what happened between Isidora and the barista, I'd have to wait to find out. I needed to get my butt to bed. After staying up late last night, I was totally pooped. Besides, tomorrow night a bunch of us were heading to Las Vegas for Christina and Ajay's wedding. I didn't want to be too wiped out to have fun.

I scooped Anne up in my arms and headed upstairs to bed.

chapter twenty-five

*P*ut in Your Batteries!

Friday morning, I scrambled around my place, rounding up a pair of jeans, shoes, and a couple of cute tops for the weekend in Vegas. I tossed a pair of heels and a red satin dress into my suitcase, too. They'd be the perfect thing to wear to a wedding in Sin City and the nightlife we'd enjoy afterward. Of course, my bikini went into the outside pocket. As hard as I'd worked all week I was looking forward to relaxing poolside, or maybe taking a late-night dip in a hot tub with a glass of wine in my hand. To hell with those warning signs about drinking alcohol in the Jacuzzi. Some risks were worth taking.

On my way out the door, I hid a key under the doormat for my neighbor, who promised not only to feed and water my cats and tend to their litter boxes, but also to give Annie some love and reassurance that her mommy would come back home shortly. Henry couldn't give a rat's ass whether he received any affection or whether I ever returned, being above such things. Nevertheless, I forced a hug and kiss on him before I left. He returned my love with a growl and hiss. "Ungrateful brat." I chucked him affectionately under the chin.

As I pulled out of my driveway, a call came in from Agent Castaneda. I pulled to the curb to speak with him. I knew he'd planned to return to the Telephone Canyon area with the infrared cameras last night. *Is he calling to tell me they'd found Nina, Larissa, and Yessenia?* My heart fluttered with hope. Then it turned to stone. It was just as possible he'd found them, but that they'd no longer been alive. *Ugh, I hate this case.*

"Good morning," I said. "Did you find the girls?"

"No," he snapped. "And we lost Salvador Hidalgo."

What?! "Lost Hidalgo? In jail?" *How the hell could that have happened? Did he tunnel out with his toothbrush? Slither out through a sewage pipe?*

"He made bail and was released in the middle of the night," Castaneda explained.

Darn. I'd kinda hoped he had to swim through sewage. It would've served the rat right. "Who paid for the bail bond?"

"Allegedly his mother," Castaneda said. "But she barely has two nickels to rub together. I bet the funds came from someone else."

"Zaragoza?"

"Possibly," he said. "We had an agent trail Hidalgo after he was released but he seemed to know he was being followed and pulled a fast one. He rented a car and drove to a twenty-four-hour restaurant in Alpine. He must've had someone meet him there with a car and change of clothes. My guy had eyes on the place, never noticed Hidalgo come out. When he didn't see him for an hour or so, the agent went inside. He found Hidalgo's clothing in the trash can in the men's room."

Dammit! "So there's no telling where he is now."

"No. He could still be in the area, or he could have snuck back into Mexico. I've got an agent watching his house in Dallas, and everyone along the border is on alert, but this guy's a slippery bastard."

The minute-by-minute evolution of an investigation is part of what kept the job of a federal law enforcement agent so interesting. But it was also part of what made it so frustrating. You never knew how things would turn out. You could luck into something and solve a case quickly, or you could work your ass off over weeks or months, years even, and have it all be for naught.

I closed my eyes and took a deep breath, issuing a silent prayer that no more lives would be lost before the guy could be tracked down and soon. The ransom on the kidnapped girls was due in three days. *If he isn't found before then . . .*

"You'll let me know once you find him?" Of course, my question assumed they *would* find him. That could be an incorrect assumption. But any other thought made me sick to my stomach.

"I sure will."

"In the meantime," I said, "I'll get over to the courthouse and see about getting a search warrant for his bank records."

"Good. Thanks."

We ended the call, and I immediately placed another, this one to Ross O'Donnell, an attorney with the Department of Justice who regularly represented the IRS. "Hi, Ross," I said. "Got time to trot over to the courthouse with me and get a search warrant?"

"No problem," he said. "What is it this time?"

"Human smuggler named Salvador Hidalgo," I said. "I need to get his bank records, see if they provide any evidence of unreported income." I was fairly certain they would.

"You got a witness for me?" Ross asked. "Or some kind of supporting documentation?"

"Of course," I said. After all, Judge Trumbull was a notorious hard-ass who leaned left. She didn't hand out search warrants unless they were clearly, well, *warranted*. "I've got notarized affidavits from four Honduran citizens testifying that they paid Hidalgo eight grand each to smuggle them into the U.S. through Big Bend National Park. He also gave the men birth certificates, social security cards, and voter registration cards so that they could work here. I can show from the tax filings that there are multiple men across the U.S. working under the same names and social security numbers."

"That ought to do us," Ross said. "Meet me at the courthouse in fifteen minutes?"

"On my way."

To speed things up at the courthouse security check, I left my gun, pepper spray, and cuffs at the office. Ross and I met in the courthouse lobby. We made our way through security together, patiently enduring the *beeps* as someone or other forgot to remove their belt or bracelet. A quick ride up in the elevator and a few steps down a hall, and we entered the courtroom over which Judge Alice Trumbull presided.

Judge Trumbull was, like my boss, a tough old broad. While Lu dyed her hair a bright strawberry blond, though, Judge Trumbull had allowed nature to take its course and let her hair go gray. She wore little makeup over her loose jowls. While she might not be the most attractive woman to ever grace a judicial bench, there was no denying she knew her business. She ran her courtroom with a practiced efficiency.

She spotted me and Ross walking in the door and raised her chin to let us know she'd get to us ASAP. When the witness who'd been testifying on the stand was dismissed, she held up a palm to the attorneys at the opposing tables facing her. "Hold on just a minute, folks," she said. "We've got a federal agent back there who looks like she needs something."

Ross and I strode quickly up to her bench.

"Special Agent Holloway is seeking a search warrant," Ross said. "She'd like to see the bank records of a suspected human smuggler."

"Human smuggler?" she repeated. "You mean like a trafficker? Sexual slavery?"

"No," I said. *Thank God.* What Hidalgo did was bad enough. "This guy gets people across the border, but then they're on their own."

She frowned. "So you're targeting undocumented immigrants? Aren't there bigger fish for you to fry?"

"I understand where you're coming from, Your Honor. The problem is, this smuggler's been leaving people to die in the desert. We also suspect he's responsible for the kidnapping of three girls who were being brought into the U.S."

She held out her hand. "Let me see what you've got."

I handed her the affidavits, tax records, and the photos of the girls, providing a quick oral synopsis of what she was looking at. "Border Patrol agents have suspected for some time that a man named Salvador Hidalgo has been smuggling people across the border, and they believe he was responsible for the deaths of several migrants found in Big Bend. The four men whose affidavits I've given you are from Honduras. They've told me that they paid Hidalgo several thousand dollars to bring them and their families across the Mexican border into the U.S. Border Patrol agents plan to arrest Hidalgo as soon as they can track him down. If I can get his bank records, I'll be able to see if his financial transactions show the types of patterns consistent with human trafficking. It's likely that he may also have failed to report the income he earned from his activities."

She nodded and flipped through the pages, her eyes skimming over them. She glanced up at me. "These guys witnessed a murder in Honduras?"

"Yes," I said. "The killers came to their homes and assaulted them a few days afterward. The men feared they'd be killed themselves if they stayed, maybe their families, too. That's why they fled."

Trumbull shook her head. "And I thought having my AC go out in my house was a life-and-death situation. First world problems, huh?"

"First world, indeed."

She came to the photos of the girls. "Pretty young things," she said softly. "Are these the girls who were kidnapped?"

I nodded. "A man phoned their aunt. She lives here in Dallas. She'd paid a man named Zaragoza to bring her nieces into the States. A gang member was putting pressure on the oldest to have a relationship with him." I paused for a moment and let the silence say what I didn't want to, what that relationship would have meant for the young woman. "They were kidnapped somewhere near the Texas-Mexico border. The ransom's due Monday. The man who phoned said if it wasn't paid the girls would never be seen again."

She closed her eyes and put her hands over her face for a moment as if to shut out the harsh reality I'd just presented her with. Only her mouth was visible. Her mouth said, "Some days I hate this job." She let out a loud sigh, removed her hands, and signed the search warrant. She handed the completed document back to me. "Go get him," she said, "and save those girls."

"Thanks, judge. We'll do our best."

With that, she turned her attention back to the attorneys waiting at the tables and the trial we'd interrupted. "The defense may call its next witness."

Ross and I slunk quietly out of the room and made our way back out of the building, parting on the sidewalk out front.

He raised a hand in good-bye as he headed off. "Later."

"Later."

On my walk back to the office, I stopped by the main downtown location of the State Bank of Dallas and spoke with the manager, showing him the search warrant.

He read over the document and looked up at me, his expression curious, though he seemed to know better than to ask any questions. While I normally didn't share information, in this instance lives were at stake and I could use the bank's help in keeping an eye out for Hidalgo. I decided to break with protocol and give him the scoop.

"The accountant holder is engaged in human smuggling," I said. "He abandoned several people in the west Texas desert. They didn't all make it out alive. We also believe his network is responsible for the kidnapping of three girls."

He eyes went wide in shock. "That's awful!"

"It is. It's also why we need to nail the guy as soon as possible."

The manager complied immediately with the warrant, taking me back to his office where he printed out a complete record of Salvador Hidalgo's account since it had been opened eight years ago. When the printer finally whirred to a stop, he pulled the warm stack off the machine, secured it with an extra-large binder clip, and handed it to me.

"Thanks. I appreciate your help." I slid the thick stack of documentation into my briefcase.

"If there's anything else I can do," the manager said, "don't hesitate to call."

Might as well capitalize on his cooperative attitude, right? "There is one more thing you could do," I said. "Can you let your staff know that if Salvador Hidalgo comes into the bank someone should call me immediately?"

"I sure can."

I handed him a stack of my business cards, enough so that he could place one at each teller station.

"Have a good weekend," I told the man as I left.

"You, too."

Oh, I would. After all, I was off for a weekend of fun in Las Vegas. It was just the thing to take my mind off work for a while. *Oh, who am I fooling? I won't be able to stop thinking of those poor, defenseless girls.*

I returned to the office and dug right into Salvador Hidalgo's bank records. Any financial evidence that was indicative of human smuggling would be the icing on the cake, as would any additional tax evasion charges. Of course, I hoped we could spread some pretty thick icing on that cake. I wanted to see Hidalgo put away for a very long time, like, say, *life*.

Sure enough, the bank statements showed a clear pattern of transactions consistent with human smuggling, including cash deposits made by third parties, presumably families in America who paid Hidalgo to smuggle their loved ones into the country. If the man surfaced again, he'd have a hard time refuting the hard evidence against him. While he made large withdrawals on a regular basis and hadn't kept a significant balance in the account, the records showed he'd received funds totaling over one hundred twenty-five thousand dollars in each of the last several years. Of course, none of that income had been reported on his tax return. Yep, looked like tax evasion could be added to his list of charges. *Neener-neener.*

I scanned the documents and sent the computer files to Agent Castaneda via e-mail, following up with a text to let him know what I'd found. *Bank records in your e-mail inbox. Clear evidence of tax evasion.*

Having done all I could on the Hidalgo case, it was time to visit Laurie Murphy at the Small Business Administration in Fort Worth, which sat around thirty miles to the west of Dallas. But first, lunch. My stomach had been growling for the past few minutes, telling me it wanted to be filled. Some sweet potato fries sure would taste good about now.

I headed down the hall to see who might be available to ride over to Cowtown with me. Eddie was busy, but Hana Kim agreed to accompany me. She and I had worked a recent case together against a catfishing Casanova who'd found people on dating sites, gained their trust, then stolen funds from them through a check-cashing ploy. We'd had some fun taking the jerk down together.

"What do you need me to do?" she asked.

"Just look tough and intimidating," I said.

She narrowed her eyes, flared her nostrils, and gritted her teeth. "How's this?"

She looked like a bull about to charge. "Perfect."

She gestured to my face as we headed out to my G-ride. "What's with the orange glow?"

"I don't know," I said. "I can't figure it out."

"You think all those wasp bites had something to do with it?"

"I don't know. Maybe."

On our way to Fort Worth, I drove through a hamburger joint to pick up an order of sweet potato fries. "You want anything?" I asked Hana as we idled at the drive-through menu board.

She leaned over and called an order into the speaker.

Once we received our food, I shoved several fries into my mouth at once, moaning in taste bud bliss. *Will I ever get tired of these things?*

A few miles out, my cell phone rang, the caller ID indicating it was Ajay on the line. I jabbed the button to put him on speaker. "What's the news, doc? Am I dying?"

He snorted. "Not hardly."

Good to know. "What's my problem, then?"

"You've got carotenoderma carotenemia."

Huh?

Hana cast me a suspicious glance and flattened herself up against the passenger door.

"Carota-what-a?" I said to Ajay. "That sounds complicated enough to kill me."

"It's a long term that simply means you've got high levels of carotenoids in your system. You've ingested too much beta-carotene. It's a harmless condition that doesn't require treatment. We see it a lot in babies and young children who tend to be picky eaters and don't vary their diets enough."

I wasn't a picky eater at all. "How did I get it?"

"Good question. Have you been eating a lot of carrots lately?"

"No." I shoved another sweet potato fry into my mouth. "I have a salad with carrots now and then, but no more than usual." I reached for another fry.

"Pumpkin? Maybe pumpkin pie?"

"No."

"Butternut squash?"

I bit off half the fry. "I like butternut squash, but it's been ages since I've eaten any."

"It must be something else, then," he said. "Most of the foods that are high in beta-carotene are orange in color."

Uh-oh. I looked at the remaining half of the sweet potato fry in my fingers and hesitated a moment.

Hana asked the question I didn't dare. "Could it be sweet potatoes?"

"It certainly could. Have you eaten an unusual amount recently, Tara?"

Only a bushel or so in the last week. "Define 'unusual.'"

Hana snorted. "I'd say it's whatever amount you've been eating."

Dang. I looked down at the remaining fries and sighed. "How long does it take to get rid of the weird color?"

"Not long," he said. "A few days at most."

At least that part was good news. "Thanks for calling," I told him. "See you at the airport tonight."

I jabbed the button to end the call. Still hungry, I eyed the fries again. Damn, they looked good. *What the hell.* Might as well finish them off, right? They'd just go to waste otherwise, and I'd already be orange in Ajay and Christina's wedding photos anyway. There wasn't time to get all the beta-carotene out of my system before tomorrow. Besides, orange was the new black, right?

I finished off the fries, pulling into the parking lot of the SBA a few minutes later. Before heading in, I figured I'd try Robin Beck's cell number again, see if maybe she'd answer today. No such luck. Rather than receiving the standard automated reply inviting me to leave a voice-mail message, this automated reply indicated the cell phone customer was temporarily unavailable and suggested the call be attempted again later. In other words, Robin was out of minutes on her prepaid cell phone plan. *Sheesh*. The girl seemed to be the queen of the deadbeats.

Sliding the phone into the pocket of my blazer, I rounded up my purse and briefcase, climbed out of my car, and headed into the building with Hana in tow. Inside the foyer, we approached the middle-aged man working the counter.

"Hello," he said. "You here for an appointment?"

"Not exactly," I told him. "We're from the IRS. We need to see Laurie Murphy."

While he looked a little leery, he didn't question our reasons for needing to see her, having been around the block enough by his age to know it was none of his business. "Let me see if she's available."

He picked up his phone and typed in a two-digit number. A few seconds later, he said, "Hi, Laurie. There's two women from the IRS here to see you." He listened for a moment, said, "Okay," and hung up the phone. "She'll be right out."

Our butts had just hit the chairs in the waiting area when the door to the back offices opened to reveal a woman around my age. She had long brown hair worn straight, no bangs. She was dressed in typical conservative government employee attire, much like me, though she'd had the fashion sense to tuck a cute polka-dot hanky into the breast pocket of her blazer.

She spotted me and Hana and said, "You're looking for me? Laurie Murphy?"

I stood. "Yes."

Hana stood, too, narrowing her eyes, flaring her nostrils, and gritting her teeth as she did so.

The woman cast Hana a bewildered look as she backed up against the door to hold it for us. "Come on back."

She led us down the hall to an office barely bigger than a closet. At least it had a small window to keep her from feeling claustrophobic. We sat down in two fake-leather-covered club chairs positioned so close together they touched. She closed the door behind us and slid into her seat behind her desk. "How can I help you two?"

I handed her one of my cards. "I'm Special Agent Tara Holloway with IRS Criminal Investigations." I raised a hand to indicate Hana. "Agent Hana Kim is assisting me today."

Continuing to glare, flare, and grit, Hana likewise handed Laurie a card.

She looked the cards over, set them down on her desk, and stood up partway, extending a hand over the desk to shake first mine, then Hana's. "Nice to meet you. What can I help you with? Is there a problem with one of our loan applicants?"

Really? She didn't realize we were here to talk about *her?* "What do you know about Bethany Flagler?" I asked.

Her expression didn't change though her hands moved to her keyboard. "I'm not familiar with that name. If you spell it for me, I could look up her file."

"No need," I said. "What about Robin Beck?" Again, there was no flicker of recognition when I mentioned the name. "Amelia Yeo? Gwen Rosenthal? Jocelyn Harris?" Nothing, nothing, nothing. Either this woman had incredible self-control, or she didn't know any of these names.

"Are they loan applicants?" she asked, looking from me to Hana. "You know that's what I do here, right? I review loan applications for small business owners."

"I understand," I said. "Actually, I'm looking into a tax fraud case, and your name came up."

Her face puckered in puzzlement. "*My* name? Why?"

"One of the victims said you might have a grudge against him."

"What?" Her mouth fell slack. "Who would have said that?"

I watched her closely. "Thomas Hoffmeyer."

Her mouth gaped even further for a brief second before it began to flap at record speed. "Thomas Hoffmeyer?" She grabbed the arms of her chair and squeezed them so tight her knuckles turned white. "That rude, insulting jerk! I can't believe he'd do this! Get the IRS after me for no reason? That man is—" She caught herself before she said something she'd regret, but she chewed on the words she didn't dare spit out, her mouth working as her cheeks flamed red with rage.

Hana arched a brow. "I take it there's no love lost between you and Thomas Hoffmeyer."

"Hardly!" the woman spat.

"So you're saying you didn't issue a false tax report in his name?" I asked.

Her face puckered again, even more this time. "A false tax report? What . . . ? How . . . ?" She raised her palms in question and squinted in my direction, as if by narrowing her eyes she could squeeze an explanation out of me. "I don't get it. What exactly are you asking me?"

Her confusion seemed sincere. My gut told me the trip out here had been yet another waste of my time. But might as well see things out. "He said you called him a bad name when he fired you."

"I was extremely upset," she said. "I worked as hard and fast as I could but he was on my back all the time. He never let up. So, yes, I called him an asshole."

The fact that she'd admitted exactly what she'd called him without any hemming or hawing told me she could be trusted. "I'm in complete agreement, by the way," I said. "He's an absolute ass."

Her face showed surprise for a moment, then broke into a smile. "Ass*hole*," she clarified.

"I stand corrected."

Eyes still narrowed, Hana looked from one of us to the other. "Gee. You two are making me sorry I never met him."

Laurie turned to Hana. "May I ask why you are looking at me like that? It's very disconcerting."

Hana glared even harder. "I'm supposed to look tough and intimidating."

I waved a dismissive hand. "You can relax now."

"Thank God!" Hana cried, her facial features relaxing. "I think I sprained an eyebrow and pulled a muscle in my septum."

I leaned forward, resting my arms on my knees. "Here's the deal, Laurie. Somebody filed reports with the IRS indicating that Thomas Hoffmeyer and several others had won prize money. We're trying to figure out who did it. It seems to me it has to be someone with a vendetta against the victims."

"That makes sense," she said. "But if you're trying to figure out who all might have a vendetta against Mr. Hoffmeyer, you'd have an awful long list. Nobody liked that man."

"Can you think of anyone at Snippy's who might have filed a false tax report on him?" I asked.

She mulled things over for a moment. "Honestly? No. I mean, a lot of the staff hated Mr. Hoffmeyer, and I'll admit that we even did some stupid things like put ketchup packets under his car tires when we came back from lunch. But filing a false tax report with the IRS could get the person who filed it in trouble, too, right? I don't think anyone would have gone that far."

"All right." I stood. "Thanks for meeting with us. If you happen to think of anyone who might have filed the reports, I'd appreciate a call."

"Okay. Should I walk you out?"

The stack of files on her desk was nearly as tall as the stack on mine. "No need," I said. "We can see you're busy. We'll see ourselves out."

Hana stood, too. We walked out of Laurie's office and were heading down the hall when I spotted an older woman ahead of me stop and call through a doorway. *"¡Ponte las pilas!"*

A laugh came from within the office and the woman continued on. Looked like that phrase was catching on everywhere, even among non-Latinas in their sixties.

A glance at my watch told me that I, too, needed to put in my batteries. It was nearly three o'clock and I had the drive back to Dallas plus a plane to catch soon. *¡Ponte las pilas, Tara!*

chapter twenty-six

$\mathcal{S}$ingles and Doubles

Nick stepped into my doorway a few minutes after five o'clock. "Ready to go?"

"Heck, yeah, I'm ready!" I grabbed my purse and out the door we went.

We drove to the expansive Dallas–Fort Worth airport, leaving our car in long-term parking. It would have been cheaper to park off-site and take a shuttle, but we were shorter on time than we were on cash. Plus, the car would only be there for forty-eight hours. The parking fee wouldn't break the bank.

After weaving our way through the security line, taking our shoes off and putting them on again, we made our way to the gate. There was no sign of Ajay or Christina.

I sent Christina a quick text. *Where are you?*

A duet of "over here!" sounded in response. Nick and I turned toward the voices to see Ajay and Christina sitting at the bar in one of the small restaurants tucked among the gates. Three other couples sat with them.

We walked over to join them.

Nick shook hands with Ajay, who was grinning ear to

ear. "You're looking awfully chipper for a man who's about to lose his freedom."

"Don't make me hurt you, Nick." Christina stood from the bar stool next to Ajay, looking gorgeous as always with her long, dark hair and generous curves tucked into a cute miniskirt and halter top. Dressed like that, she looked more like a cocktail waitress than an agent for the DEA. Still wearing my beige dress pants and basic black blazer, I felt relatively frumpy, but as soon as we got to our hotel I'd shed these work clothes and join everyone else in their party attire.

She gave Nick a hug and turned to me, giving me one, too. "I'm so glad you two could make it!"

I gave her a smile. "I wouldn't miss your wedding for the world!"

She introduced us to the other couples. One included a fellow DEA agent. The second included a good friend from Christina's childhood in Houston. The third were Ajay's older brother and his wife, who'd been sworn to secrecy.

"If my mother knew I was eloping," Ajay said, "she'd fly out to Vegas and give me a spanking."

The bartender, who'd been pouring drinks nearby, couldn't help himself. "If I gave your mother a call, you think she'd spank me?"

Ajay raised his near-empty glass. "You can count on it." He tossed back what little alcohol remained.

Nick pointed at Ajay's drink. "Ready for another?"

"You buying?"

"Hell, yes!" Nick said. "The wedding couple never pays for their own drinks."

"In that case," Ajay said, "make it a double!"

By the time the ten of us boarded the plane, we were already flying high. The three-hour flight to Vegas passed in a flash, and with us gaining two hours between the central time zone in Dallas and the Pacific time zone in Sin City, we arrived only an hour after we left. That meant there was plenty of time for fun tonight!

We checked into Caesars Palace and went up to our rooms to freshen up. I slid out of my boring work clothes and into my jeans and a brightly colored blouse paired with a pair of cute wedges. Everyone met downstairs by the craps tables, where we split into two groups, the girls and the boys.

"Don't be too naughty!" Christina called over her shoulder to Ajay as we girls headed out.

"You're not the boss of me!" he hollered back. "At least, not yet!"

We took a cab for the short ride from Caesars to the Excalibur, securing yet another round of drinks before taking our seats for the show. The Thunder from Down Under proved to be a perfect choice for an impromptu bachelorette party. The male dancers sure knew how to entertain. We whooped it up, took our photo afterward with a group of the dancers, and headed back to Caesars, all of us wiped out from the travel and excitement.

As we traipsed past the sports book, Christina threw out an arm to stop us. "Look!" she cried. "There's the guys."

Rather than go out for a show, they'd apparently opted to hang out and watch sports on the dozen or so oversized television screens that covered the walls. At the moment, all of their eyes were locked on two enormous sumo wrestlers engaged in combat on one of the screens. Japan was one of the few countries televising live sports at this late hour.

Ajay's older brother and Nick leaped from their seats, cheering. "Go, Kanji!" they yelled. "Take him down!"

In response, Ajay and the two other men pounded their fists on the arms of their club chairs, chanting, "Tom-o-yor-i! Tom-o-yor-i!"

I exchanged glances with Christina. Looked like our

men were growing up and settling down, more interested in sports than peep shows.

I nudged her with my elbow. "You know we have to give them crap for this."

"Of course!"

The five of us women entered the sports book and stopped in front of the men.

Christina plopped down on Ajay's lap, wrapping her arms around his neck. "I thought you boys would be at a topless show."

"We are." He gestured to the screen. "Those guys have the biggest bare breasts in town!"

One glance at the screen told me he was right.

A few seconds more and Tomoyori defeated Kanji.

Nick and Ajay's brother booed the screen, while Ajay shifted Christina off his lap and went with the others to the counter to collect their winnings. "Half of that's mine!" she called after him.

When they returned, we all agreed to call it a night.

"See y'all in the morning!" Nick called, wrapping an arm around my shoulders.

We went up to our room. As I took off my makeup and slipped into my nightgown, I couldn't help but think of Nina, Larissa, and Yessenia. Where were they tonight? Held captive in a cave somewhere, hoping a bear, mountain lion, or coyote wouldn't get them? Or had they succumbed to the intense desert heat and been left to decompose somewhere in the expanse of west Texas?

Nick eyed me intently. "You're thinking of those girls, aren't you?"

"I've been trying not to," I said. Thanks to the alcohol and half-naked men, I'd been fairly successful at pushing the kidnapping to the back of my mind for most of the evening. But it was harder now.

Nick stepped over and enveloped me in his arms. "It's going to be okay."

"You don't know that," I said softly, grabbing his T-shirt in both fists and burying my face in his chest as if to hide from my feelings.

"You're right," he acquiesced. "But I do know this. You've done everything in your power to help those girls."

It was true. I only wish I knew if it was going to be enough.

I spent a restless night worrying about the girls, but when I woke the next morning I was determined not to let it ruin Christina and Ajay's special day. I forced a smile to my face, and soon it became a real one. The wedding was a beautiful event.

Ajay wore a stylish three-piece suit, and Christina looked stunning in a strapless satin ivory gown that hung to mid-calf. She'd chosen to forgo a veil, instead wearing a head-band of fresh white roses. While Caesars offered a variety of wedding venues for ceremonies of all sizes, the two had opted for the smallest chapel, the Romano, given the circumstances. We headed down to the chapel en masse and, as we approached the room, we discovered both Ajay's and Christina's parents and extended family waiting, broad smiles on their faces.

"Surprise!" they called.

Christina gasped, and she and Ajay stopped in their tracks.

Ajay's mother stepped forward, Christina's mother flanking her.

Ajay's mom spoke first, looking from Christina to her son. "Your brother called us. He told us that we were putting too much pressure on you two and that we better back off and let you do things your way or we'd miss out on the entire thing. We are so sorry for interfering. I hope you can forgive us."

"Us, too," Christina's mother said, taking her daughter's hands in hers. "We certainly don't want to start things off on the wrong foot."

Christina misted up, waving a hand tipped with pearlescent polish in front of her face to dry the tears that were forming in her eyes. "I'm so glad you're here!" she choked out. "I really hated to do this without you!"

"Me, too," Ajay told his parents, giving his mother a hug and his dad a squeeze on the shoulder. He turned to Christina. "You ready to become the next Mrs. Maju?"

She nodded vigorously, still too emotional to speak.

Ajay's brother opened the double doors and we stepped into the chapel. The room was pretty, with marble columns and arched accents, as well as carpet in a colorful, traditional print. A black grand piano sat at the back of the room, a pianist ready to start.

The officiant was a gray-haired man in a stylish suit a shade lighter than his hair. He stood at the front next to a white, wooden podium, his hands clasped behind him. While the rest of us took our seats, Ajay walked up to stand to the man's left. Once everyone was in place, the pianist launched into an abbreviated version of the traditional wedding march. Christina's father, a tall man with her same dark hair and fit build, escorted her up the aisle. He gave her a kiss on the cheek and took a seat next to her mother in the front row.

When Christina and Ajay turned to each other with such love in their eyes, I found myself tearing up, too. Unlike the *amor* portrayed in *Amor y Vengaza,* the love between these two was real and lasting, the way it should be, the way it was when it was meant to be. You know, without the fake smiles and backstabbing and attempted murders and stuff.

Nick cut a glance my way, smiled softly when he saw my tears, and whipped a tissue out of his jacket pocket. He must've known this was coming and slid a package into his pocket when we were getting ready at the hotel. He wrapped a warm hand around my shoulders as I dabbed my eyes.

After the usual preliminaries, the officiant got down to business, turning to Ajay. "Do you, Ajay, take Christina to be your wife? Will you always love, honor, and cherish her, in sickness and in health, for richer and for poorer, for as long as you both shall live?"

Ajay said, "I do." His voice broke when he added, "And I always will."

Christina smiled at his improvisation, repeating the sentiment when it was her turn. "I do, and I always will."

They exchanged rings and the officiant pronounced them man and and wife, the rest of us cheering and applauding. They sealed their future with a warm kiss.

After a celebratory meal topped off with champagne and wedding cake at one of the casino's upscale restaurants, we spent the rest of the day enjoying the city. We gathered around a craps table, some of us winning and some of us losing, our money basically being redistributed among us time and time again. Just three hours into their marriage and Ajay and Christina had already gone through three or four rounds of richer and poorer.

When we tired of craps, we moved on to blackjack. The waitress brought us another round of drinks as we slid onto the stools. In the first game, the dealer dealt me the queen of hearts. "Hit me," I said, tapping my card.

He gave me a second card. The ace of spades. I threw my hands in the air. "Twenty-one!"

"Rub it in, why don't you?" snarled Ajay jokingly. He'd gone over. He shouldn't have asked for that fourth card.

After an hour or so, we moved on to the slots.

Christina's mother chose a machine next to me. "I remember back in the day when the machines gave you actual money instead of a ticket to redeem," she said. "We'd all carry around these little plastic buckets of money and the coins would turn our fingers black. It wasn't as convenient, but it sure was fun watching those coins fall into the tray." These days, that sound was simulated by the machines when they paid out.

She pulled the lever to play the machine. A red seven popped up in the first column. Another red seven popped up in the second column. She raised clenched fists. "Come on, red seven!" As if she'd willed it, a third red seven popped up in the third column. A light at the top of the machine began to spin like a police beacon. "I won!"

"Congrats!" I said. "How much?"

She consulted the screen. "Two grand! Woo hoo!" She cashed out and grabbed her payout ticket from the machine. Leaning in to me, she said, "Don't tell my husband I won. I'm going to surprise him with a new sofa, maybe one with a built-in recliner. We've had the one we've got since Christina was a little girl. It's time for an upgrade."

I gave her a smile and pretended to zip my lip.

Nick walked up. "These machines are robbing me blind. How about we go for a swim?"

We bade good-bye to Christina's mother, went up to our room to change into our bathing suits, and spent the next couple of hours lounging by the pool, me with a frozen margarita in my hands, Nick with a cold beer. My odd skin tone garnered me a few odd looks as I lay sprawled on the padded chaise, but I didn't care. I was having too much fun.

That night, we regrouped to go see the Blue Man Group together. Sitting in front of me at the performance, Ajay turned his head and caught my eye over his shoulder. "With your skin, you could star in the Orange Woman Show."

I took his razzing in stride, responding only by sticking out my tongue.

The show was a lot of fun, an unusual but entertaining mix of music, science, dancing, and comedy. Afterward, Nick and I returned to our room, tired from the busy day, but not too tired to continue the party on our own.

"I may have lost at the tables and slots," Nick said with a naughty grin as he swept me up into his arms and carried me to the bed, "but I know I'll get lucky here."

"I owe you that raunchy makeup sex, don't I?"

"Hell, yeah!"

By the time we were finished, the pillows were on the floor, the sheets were tangled up around us, and we were both panting as if we'd just run a marathon.

Nick turned his head to look at me. "This Vegas wedding has been fun. Maybe you and I should get married here."

"It's much too late for that," I told him. "Our mothers have nearly all the details hammered out already."

"They didn't waste any time, did they?"

"Not a second."

He turned to face me full on, propping himself up on an elbow. "Those two are going to spoil our kids."

"I don't doubt that for a second."

He reached out a hand and rubbed a warm thumb down the side of my face. "I love the hell out of you, Tara Holloway."

"Back at you, Nick Pratt."

Everyone was much quieter on the flight home Sunday, worn out from the nonstop action and excitement. The closer the plane got to Texas, the more my anxiety about the girls returned. I'd hoped Agent Castaneda would have contacted me over the weekend to tell me that they'd either found the girls or put eyes back on Hidalgo, but he hadn't been in touch. My heart shrank into a hard, painful ball in my chest. Only twenty-four hours remained before the ransom was due. If the girls weren't found before then, their lives could be over. God, I didn't want to think of that horrific possibility.

While Nick dozed next to me, I took advantage of the airplane's Wi-Fi system to watch the next episode of *A y V*. I'd been going nuts wondering what would happen between Isidora and the barista, and I figured the show might help take my mind off my worries.

The episode began by repeating the previous scene, the one on which the preceding episode had ended.

"Isidora?" the barista cried, his expression incredulous. *"You are my new boss?"*

The deceptive smile spread across her face once again, just as it had in the last episode. *"Indeed I am."*

"But what we had was so special! Why do you treat me so poorly? Do you love me no longer?"

"I never loved you," Isidora lied. *"You were merely a plaything to me."*

Ooh, that did it. The sexy barista threw down the gauntlet—or, rather, he threw down his bar towel. I watched the screen, one eye on the actors, the other on the subtitles. *"I refuse to work for such a pittance!"* he cried to Isidora. *"Or for such an evil woman as you! I quit!"*

As he stormed out of the room, she had a vicious thought that ran across the bottom of the screen. *Nobody makes a fool of Isidora Davila without thoroughly regretting it.*

She sat down at her computer and doctored the coffeehouse's financial records, smiling deceptively as she reported an enormous amount of income for the barista to the SAT, or Tax Administration Service, the Mexican equivalent of the IRS.

Holy guacamole!

The situation was too similar to the fake prize case I was investigating to be coincidence, wasn't it? Had I just been handed an inadvertent clue? Could the person who issued the fraudulent 1099s have been inspired by Isidora Davila? Had the telenovela star given a viewer the idea of using the tax reporting system as a means of revenge?

It was certainly possible, likely even. But with seemingly everyone I'd spoken to lately being hooked on the show, including all of the victims, this potential lead didn't narrow things down much, if at all. Still, it gave me something to think about.

Think, Tara. Think. Think . . .

Could the perpetrator be someone like Isidora, a seemingly sweet woman to everyone's face, but a conniving backstabber when she felt she'd been wronged? If so, who was this person?

chapter twenty-seven

$\mathcal{M}$aking the Connection

When the plane landed at DFW at 9:30 Sunday evening, I still didn't know who was responsible for issuing the fake prize reports, but I felt certain it was someone who watched *A y V.* That person had to have a connection to all of the victims. But whatever the link was, it still eluded me.

Ugh!

The nap Nick had taken had given him a second wind, and my frustration seemed to be fueling me. Like the connection between the 1099 targets, Salvador Hidalgo was nowhere to be found. On the drive home, I asked Nick if he'd mind taking a quick detour.

"Just tell me where to," he said.

I inputted Hidalgo's address in Pleasant Grove into my GPS. A half hour later, we rolled up his street. When the GPS told us we'd arrived at our destination, I gave the house a quick but thorough once-over as Nick kept the car moving. Didn't want to inadvertently tip the guy off that his house was being cased or he might not return to it. Of course, given that the house was totally dark and there was no vehicle in the carport, it appeared no one was home anyway.

We continued on down the street. When we turned the corner at the next intersection, I spotted a man sitting in an old muscle car, smoking a cigarette. I glanced back, noting he could keep eyes on Hidalgo's house from his position.

Nick picked up on the guy, too. "A hundred bucks says that guy in the GTO is a fed."

"That's a bet you might actually win," I teased. Nick had lost every cent he'd brought to Vegas. First Kanji the sumo wrestler let him down, then it was the shooters at the craps table, then it was the blackjack dealer. Heck, even the cherries conspired against him at the slot machines.

Being a good sport, Nick chuckled. "I hope you won't mind working until you're eighty because I lost all of my retirement savings."

"Time for me to start looking for that second husband, huh?"

"Don't you dare."

The fact that Border Patrol had an undercover agent keeping eyes on Hidalgo's house here told me they still hadn't tracked the guy down. *Damn.* I'd been hoping to hear some good news when I got back in town, thought maybe Castaneda has been saving it for after I returned from my trip. So much for that.

Where was Hidalgo hiding? Whether he was north of the border or south was anyone's guess at this point. Hell, for all we knew he was in a kayak, taking a nice pleasure trip down the Rio Grande River. Was it wrong of me to hope he capsized and got eaten by a bear?

When I arrived home, Annie met me and Nick at the door, mewing nonstop as if to say *Mommy! Mommy! Mommy! I thought you'd never come home!* While Nick carried my suitcase upstairs to my bedroom, I scooped the cat up in my arms and cuddled her tight, scratching behind her ears with my fingers. She craned her neck and purred in appreciation.

From atop the armoire that housed my TV, Henry lay with his eyes closed, though he swished his tail to let me know he was angry I hadn't been here to give him his treats on demand. I stepped over and gave him a rub down his back. "Come on, boy. I'll give you a treat."

He stood, stretched, and made his way down from the perch, hopping first to a bookcase, then onto the coffee table, then onto the floor. He followed me to the kitchen, where I gave each of the cats three treats each. Henry gobbled his down, swished his tail one last time, and returned to the living room to sharpen his claws on my sofa.

Nick left me with a chaste kiss. "See you in the morning."

I tossed and turned all night, my mind troubled with the niggling thought that there was something I was missing, some clue I'd overlooked. When I woke on Monday morning, groggy and grumpy, I started the coffeepot and took a shower.

As the warm water ran over me, I realized that while I'd asked the prize scam victims for their personal information and compared their lists of churches, banks, gyms, and the like, and while I'd asked them about their coworkers, I hadn't gone so far as to compare a list of employees for each of the companies. Really, it was the only thing left I could do before throwing in the towel and telling the victims and the senator that all leads had been exhausted to no avail.

I dried off, got ready for work, and drove to the office. After logging into the system, I pulled up the W-2 data for

Sweet Melody Music, MetalMasters, Eternal Summer, and Snippy's. I printed out a list of people for whom each company had filed 1099s in the past five years. Fortunately, the lists for all of the companies but MetalMasters were relatively short. Being strategic, I focused on the lists for the other three companies, searching for any overlap of names. I set the three lists side by side, going through the names one by one.

Adamson, Bradley. *Nope.* That name appeared only on the Sweet Melody list.

Anders, Mary. *Nope.* That name was not repeated elsewhere, either.

Archer, Nicole. *Nope.*

I continued on down the list. The only overlap among the three was the name John Smith. Not a surprise, I supposed, given that both the first and last names were extremely common. While the name did not show up on the Sweet Melody list, it appeared on both the list for MetalMasters and the one for Snippy's. A quick glance at the employee's social security numbers, however, told me it was two different John Smiths.

Ugh.

I continued on until I reached the end of the list. Zaruba, Zachary. *Nope.*

Dang it! Dang, dang, dang!

I rounded up my notes from my briefcase. Maybe if I took a look at them one more time, something would pop out at me. If not, the file would go into archives along with the other cases agents had been unable to solve. I didn't like that idea, though. I mean, on a realistic, practical level, I realized I wouldn't win them all, wouldn't always figure things out, wouldn't catch every bad guy. But on another level, I didn't like to lose, especially to someone who'd used the IRS as an unwitting pawn. If I couldn't determine who had issued those fake 1099s for the prize winnings, it was going to bug me, to sit in a tiny little corner of my gut and fester. And I sure didn't like the fact that I'd be letting Lu down. She'd have to call Senator Perkins's office and tell him that I'd been unable to find the clues I'd needed or put together the clues I'd gathered. She'd have to tell him that I'd failed. Maybe I'm a bit of a perfectionist when it comes to my work, and maybe I put undue pressure on myself, but I didn't like to be a failure.

I ripped the pages of notes from the notepad and laid them out on the desk where I could see them all at once. I ran my gaze over the pages, various words randomly catching my eye. I circled the ones that could be important. *Stolen checks. Payroll service. Franchisee.*

Wait a second . . .

My eyes and mind went back to *payroll service.* Jocelyn had mentioned that the woman sent out by Eternal Summer's payroll service had made some mistakes. I'd dismissed the information at the time because Jocelyn said she'd never complained about the worker to the payroll company. I'd assumed, then, that the worker wouldn't have known Jocelyn was dissatisfied and would have suffered no consequences as a result, and would therefore have no reason to seek revenge on Jocelyn. That logic still seemed to hold. But hadn't Thomas Hoffmeyer also mentioned that Snippy had outsourced its payroll?

My eyes scanned the pages, stopping on the notes I'd taken during his interview. Yep, I'd jotted a note that Laurie Murphy and his other staff members had taken turns handling payroll on a four-week rotation before the payroll handling was sent "out of house."

My nerves began to buzz with excitement, but I tried my best to ignore it. This could be nothing, a mere coincidence. After all, it wasn't at all unusual for companies, especially smaller ones, to hire a third-party service to handle their payroll. Collecting and paying taxes could be complicated, and it was often cheaper to have a specialized company take care of the task than to hire an experienced employee to handle it. In fact, payroll processing services were on the rise, with many to choose from. Heck, one of the CPAs I'd worked with at Martin & McGee had left the firm to start his own payroll service outfit. Last I heard, he was making money hand over fist.

Could the payroll service be the missing link, the connection between the victims that I'd been missing? Neither Bethany Flagler nor either of the accountants at Metal-Masters had mentioned a payroll service. But I hadn't asked them about their payroll, either. Looked like it was time to do just that.

I grabbed my phone and placed a call to Sweet Melody Music. "Bethany Flagler, please," I said when the male voice answered again. When he put me on hold, the music this time was a marching band's version of Rick Astley's "Never Gonna Give You Up." Yep, I'd been Rick-rolled.

I sang along with the music for a minute or so until Bethany picked up the line. "Bethany Flagler. How may I help you?"

"Hello, Bethany," I said. "It's Special Agent Holloway from the IRS."

"Oh. Hi. Did you figure out anything about the prize scam?"

"You may have the answer to that question."

"Excuse me?"

I couldn't blame her for being confused. My words had been a bit cryptic. "I'm working on a theory," I told her. "Can you tell me who does the payroll for Sweet Melody Music?" I held my breath, hoping her answer would give me the break I'd been looking for.

"It's handled by an outside company," she said.

Break! Or, at least *potential break!*

"Which one?" I asked.

"I'm not sure what their name is, but their logo is printed on our paychecks. It's two white letter *F*s outlined in black with flames coming out of the bottom. I think they're supposed to look like rockets or something."

"Hold on a second." I performed a quick Internet search. In less than fifteen seconds I had my answer. Sweet Melody's payroll service was Financial Force Ltd. "Got it," I said. "Looks like it's Financial Force."

"That sounds right."

"Did you ever come in direct contact with anyone from the company?"

"Yeah," she replied. "They sent someone out to set up the payroll system for Sweet Melody."

"Male or female?"

"Female. A girl about twenty-five."

"What was her name?"

"I can't remember off the top of my head. Sorry. She was only here a day or two, and that was a couple years ago. But I'll never forget her. She's the one who introduced me to *Amor y Vengaza*. She was watching it on her break and told me how good it was."

"Did you and she ever butt heads?"

"What do you mean?" Bethany asked.

"Did you argue about anything? Maybe have a disagreement?"

"No. We didn't really talk a whole lot, other than about the show. Anything else was just small talk. The weather. The traffic. Stuff like that. But we never had an argument."

Hmm. There seemed to be a lack of motive here, but I'd worry about that later. Even if the young woman hadn't been the actual one to issue the false reports, she was the common denominator. Maybe someone had used her log-in credential to steal the client's personal data. "Do you think anyone else at Sweet Melody might remember her name?"

She was quiet for a moment, probably thinking. "Maybe Ronnie," she said. "The girl looked just like Isidora from *A y V*." Again she pronounced it *ah ee vay*. "Ronnie joked that he'd always wanted to date a TV star and that she was the closest he was likely to ever get. I think he might have asked her out. I'm not sure whether they ever went out or not, but I can check."

"Please do. Call me back once you hear, okay?"

"Okay."

As we hung up the phone, I remembered that Gwen and Amelia had mentioned having a coworker who dyed her hair black and dressed like Isidora. It had to be the same person, right?

I phoned MetalMasters and asked to be transferred to the office of Amelia Yeo and Gwen Rosenthal.

Amelia answered the phone. "Hello, this is Amelia Yeo."

After identifying myself, I said, "Is Gwen there with you?"

"Yes. She's at her desk, too."

"Can you put me on speaker?"

"Sure. Just a sec." A moment later there was a *click* and Amelia's voice came back. "Gwen and I are both listening now."

"Great. I have a few follow-up questions for you two."

"All right," Gwen said.

"When I came to MetalMasters to interview you, you mentioned you had a coworker who was hooked on *Amor y Vengaza* and had dyed her hair to look like Isidora. What was her name?"

"She wasn't actually a coworker," Amelia corrected me. "She worked for an outside company and was only here for a week."

"What outside company did she work for?"

"Our payroll processor," Amelia said. "She came out to install the software and input the employee information."

"And is your payroll processor Financial Force?"

"Yes," Amelia replied. "That's the one."

Woo hoo! This *potential break* was looking more and more like a *real break!* Whoever this girl was would have had access to the employees' names, social security numbers, and home addresses when she set up the company's payroll system.

"What was the girl's name?" I asked.

"Cassidy . . . something," Amelia said. "I'm not sure I ever knew her last name."

Gwen's voice called out, "Briscoe! Her name was Cassidy Briscoe."

"Got it." I wrote the name down on my pad and, in my excitement, underlined it three times in quick succession. "Did either of you have any trouble with her?"

"Not at all," Amelia said. "She was very sweet."

"She was one of those people who smiles all the time," Gwen added. "Always happy."

But did Cassidy's smile hide a thousand feelings? Some of which might be anger, irritation, or jealousy?

Again, if Cassidy Briscoe was the one who'd filed the false 1099s for Amelia and Gwen, there seemed to be a lack of motive. But perhaps there was a motive the victims weren't aware of. Or, again, maybe Cassidy had been a pawn in the scheme, too. Maybe someone had used Cassidy to get access to the victim's data. But who might that person be and why would they issue the reports? Only Cassidy herself could tell me that.

"Thanks," I said. "That's all I need for now."

As I hung up on the two, a call came in from Bethany Flagler.

"I got the name from Ronnie," she said. "The girl's name was Cassidy. He said they didn't actually go out or anything, just flirted a little."

"Thanks."

I called Jocelyn next. Unfortunately, she was with a client and was unable to take my call. Thomas Hoffmeyer wasn't available when I tried his home number, either.

"He's out at the driving range," his wife said. "You could try his cell, but you're not likely to have any luck. He turns his phone off when he goes out there."

"Maybe you can help me," I said. "Where'd you first hear of *Amor y Vengaza?* Any chance it was from a young woman named Cassidy Briscoe?"

"How'd you know?" she replied, surprise in her voice.

"Several others involved in the bogus prize investigation have mentioned her name."

"They did? Well, she sure was a sweet little thing. Always cheerful. She spent a couple of weeks at Snippy's helping set up the payroll systems for both the corporate office and the franchisees. The company wasn't very big at that time and they hired me to help out with a few administrative things now and then. I'd been an executive secretary years ago. Cassidy and I shared an office for a few days."

"Would she have any reason to want to get back at your husband?" I asked.

"I can't think of any reason in particular," she said. "Even though he wasn't technically her boss, he was as hard on her as he was on the employees. He never seemed to think anyone worked fast enough or put in enough hours. But there wasn't any specific incident or problem if that's what you're asking. Besides, she and I got along just fine. I even took her out for lunch one day."

I thanked her for the information. "Enjoy the rest of your day."

"You, too."

My next step would be questioning Cassidy Briscoe in person. Every nerve tingled at the thought. Either she was the person I was looking for, or she could probably lead me to the culprit. Either way, I'd better take my handcuffs.

chapter twenty-eight

$\mathscr{Y}$ou Can't Spell Smile Without L-I-E-S

I slid my handcuffs into my briefcase, gathered my things, and stepped out into the hall, glancing into Nick's office. He was talking on his phone and leaning back in his chair, his boots propped on his desk. His silver belt buckle reflected the fluorescent light from overhead. He cut a glance my way and shot me a wink. I blew him a kiss and he pretended to snatch it out of the air with his teeth.

I snagged Josh as he came up the hallway. "I'm on my way to question someone who likely obtained social security numbers and other personal information from office computers. Can you come along in case she gets technical on me?"

I could use computers, but I didn't really understand how they worked. If Cassidy started in on access issues or password protection or encryption, I could quickly get in over my head. Better to have the office tech specialist along in case the conversation went in that direction.

"Sure," Josh said.

I wasn't surprised he'd agreed. He liked to lord his technical superiority over the rest of us. But we couldn't much blame him. He was short and small and had only recently lost his virginity. His technical savvy was one of the few things he had going for him. At least he was no longer the obnoxious dweeb he'd been when I'd first joined the IRS.

While Financial Force was a national corporation, they maintained regional offices. The Dallas office was in a business district near the Galleria. Of course, it was possible that Cassidy would be out at a client's office setting up their new payroll system, but I preferred to go to the office and speak with her supervisor rather than discussing the matter on the phone. I wanted to make sure that the supervisor understood the seriousness of the situation and didn't try to interfere by giving Cassidy a heads-up. As well as Robin Beck had been able to stay out of my sights without even trying, and with Hidalgo on the lam, too, I didn't want Cassidy to go into hiding as well. I needed something to show for all the effort I was putting in.

We climbed into my G-ride, wound our way out of downtown, and merged onto the tollway, heading north. As always, the tollway was a virtual free-for-all, the posted speed limits considered a mere suggestion by the motorists who thought paying a fee to use the road gave them the right to drive as fast as they wanted. Fortunately, despite a couple of motorists who cut me off, seemingly intent on knocking off my front bumper, Josh and I made it unscathed to the office building where Financial Force Ltd. had its offices.

We rode the elevator up to the fifth floor and stepped out, glancing up and down the hall. *There it is.* The logo with two flaming *F*s graced the glass enclosing a small reception area.

We went inside and checked in with the woman behind the desk. She had the shiny hair and practiced pleasantness of a flight attendant. "Good morning. How may I help you today?"

Though nobody was in the reception area, I nonetheless kept my voice quiet as I handed her my business card. "I'm Special Agent Tara Holloway from the Internal Revenue Service." I hiked a thumb at Josh. "Agent Schmidt, also from IRS. We need to speak to whoever is in charge of this office."

The women seemed nonplussed. I supposed it made sense for a business that was used to dealing with tax matters on a regular basis. *IRS? No problem.* "That would be Nancy DeWitt," she said. "She's the regional manager. I'll let her know you're here. Feel free to take a seat."

While she phoned the office's grand pooh-bah, Josh and I perched on an ugly yet functional vinyl loveseat and looked over the magazine selections. All were financial rags, their taglines intended to entice readers to purchase them, promising secret day-trading tips and how to make millions working part-time from home. *Yeah, right.*

I'd just begun to read an article on the top ten money mistakes newlyweds make when Nancy DeWitt opened the door that led back to the offices. She was fifty-plus, sturdy, and carried herself with the confidence of a woman who'd weathered enough crises to know nothing short of a nuclear bomb could take her down. "Agents Holloway and Schmidt?"

We stood and walked over to shake her hand.

"Let's talk in my office." She turned and led the way down the hall. She walked through a set of double doors at the end of the corridor, stopping to close them behind us once Josh and I stepped through.

Her corner office was large and nicely decorated with cherrywood furniture and prints of famous paintings that I recognized, though I could name neither the artists nor the titles. *I should work on becoming more cultured, huh?* Her two walls of windows faced east and south, giving her a view of the downtown Dallas skyline and the Galleria Mall next door.

She held out a hand to indicate the two Queen Anne chairs placed before her desk. I took a seat in one and Josh took the other. To my surprise, she plunked one butt cheek onto the front of the desk rather than sitting behind it. Looked like she wanted to keep things more friendly and casual. I didn't often get that kind of reception. Most people wanted to put as much distance as they could between themselves and an IRS agent.

As she leaned against the desk, her brows rose, disappearing under her curly bangs. "We've never had a visit from the criminal department of the IRS," she said. "I'm guessing there's a problem?"

"There is," I said. "Someone filed false tax reports on several people in the Dallas area a couple of years ago. The bogus reports indicated the people had won prize awards. I've interviewed all of the witnesses and looked for a common denominator that might tell me who filed the reports."

DeWitt lifted her chin. "I take it Financial Force is the common denominator?"

"It is," I said. "One of your staff installed payroll software at the workplaces of each of the victims and interacted with each of them."

"Which would give the staff member access to the victims' personal information," DeWitt supplied for me.

"Exactly."

Her brows returned to their normal position but her lips pursed. "I can't imagine who on my staff might have misused sensitive data like that, but it would be naive for me to assume I know people as well as I think I do. Who do you think it is?"

"Cassidy Briscoe."

The woman's head snapped backward as if she'd been slapped. She raised her palms. "Whoa, whoa, whoa. *Cassidy?*" She shook her head. "No. Not her."

I gave her a pointed look. "I thought you weren't going to make any assumptions."

"I did say that, didn't I?" Her expression bordered on pained. "It's just that Cassidy is the office sweetheart. She's a ball of sunshine."

I cocked my head. "Always wears a smile?"

"Well, yes. She does. Why?"

"Ever heard the expression, *a smile can hide a thousand feelings?*"

"No."

"Neither have I," said Josh.

Okay, so I hadn't, either. At least not until I'd read the slip of paper that came inside my fortune cookie. Still, it was a profound, even ugly truth. Especially for women. How many times were we told to "put on a happy face" when we were upset? To fake it 'til we make it? Such unhealthy bullshit. When something was bothering me, I'd found taking my Glock to a firing range and squeezing off a few rounds provided welcome relief and was much better for my psyche than pretending my feelings weren't warranted and didn't exist.

The woman's face creased along the edges of her eyes and mouth, showing how perplexed and conflicted she felt. "Even if Cassidy had access to all of the victims' personal data," she said, "why would she want to cause them trouble?"

"Honestly? I don't know that," I admitted. "But I'm hoping to find out."

She was quiet a moment, her expression thoughtful. "Even though Cassidy might have been the one to set up the relevant client accounts," she said, "she would not have been the only Financial Force employee to have access to their information. If there were updates or a client had technical problems, someone else might have helped them."

"It might very well be an employee other than Cassidy," I acknowledged. "But I have to start somewhere and she seems to be the logical place." Especially since the heroine of her favorite telenovela had herself filed false tax reports as a means of revenge, and Cassidy seemed to be modeling herself after the woman. "Is she out at a client's office?"

"Not today," DeWitt said. "She's updating direct deposit information for workers who have switched banks." She sighed and stood slowly, reluctantly. "I'll take you to her office."

"Great." I stood, also, and Josh followed suit.

She pulled open the double doors and led us down to the end of the hall. We passed an open door where a young man sat with earbuds in his ears, bobbing his head to music as he worked on his computer. She stopped at the next door, the last one on the hall, which sat next to the door that led to the stairwell. Cassidy's office door was wide open, though I couldn't see around DeWitt. All I could see was the door, adorned with a poster of a tiny gray kitten staring up the trunk of a big tree. The caption read, *You can do it!*

I hesitated briefly. Would someone who displayed this type of cheesy inspirational poster file false tax reports? Josh must've been having the same thought, meeting my gaze then cutting his eyes to the kitty.

DeWitt tapped a knuckle on the door of the office. "Cassidy? I need to speak with you."

"Come on in!" called a cheery voice.

DeWitt walked into the office, stepping aside to reveal an Isidora Davila clone sitting behind a desk. *Whoa.* The resemblance was truly uncanny, as close as any of the celebrity impersonators I'd seen on the billboards and posters in Vegas. The hair color and makeup were the same, and the black dress Cassidy wore was precisely Isidora's trademark mix of professional and feminine, its sheer sleeves providing a subtle hint of sex appeal. A bowl of strawberry-flavored candy in shiny wrappers on her desk offered a treat to those who visited her office. A laptop computer sat in front of her, its cord plugged into a power strip on the edge of her desk, along with a printer and a desk lamp.

When Cassidy caught my eye, her lips spread in a warm smile that, ironically, froze the blood in my veins.

I know that smile. And it hides pure evil.

Okay, perhaps I was being melodramatic. Maybe I'd been watching too much *A y V.*

She stood and offered her hand. "Hi, there! I'm Cassidy."

While I shook the young woman's hand, her boss introduced me. She did the same for Josh.

Cassidy blinked a couple of times, the smile never faltering. "How can I help you two?"

Before I could answer, DeWitt excused herself. "I've got some matters to tend to. I'll check in with y'all in a bit." She left the office, shutting the door behind her.

I looked Cassidy in the eye. "Miss Briscoe, I'll be upfront with you. Someone filed fraudulent 1099s reporting prize winnings to several people in the area."

"They did?"

"Yes."

She tilted her head, her expression innocent. "I don't understand. Why are you here?"

"Because you're the primary suspect."

chapter twenty-nine

Stairway to Hell

Cassidy's eyes flashed. But whether it was from alarm, fear, or anger was unclear.

"Me?" Her voice sounded incredulous as the words slipped past her smiling lips. "Why am I a suspect?"

"Because you installed payroll software at the companies where each of the victims works. That can't be mere coincidence."

She put a hand tipped with red nails to her chest, her gaze going from me to Josh as if seeking an ally. "But filing false tax reports? I'd never do such a thing!"

"I think you might."

Her mouth fell open. "Why? What reason would I have to file false reports for anyone?"

She had me there. I'd yet to determine her motive, at least where everyone other than Thomas Hoffmeyer was concerned. He was a jerk and it was obvious why anyone would want to give him a little hell.

"Why?" I said. "Maybe because it's the type of thing Isidora Davila would do if someone upset her. After all, she filed a false tax report on her barista boyfriend."

Cassidy's eyes flashed again. Was she angry she'd been found out, that the show she loved and the character she idolized had betrayed her? Or was she was simply scared of being wrongfully convicted for something she didn't do? "I'm innocent!" she insisted. "Ask anyone! They'll tell you. I'm not like that. Besides, why would I do something that could get me in trouble, too? I love my job and my boss, and I certainly don't want the IRS coming after me."

Why, indeed? Maybe I was like the kitten from the poster, looking up the wrong tree. "If it wasn't you," I said, "then who could it be?"

"I have no idea," she said. "It could have been someone else at the clients' offices, or maybe someone else here, even. The account representatives have access to all the client files."

"That's what your boss told me, too." That tingle I'd felt earlier, the one that told me I was getting close to solving the case, had disappeared, replaced by a niggling feeling that I was off base here. "How many account representatives are there?"

"Sixteen," she said, "not including the tech staff. If you add them in it's twenty-one."

In other words, twenty other potential suspects. But before I moved on to them, I needed to be convinced that Cassidy wasn't the wrongdoer.

"If it was one of your coworkers who filed the fake reports," I said, "why would they have done it?" I was still searching for the elusive motive here.

"I hate to say this," she said, cringing. "But someone here might be trying to frame me."

Was it possible? Or was this just some telenovela-style melodrama? "Why would anyone want to frame you? By all accounts you're the office sweetheart."

"That's exactly why!" She let out a slow breath. "I'm young and attractive and friendly and everyone likes me. One of the other women around here is probably jealous and wants to get me fired. Or maybe one of the guys. There are some pretty ambitious types here, and they might not like that Nancy and I get along so well."

I'd come here convinced that Cassidy Briscoe was the guilty party, but now I wasn't so sure, not at all. I mean, sure, she looked like Isidora and Isidora was no saint, but I'd found myself drawn to the character, too, admiring her determination, the fact that she didn't take crap from anyone, at least not without getting even somehow. Who was I to judge Cassidy so harshly? And there was no denying that Isidora was a knockout with a dazzling style. Maybe this young woman just wanted to look like Isidora, not act like her.

Whether I was right or wrong, it was clear I'd get no further talking to Cassidy. She'd made no confession, given me nothing more to go on. I figured I might as well speak to her coworkers, see what they had to say. Heck, one of them might even break down and confess. It happened on occasion, especially if a suspect thought they could get off easy by cooperating.

"Who are the people you think would be most likely to try to frame you?" I asked, pen at the ready to take notes. "Can you give me some names?"

"Okay," Cassidy said softly, her expression reluctant and resigned. She proceeded to give me three names of coworkers who just might be envious enough of her to try to frame her for tax fraud. Two were female, one was male.

"What do these people do?" I asked.

She indicated that the two females were customer account representatives like her, but that the male coworker was a programmer who handled the technical end, troubleshooting software issues and customizing software for bigger clients.

"Did all of these people work here two years ago?" I asked.

"Yes," she said. "Why?" She seemed genuinely in the dark.

"That's when the false tax reports were filed."

She cupped her hands under her chin and put her elbows on the desk, her expression saying that she was thinking things through. "We've had a few people leave since then," she said. "What if it was one of them?"

Ugh. I came here for answers, not more questions. "Whoever it was," I said, "I'll figure it out eventually." Isidora Davila wasn't the only one with determination. I held up the list of names she'd given me.

"Can you show us to their offices?"

"I'd be happy to."

Josh stepped out in the hall. As I turned to exit, too, I heard a noise behind me. I glanced over my shoulder to see that Cassidy had ripped the electrical cord from her laptop and the socket. The next thing I knew, she'd flung the cord over my head and yanked back on it with all the force she could muster.

Holy shit! I thought as the cord tightened around my neck. *I can't breathe!*

I tried to holler to Josh, who was out in the hall, but I couldn't get a scream out. My voice came out no louder than a soft whisper. "Josh!"

I dropped my purse and briefcase to the floor and clawed reflexively at the cord, falling backward against Cassidy's desk as she pulled. Her hands whipped around my head, wrapping the cord around my neck a second time.

No!

I tried desperately to suck in some air, any air! But there was no air to be had.

Still trying to pull the cord loose, but unable to get a finger under the strand digging into my neck, I kicked out at the chair I'd been sitting in. I'd hoped to make enough noise that Josh would turn around to see what the ruckus was all about. Unfortunately, the lightweight chair simply fell over quietly on the carpet, hardly making a sound. *Shit!*

Giving up on the cord, I reached down to my waist, attempting to access my gun. Cassidy beat me to the punch, grabbing my wrist and yanking my arm up behind me. *OW!* I wanted to scream in pain, but couldn't.

I struggled to free my arm, but with sparks starting to dance in my peripheral vision, I was losing both consciousness and strength. *What can I do? I don't want to die here!*

Fortunately, I'd studied martial arts very briefly when a recent case squared me against a black belt. I remembered that self-defense often required a person to act against instinct, to sometimes run toward danger rather than to retreat. While my instincts were telling me to pull against the cord, maybe I should instead be forcing myself backward, toward Cassidy.

I did just that, using my left hand to leverage myself up onto her desk. I put the rubber soles of my Doc Martens on the surface and pushed with all my might, forcing myself backward.

The candy dish!

As I pushed myself back, I kicked the candy dish as hard as I could. It sailed off the desk and through the air, crashing into the wall, strawberry candies raining down on the carpet.

Josh peered back through the door as I flew off the desk

on the other side. "What's going on here!" he yelled, re-flexively raising his hands in the air. "Stop! Help!"

Unfortunately, with everyone in the immediate vicinity wearing earbuds, Josh's cries weren't likely to rouse anyone. Besides, he was the federal agent. He was the one with the gun. He was the one who was supposed to stop this, to be my help. Sometimes he seemed to forget that his technical skills weren't his only skills.

My back impacted Cassidy's chest and she released my arm. The cord loosened for a split second as we fell to the floor behind her desk, just long enough for me to gasp a single breath of air. *Uh!*

Cassidy wriggled out from under me and managed to get to her feet, both hands still grasping the cord. Backed against the wall behind me, she yanked up on the cord, lifting me by my neck.

"Let her down!" Josh ran over and grabbed my legs, trying to pull my feet back down to the floor. I bobbed up and down on the floor like a human yo-yo on a tangled string. My entire face throbbed, the blood trapped, unable to circulate. Again, lights flared around the edges of my vision, darkness closing in after them.

One thought went through my oxygen-deprived brain at the moment. *If I lose consciousness, I'll lose my life.* Nick and I would never marry. He'd never become father to Hank or Waylon or Reba or Dolly, at least not with me as their mother. All that work and time my mother and Bonnie had put into planning the wedding would be lost. My cats would wonder why their mommy had never come home. I'd never be able to enjoy sweet potato fries again. *I can't let that happen.*

With my right arm free, I began to go for my gun again, but then I realized it wasn't the right weapon for the situation. At least not yet. I couldn't shoot someone who was behind me. How would I aim? And with Josh and Cassidy jerking me back and forth and up and down like a tangled mini-blind, a bullet could end up going through the floor, ceiling, or wall and hurting or killing Josh or one of Cassidy's coworkers. I couldn't take that risk.

A file folder with the Financial Force logo caught my eye, providing me with inspiration. If those *F*s could take off like rockets, so could I, right? When Josh managed to pull me down, I got my feet under me, my knees bent, and summoned all the strength I had left, pushing against the floor and shooting up like a rocket, my feet momentarily leaving the ground.

The force nearly broke my windpipe and failed to free me from Cassidy's clutches. The only thing it managed to do was knock Josh back on his ass. *Dammit!* Beyond desperate now, I flung myself back against Cassidy again, slamming her against the back wall. I heard a soft *thud* as her skull hit the wall. *Good.* Maybe I'd knock this crazy bitch out.

I slammed her back again, this time throwing my own head back, the upper part of my skull impacting what felt like the bridge of her nose. Her head hit the wall again. *Thud!*

The cord loosened for a split second, but I wasn't about to wait for a second chance. I twirled toward her, the motion unwinding the cord one rotation. Another spin and my neck was free. *Glory hallelujah!* I gulped air through my mouth. *UH-UH-UH-UH!* My God, why had I never realized how wonderful oxygen is?

Having caught my breath, I threw a punch at Cassidy's face, my fist hitting her right in the mouth. Both she and Josh screamed as her lower lip exploded in blood. *Her smile will never look the same. Ha!*

Dropping the cord, she put her hands on my shoulders

and shoved me backward into Josh before running to the door. She turned left, wrenching open the door to the stairwell. I was after her in an instant. I leaped onto her back, hoping to take her down.

And take her down I most certainly did.

Thump-thump-thump-thump-thump! With Josh scurrying after us, trying ineffectively to pull us apart, Cassidy and I rolled head over heels down the first flight of stairs, careening toward the landing. No doubt I'd have a nice assortment of bruises tomorrow, but for now there was too much adrenaline going through my system for me to feel the pain.

Luckily for me, I ended up on top when we came to a stop. I leveraged myself to a stand and whipped my gun from my holster, pointing it at her face as she sat up. "Don't move!"

Josh glanced over at me, saw my weapon, and pulled his, too. "Don't move!" he shouted, too. A little redundant, but what the heck.

Cassidy looked up at us, her split, bloody lip quivering, and began to blubber. She put her hands over her face to cry into them. *Good.* With her wrists easily accessible, it would make it that much easier to cuff her.

"I'm so sorry!" she cried. "I'm so, so sorry!"

"Save it for the judge." I shoved my gun back into the holster, grabbed one of her hands, and slapped the cuff on it—*click*—pulling it behind her. I grabbed the other and pulled it up behind her, too. But before I could get the cuff on, she twisted her hand to grab my wrist and dove down the next flight of stairs, tucking into a roll and taking me with her. *Thump-thump-thump-thump-thump!* Sorry, my ass. I prayed Josh wouldn't take a shot. With Cassidy and I engaged in this catfight, he had just as much chance of hitting me as hitting Cassidy.

We scrabbled briefly on the next landing before tumbling down the next flight of stairs. *Thump-thump-thump-thump-thump!* This process repeated—*thump-thump-thump-thump-thump!*—until finally we reached the bottom floor. *It's about damn time!* Good thing Financial Force wasn't on the top floor of a skyscraper or Cassidy and I would be nothing but broken bones and mashed flesh.

Though we were both disoriented, my brain righted itself quicker than hers did. I clicked the other handcuff onto her wrist, ordered her not to move, and whipped out my cell phone, dialing the marshal's office. "I need transportation for a female suspect," I told them, my voice so hoarse it was barely audible. It was no wonder. My windpipe had nearly been crushed.

"Sorry," the woman said. "I'm having trouble hearing you. What did you say?"

I repeated the request.

"Is she violent?" asked the dispatcher.

"Little bit," I said. "She tried to choke me with an electrical cord and dragged me down five flights of stairs."

"My goodness! Sounds like you've had your share of drama."

"And then some." Frankly, I'd had all the drama I could take. Then and there, I swore off *Amor y Vengaza*. From now on, I'd stick to sitcoms and my favorite shows on the BBC network.

"I'll send two marshals," the woman said, "just in case she hasn't gotten everything out of her system."

The door to the stairwell opened and three faces—two male, one female—gaped at us.

"We heard some noise," one of the men said. "Are you three okay?"

I looked to Josh to explain. It hurt too much for me to speak. When he finished telling them how he and I had come to interrogate Cassidy and she'd gone berserk, their mouths fell open even further.

"That's crazy!" the woman said.

"Believe it or not," Josh told them, "this isn't even close to the strangest thing that has happened to Tara on the job."

They looked to me. "Seriously?" asked one of the men.

I shrugged. What could I say? Something about me brought out the crazy in people.

Twenty minutes later, everyone from Financial Force gathered in the parking lot to watch as the coworker they'd all thought was so sweet was taken off to the klink. There was lots of murmuring and exclamations of disbelief.

Nancy DeWitt shook her head, her eyes wide in shock. "I never thought she had it in her to attack someone!"

"I feel like this can't really be happening," the guy from the office next door to Cassidy said. "It's like we're trapped in some warped dream."

A woman who was pushing forty offered a wry shrug. "I never much liked her. She seemed like a phony."

Yep, she was one of the women Cassidy thought might be jealous of her. Looked like the little criminal had been right.

I raised a hand in good-bye and Josh and I returned to my car. I slipped gingerly into the driver's seat. After the tumble I'd taken, my entire backside felt like one big bruise. My neck and throat were sore, too. It had been worth it, though. I'd done my job, taken another criminal off the streets.

I phoned Lu. "You can call Perky Ernie," I rasped, "and tell him I just arrested a young woman who works at a payroll processing firm."

"Tara?" Lu asked. "Is that you?"

"Yeah."

"Why does your voice sound funny? I can hardly make out what you're saying. You're not getting sick, are you?"

I handed the phone to Josh. He put it on speaker.

"Hi, Lu," he said. "It's Josh. We've arrested Cassidy Briscoe. We'll explain it all when we get back to the office."

"Okay," she said, curiosity in her voice. "This girl you two arrested? You're sure she's the one who did it?"

"Oh, yeah," he said, cutting a glance my way. "She did it all right."

"Okeydoke. See you in a bit."

He ended the call and handed my phone back to me. I slid it into the cup holder, started the engine, and exited the parking lot to head off in victory, another case solved. While the tax fraud charges might not have gotten her much, if any, jail time, Cassidy would now face indictment for attempted murder of a federal agent or, at the very least, for assault. If she'd been looking for a way to add more drama to her life, she'd certainly found it.

chapter thirty

$\mathcal{U}$p, Up, and Away

Before heading back to the office, I swung by the medical clinic. I was seen to today by one of Ajay's medical associates, given that he and Christina had taken a week off to spend together, a sort of "honeymoon at home."

The tall female doctor came into the room, her laptop perched on one arm. She looked from her computer screen to me. "You have quite the large file, Miss Holloway."

My medical records chronicled my investigations, starting with minor burns and working their way through a litany of assorted injuries leading up to today's throat injury.

She stepped over to the examination table. "Judging from your records, working as an IRS agent is clearly not as boring as one might think."

A painful laugh burst from my esophagus. "There's never a dull moment." Frankly, I'd have appreciated some dull moments about then.

The woman examined my neck, apologizing when she had to feel around the sensitive area with her fingertips.

She also shined a light down my throat and listened to me breathe in and out. "You'll be sore for a while," she said, "but you should eventually make a full recovery. For the next few days, eat only soft foods that are easy to swallow."

A diet of chocolate pudding and milkshakes? I could deal with that.

She looked into my eyes next, shining the flashlight in them. When the receptionist had looked startled by my appearance a few minutes before, I'd whipped out my compact to take a look. My eyes were bloodshot, the capillaries therein strained by the incident, the whites looking more pink than white. They looked like the kind of eyes you'd see in a Halloween mask. At least my skin wasn't so orange anymore, the carotenoids having mostly processed out of my system by now. I had to admit I was missing those sweet potato fries, though.

"I'll write you a prescription for some eyedrops," the doctor said. "That'll soothe the pain. You can take aspirin for the aches and bruises, apply some cold packs." She pulled a pad out of her pocket, scribbled on it, and tore the sheet from the pad, handing it to me. "Anything else?" she asked.

"Ajay usually gives me a lollipop," I rasped.

She reached into her other pocket and pulled out a green sucker. "Here you go. Be a good girl, okay?"

"I will."

Back at the office, I sucked on my lollipop as I took a look at the links my mother had sent me to possible mother-of-the-bride dresses for her. While all of the dresses were pretty, most were very conservative. The one that caught my eye was a taffeta number with a fitted bodice, a flirty peplum, and three-quarter sleeves. Small purple beads trimmed the neck and hemlines. It looked like a dress she couldn't help but have fun in. I sent her a reply. *Get this one. You'll be stunning in it.*

Monday night came with no sign of Hidalgo or the missing girls. Nobody called their aunt to tell her where to deposit the ransom, either. I downed a couple of aspirin and went to bed wondering whether the girls would ever be seen or heard from again. Why hadn't the kidnapper called? Were the girls dead? Had something else happened?

Knowing I'd be sick with worry and that I was in pain from the day's takedown, Nick stayed at my place that night in case I needed a nursemaid or a shoulder to cry on. Henry was none too happy about Daffodil invading his territory, but Anne didn't mind sharing the bed with the dog. In fact, the two curled up together nose-to-nose at the foot of the bed.

"Maybe no news is good news," Nick said, trying to lift my spirits.

I wasn't sure he was right, but I chose to believe it. I simply wasn't willing to accept the alternative. I reached over and turned out the light. It felt symbolic. If the girls were no longer with us, I'd rather be in the dark.

At the office Tuesday morning, my cell phone rang with an incoming call. The readout told me it was Agent Castaneda.

I jabbed the button to connect us. "Good morning, Age—"

Before I could finish he interrupted me. "My counterpart in Mexico says they just found a rental car hidden in some brush alongside Mexican Highway 53, a few miles southeast of the Boquillas Crossing Port of Entry. They've confirmed it was rented in the name of Salvador Hidalgo. We believe he's smuggling people across as we speak.

They can't use the checkpoint without passports, but we're guessing he's going to bring them over a few miles away. We're just not sure in which direction. The car's engine was still hot, so he couldn't have gotten far yet."

"I hope you get him," I said, thinking of the orphaned toddler whose parents had trusted Hidalgo with their lives. If only they'd known he couldn't be counted on.

"We need you to come with us," Castaneda said. "If we finally catch him with undocumented migrants, we've got him. But if we find him alone like the other times, we'll need you there to testify about your investigation, about the people you spoke with. You can vouch for the affidavits."

"But it'll take me hours to drive there. Won't that be too late?"

"There's a flight to the Midland-Odessa airport leaving in an hour from Love Field," he said, referencing the smaller of the two airports in Dallas. "Get on that flight. I'll pick you up in Midland and fly you down in my helicopter."

"Gotcha. I'm on my way." I grabbed my purse and briefcase and rushed out of my office, pausing for only a moment to tell Nick my plans.

"Good luck," he said. "Hope you get him."

"You and me both."

I drove like a bat out of hell to the airport, leaving my car in the expensive short-term parking lot and sprinting toward the counter. I bought a ticket on Southwest Airlines, my late purchase earning me the dreaded middle seat. But at least I was able to sit in the front row, deemed by most to be undesirable due to its lack of under-seat storage to the front. Not a problem for me. All I had was my briefcase and purse, which fit in the overhead bin.

With no time to get the clearances I'd need to bring my

weapon on the plane, I'd had to leave my gun in the glove compartment of my car. But that shouldn't be a problem. I was armed with original affidavits from the men who worked for Brett. That should be all I needed, right?

The cheerful flight attendant read us the safety information, including the information about water evacuations even though there was little water between Dallas and west Texas. When she finished and took her seat, the plane pushed back from the gate, taxied down the runway, and off we went into the wild blue yonder. We were in the air just long enough to down a few ounces of soda and a foil bag of peanuts before the plane landed in Midland. Gotta love those short flights. I was the second one off the aircraft, saying a quick "thanks" to the flight attendants and dialing Agent Castaneda on my cell phone as I sprinted up the Jetway.

"Where are you?" I asked as I jogged through the main concourse.

"Exit the front of the airport and turn right," he said. "You'll see me waiting on the helipad."

Luckily, the Midland-Odessa airport handled much less air traffic and was infinitely smaller than the Dallas–Fort Worth airport I was used to. A single terminal was so much easier to navigate than the five expansive ones at DFW.

I darted out the door and into the dry, west Texas heat. I could almost feel the moisture being sucked out of my skin as I ran for the Black Hawk up ahead. A TSA agent stopped me at the gate, but once I showed my identification he waved me through to the helipad.

Through the windshield, I could see Castaneda at the controls, his sunglasses and headset on. Another agent sat next to him up front. The open door revealed a third Border Patrol agent seated in the back, while a fourth stood at the door to help me in.

The instant I was buckled, the door was closed, the propeller began to spin, and we lifted off, my tummy once again tumbling inside me. Those peanuts had been a bad idea. My stomach was churning them into peanut butter.

Fortunately, we leveled off a minute or so later, shooting across the sky, our view an occasional far-off mesa and hundreds of pumpjacks moving up and down, sucking oil up from the Permian Basin, looking like big metal birds pecking for seed in slow motion.

Now that we were settled, the agent who'd helped me into the Black Hawk handed me a headset and we exchanged names. The tall, thinner one who'd assisted me was Agent Armbruster, a fellow gringo. The beefier but shorter one in back was Agent Peña, while Agent Ochoa, an average-sized guy, sat in the other seat up front. All three appeared to be seasoned agents in their late thirties to early forties. They wore uniforms, weapons, and sunglasses, but no smiles, like soldiers on a dry, desolate frontier. In a rack between the agents were more guns, both short- and long-range rifles. While I was most accurate with my Glock given that I practiced on it routinely at the firing range, I was no novice when it came to larger guns. In fact, I'd once used such a gun to put a bullet between the eyes of a narcotics dealer. When he'd been about to shoot Nick in the back of the head execution-style and shove the love of my life into a shallow grave, the man had left me no choice but to end his life. I didn't take pride in the fact that I'd killed a violent cartel member, but I didn't dwell on it, either. I did what had to be done.

I kept my focus out the front window, watching as hazy apparitions appeared in the distance, rising from the flat desert floor like towering gray monsters. As we drew closer, the mountains became more discernible, as did canyons and cactus and scrubby trees and clear creeks. It was rough, rugged country, but it was undeniably beautiful country.

Castaneda dropped lower and the other agents fished binoculars out from under their seats and put them to their eyes, looking out the side windows, scanning the brush for any signs of Hidalgo or other members of his smuggling network, as well as the desperate people they'd snuck over the border. I reached down and felt under my seat, finding a pair of binoculars and putting them to my eyes, too.

I found it difficult to focus at first, with the helicopter moving and so much of the landscape being similarly colored in muted shades of brown and green, like natural camouflage. We flew over an impressively deep canyon, its steep walls tall and treacherous, the bottom littered with large boulders.

When a glint sparked on the horizon a second or two later, I realized it could be a sign. I squinted through the lenses. Yep, something metal had reflected the sun. And whatever it had been was situated behind a scrubby bush.

"Over there!" I called through the headset, using my outside voice to be heard over the *whop-whop-whop* of the propellers. Instinctively, I pointed, but quickly realized giving a clock position would be more helpful to the pilot up front. "At eleven o'clock. I saw something reflect the sun."

Swoop.

My stomach seemed to swing inside me as the Black Hawk banked and headed in the direction I'd indicated. Given that we'd changed position, I could no longer see the target out of the side window. With the control panels and seats in the way, I couldn't see very well out the front, either. But a moment later Agent Ochoa verified my suspicions as he spied through his binoculars. "There's a dozen people in that dry creek bed up ahead."

I shifted in my seat for a better view. Sure enough, I could see a dry, shallow rivulet in the earth. Several people were crouched down against the edge as if trying to hide. Unfortunately, none of them appeared to be Nina, Larissa, or Yessenia.

Castaneda pulled to a stop in the air, hovering close enough to the crowd that they'd know we spotted them, but not so close that the helicopter would pose a risk to their safety.

Ochoa reached for the microphone on the dash, flipped a switch, and pushed the button to speak. His voice came over a loudspeaker outside. He said something in Spanish, and immediately thereafter the people climbed out of the creek bed, dropped to their knees, and put their hands in the air.

Well, all of them but one.

That one—*Hidalgo, no doubt*—rushed out of the bed and ran off to the left, heading directly for the deep canyon we'd just flown over. While he might not realize the danger he was in, those of us in the air could see it clearly. Unless the guy had a parachute, he was about to be like Wile E. Coyote from the old Road Runner cartoons and plummet to a painful, dusty end on the hard-packed earth.

As Castaneda turned the aircraft to follow Hidalgo, Ochoa shook his head. "That man's got a death wish." He pushed the button for the microphone again and said something else in Spanish. I recognized only two words. The first was *cañon,* which was clearly the Spanish word for "canyon." The second was *peligro.* I knew that word, too. *Danger.*

Hidalgo ignored the warning, continuing to run, his footsteps kicking up dust clouds.

Castaneda sighed through the headphones as he watched Hidalgo make a beeline for the cliff. "As little as that guy deserves to live, I don't want to see anyone else die out here."

He took the helicopter up and over Hidalgo, descending in front of the man, the rocks and dust kicked up by the twirling propeller serving as a deterrent, stopping Hidalgo in his tracks as he threw up his hands to protect his face.

Ochoa issued the same order he'd issued earlier, and Hidalgo obeyed this time, dropping to his knees. But rather than raising his hands in the air as the others had done, he lifted his shirt and pulled a semiautomatic from the waistband of his jeans. Before any of us could process his movements, he'd raised the weapon and begun to fire at the helicopter.

Ping-ping-ping-ping-ping!

Bullets ricocheted off the propeller and tore through the floor at my feet, daylight visible through the tiny holes. *Holy crap! He's going to kill us!*

I flattened myself back against my seat and tried my best to breathe normally.

Ping-ping-ping!

While Castaneda soared up and off and I tried not to hyperventilate, the other agents grabbed two of the rifles and slid their side door open, a rush of air blowing in. The agents leaned as far out as their straps and courage would allow, trying to get a bead on Hidalgo so they could return fire.

Ping-ping! Crack!

Before they could shoot back, a spiderweb of cracks spread across the windshield of the helicopter and dark smoke began to pour out of the engine, trailing past the open window.

"Holy shit!" Ochoa cried. "We're fucked!"

As the others issued similar cries of alarm, panic seized my brain and the world went fuzzy. Given that I was about to crash to a fiery death in the middle of an unforgiving desert, it was tempting to let the fuzz take over and drift into the oblivion. But as my eyes slid closed, the sun glinted off my engagement ring and I realized I had too much to live for to accept this fate without a fight. It was likely futile, but I had to try. For Nick. For my mother and Bonnie, who'd put so much time into planning our wedding. For my future children, Hank and Waylon or Reba and Dolly. And, if for nothing else, I had to live so I could eat another platter of sweet potato fries. You know, just in case they didn't serve them in heaven.

I grabbed the handle for the door on my side, threw it open, and yanked a rifle from the rack next to me. Holding the scope to my eye, I scanned the area, quickly sighting Hidalgo from the muzzle flashes.

I took aim. *"Adiós, amigo."*

Bang!

My shot went through the middle of his right hand, and he dropped his gun to the ground. *Daddy had taught me well.* Still, Hidalgo didn't surrender, instead beginning to run again.

Bang!

My second shot got him right below the knee. Hidalgo didn't go down, but he reached down with his left hand to grab his wounded leg.

Though cries of victory resounded through my headset, Hidalgo continued to hobble through the desert below, limping his way toward the top of the canyon as fast as he could go, leaving a trail of blood behind him.

Ochoa again issued the warning over the loudspeaker, telling Hidalgo what lay ahead. *"¡Cañon!"* he shouted. *"¡Peligro!"*

But Hidalgo wouldn't listen. He continued hobbling at surprising speed until he reached the edge, his mouth opening to emit screams of terror we couldn't hear over the sounds of the helicopter. He windmilled his arms in a desperate attempt to stop his forward momentum.

But it was too late.

Over the edge he went.

chapter thirty-one

*A*nother Puppet
on a String

The helicopter had become harder for Castaneda to control, but he was able to swing it around over the canyon as he aimed for a flat place to set it down. I closed my eyes as we passed over, not wanting to see the gooey blob that had once been Salvador Hidalgo at the bottom.

"You've gotta be shitting me!" Peña shouted. "That son of a bitch is still alive!"

I opened my eyes to see Hidalgo lying on a small outcropping of rock fifteen feet down from the top of the canyon. Landing on such a hard surface must have hurt like hell, but it had saved his life. He writhed in agony for a moment or two, then lay still, his head turned our way. I put the rifle scope back to my eye to take in his nasty scowl. I had to give the bastard credit. Even after taking two bullets and a significant fall, he had the ability to muster up enough hate to send a glare in our direction.

Castaneda set the smoking helicopter down as softly as he could, but the landing was nonetheless hard. My teeth and vertebrae slammed into each other, threatening to crack. But after a moment or two, I realized that I'd be sore but nothing had broken. *Thank goodness.*

"Out! Now!" Ochoa shouted.

Grabbing the buckle to unclip my seat belt, I yanked off the strap and hopped out of the side door, the rifle still clutched in my hand. I followed the lead of the others as they abandoned the helicopter and ran as fast as they could across the desert in an attempt to put as much distance as possible between themselves and the Black Hawk. None too soon, either. As I dared a glance back, the smoke turned to flame, the dry desert wind fanned the flames backward across the aircraft, and the fuel tanks ignited.

KABOOM!

The propeller flew straight up into the air like a giant-sized whirligig, while smaller, blazing pieces of the helicopter and equipment flew through the air, falling into the canyon or to the sandy soil all around us. I ducked behind a boulder for protection and clenched my eyes closed, cringing at each whizzing sound that passed by. The explosion echoed off the mountains and through the canyon. *Kaboom-boom-boom!*

When the clinging, clanking, whizzing, and booming stopped, I popped my head up and peeked over the boulder. The faces of Agents Castaneda, Ochoa, Peña, and Armbruster peeked over other boulders nearby. Fortunately, all seemed to have intact eyeballs, and ears and noses remained attached.

Castaneda stood. "Anybody hurt?"

When everyone had responded in the negative, he pulled a radio from his pocket and requested another helicopter. "Just look for the smoke a few miles from the Boquillas Crossing," he said. "You can't miss us."

While we waited for the aircraft and backup to arrive, we stepped closer to the edge of the canyon, stopping far enough back to ensure we wouldn't fall in. Across the expanse, Salvador Hidalgo had backed up into the small sliver of shade against the canyon wall. He sat in what appeared to be an odd yoga pose with one arm wrapped around his knee, applying pressure with his forearm while clenching his injured hand in the other. His pants were soaked with blood, though not likely enough to cause him to lose consciousness.

Twenty minutes later, my ears picked up the *whop-whop-whop* of an approaching helicopter. We looked up to see another Black Hawk approaching. It made a wide circle of the area once as if getting a read on the situation, then set down not far from where we had crash landed.

"Agent Holloway!" barked Castaneda as he headed toward the helicopter. "Keep that gun trained on Hidalgo. If he tries any funny business during the rescue, shoot him again."

"Got it!" I hollered back. I sat down in the sandy soil and scooted closer to the edge of the canyon, aiming the rifle at Hidalgo across the divide. Any funny business, and he'd find himself with a third fresh hole in his flesh.

Castaneda climbed aboard the other Black Hawk. As the rest of us watched, the helicopter eased out over the canyon, positioning itself directly above Hidalgo, hovering high enough that the wind created by the blades wouldn't blow the guy off the ledge. A moment later the side door slid open and Castaneda appeared, a nylon harness strapped over his uniform. Hanging from a rope, he dropped slowly toward the ledge, his eye on Hidalgo all the while. When he was a few feet above Hidalgo, he stopped his descent and yelled something at the man that I couldn't hear. Apparently it was an order for Hidalgo to raise his hands and turn around, because that's the next thing the smuggler did, blood from his wounded hand running down the rock to form a small pool at his feet.

Castaneda lowered himself tentatively the rest of the way, a spotter from above watching carefully in case Hidalgo did something stupid and tried to harm the agent rescuing him.

When Castaneda's feet hit the rock of the ledge, the spotter lowered another harness down. Castaneda stepped forward and fastened the second harness to Hidalgo. He said a few words, probably giving the guy instructions, before ascending back up to the helicopter. Hidalgo was pulled up next, like a limp puppet in a brutal, bloody show.

As soon as he was inside the aircraft, I lowered my gun, my services no longer needed. Through the open door, I saw Castaneda grab Hidalgo's hands and pull them behind his back to be cuffed. He also said something to the guy, probably asking about the kidnapped girls. Hidalgo's mouth never moved. If he knew anything about the girls, he wasn't talking. *Bastard.*

While a few of the migrants had run south, evidently hoping to make it back across the border into Mexico before they could be apprehended, others had complied with the instructions they'd been given and were waiting for the agents. The Black Hawk set down near them. Two agents emerged and stood watch while half of the group was loaded onto the helicopter.

A second helicopter arrived then, picking up me, Ochoa, Peña, and Armbruster, as well as the remaining migrants. Though I attempted to make eye contact with them, to acknowledge their situation with at least a nod or soft smile, all of them stared at the bottom of the helicopter, their shoulders slumped in defeat and despair. Two of the females cried openly, their tears leaving a track in the dust on their faces. I couldn't help but wonder what would become of them now. Would they be returned to their countries, where they might face danger? Would they be granted some type of asylum here? I suppose it all depended on their particular situations. The only thing I could be sure of was that I'd never take my relatively easy and secure life for granted ever again.

The pilot began to work the controls. As the helicopter lifted off, I glanced out the window. Off in the distance I thought I saw something moving. Of course, it could simply be the breeze, or an animal who'd been scared off by the gunfire, explosion, and helicopter noise.

I grabbed a pair of binoculars and held them to my eyes. To my surprise and delight, I saw three girls running in our direction, waving their arms over their heads. They had to be Nina, Larissa, and Yessenia. I looked up to sky. *Thank you, Lord!*

"Hold up!" I cried to the pilot. "I see the missing girls!"

He looked back at me, his eyes bright with hope. "You do?"

I pointed out the window and took another look. "Over there. They're running this way."

He grabbed his own pair of binoculars and looked through them. "Well, I'll be damned." He lowered the glasses, returned them to their placed under his seat, and shut off the engine.

While the pilot used the radio to notify Castaneda, I climbed out of the helicopter and stepped a few feet away to wait. Castaneda climbed out of the other helicopter and came over to stand beside me. When the girls ran up, they were dirty, exhausted, emaciated, and thirsty, their throats so dry and their voices so raspy it must have hurt to speak. After what had happened to me at Financial Force, I could relate. The sounds they made told me they were crying, but they were so dehydrated that the tears barely came.

Castaneda and I quickly loaded them into the aircraft and brought them bottled water from the cooler.

The agents flew the girls to the hospital in Presidio for treatment, and took the other migrants to the Border Patrol station. Afterward, Castaneda returned me to the Midland-Odessa airport. Once he'd turned off the engine and we'd stepped out onto the helipad, he held out a hand. "Great working with you, Special Agent Holloway."

"Ditto," I said. "I'll send your office a bill for my new teeth and spine."

He chuckled and gave me a chuck on the shoulder before turning to head back to his aircraft. I went into the concourse, purchased a ticket on the next flight back to Dallas, and headed straight for the bar. I wasn't sure if the drink would be to calm my frayed nerves or to celebrate surviving a close call in a remote desert, but either justification worked.

I laid a twenty-dollar bill on the bar. "A glass of your house red," I told the bartender. "With a cherry."

chapter thirty-two

*H*ome Sweet Home

I received a lot of news over the next few days from Agent Castaneda. Fortunately, all of the news was good.

Based on the affidavits provided by the men who worked for Brett, as well as their willingness to testify at a later trial, Salvador Hidalgo was being held without bond. His days of luring people to their deaths in the west Texas desert and kidnapping vulnerable migrants were over.

The migrants that had been rounded up in the desert would likely be allowed to stay. All were shop owners whose livelihoods and very lives had been threatened by violent gangs in Guatemala. Because they could not return without facing possible harm or even death, the judge had stayed deportation pending a full hearing. As victims of crimes willing to testify against Hidalgo, the three girls would also be permitted to remain in the United States. They were united with their aunt and uncle in Dallas, where the younger girls had been enrolled in school and Yessenia had begun helping out in her uncle's custom cabinet business. Zaragoza was rounded up in the desert, not

far from where we'd found the girls. They'd been trailing
the other group of migrants being led by Hidalgo. When
Zaragoza had seen the helicopters ahead, he'd abandoned
the girls, turned tail, and run in the opposite direction. He
just hadn't run fast enough. *Neener-neener.*

Brett's men asked around and finally determined the
whereabouts of Julio Número Uno, his wife, and young
son. Nick and I went to their new apartment to return the
dog to the little boy in person. When his parents answered,
he ran up behind them. Spotting the stuffed toy in my
hand, he cried out in glee, "Pepito!"

He grabbed the dog from me as quickly as he could, and
clutched it to his chest with both hands, turning side to side
with emotion.

His mother, the woman I'd spoken to at the mobile
home several days ago, gave me a teary-eyed smile. *"Muchas gracias."* She said more, which Nick translated for
me. "That little dog meant so much to my son. He's been
crying and crying. We appreciate this more than you could
ever know. You've made three people very happy today."

About time someone was happy to see me, huh?

Cassidy Briscoe was released, but only after her attorney and lawyers at the Department of Justice negotiated a
deal whereby she would wear an ankle monitor and live
with her parents under house arrest until her trial. A diary
found in her apartment revealed her motivations for filing
the bogus tax reports, all of which, like Isidora's motives,
were petty. Bethany Flagler had apparently failed to offer
Cassidy any of the cookies she'd bought from the vending
machine in the break room, even though Cassidy had
shared her chips the day before. Amelia and Gwen had
made plans to attend a rock concert without inviting Cassidy. Jocelyn hadn't returned a compliment when Cassidy
had commented on her cute shoes. As for Thomas Hoff-

meyer, the diary simply said he'd acted like "an arrogant asshole." She'd get no argument from me there.

Robin Beck never surfaced. Looked like she'd decided to forgo her final paycheck from the store in the mall rather than suffer the humiliation of returning to the store to pick it up. Or maybe she feared her boss might change her mind and decide to press theft charges. Who knows?

I cut back on the sweet potato fries, and my weight and complexion returned to normal. There'd be no need to re-size my ring or order a wedding dress in a larger size. Nonetheless, I asked my mother and Bonnie to add sweet potato fries to the selections they planned to offer at our wedding buffet dinner. The two graciously agreed.

With my major cases resolved and Bonnie and my mother on top of the wedding plans, I was able to relax and enjoy a girl's night out and frozen margaritas with Christina and Alicia, who'd just returned from their honeymoons. It was just what I needed.

The following Sunday evening, Nick and I pulled to a stop in front of his mother's house. She'd invited us over for dinner and to go over some of the wedding ideas she and my mother had come up with.

As we climbed out of the pickup, Nick gestured to the house next door. "Would ya look at that? There's a FOR SALE sign in the yard."

I glanced over at the house. It was a single-story Tudor style with a two-car garage, mature Bradford pear trees on either side of the drive, and a row of yellow roses along the front and sides.

Before I could respond, Bonnie rushed out of her front door. "They're moving!" she cried, pointing to the sign Nick had just pointed out. "I saw the realtor putting the sign in the yard this afternoon when I was watering the plants on my porch. You two should take a look. It would be great to have y'all so close! Aren't those roses pretty? And that backyard is big enough for kids and a dog, too. Plus it's got fresh paint and new carpet. I've seen the crews over there working on it."

While many women might cringe at the thought of living so close to their mother-in-law, I wasn't one of them. Bonnie had never butted into our business—well, until now, when she was trying to sell us on buying the house next door. She wasn't critical, either, accepting both her son and me as we were without judgment. And she made a great glass of peach sangria and a delicious spinach lasagna. I bet she'd have us over for dinner all the time, and when we had kids she'd be a convenient babysitter. Yep, living next door to her could definitely have its advantages . . .

Of course, my motives weren't entirely selfish. With Nick's dad having passed on some time ago, Bonnie lived alone, which wasn't easy for anyone, let alone a woman her age. If we lived next door, Nick would be able to take care of her yard and help her maintain things. We'd all be able to enjoy each other's company more often.

Bonnie waved for us to follow her. "Let's see if they're home. Maybe they'll let you take a sneak peek."

We followed her up the driveway to the front door, where she rang the bell. *Ding-dong!*

A moment later, the door was answered by a man in his late fifties. He pushed his glasses back on his nose and offered us a smile. "Hello there, Bonnie." He nodded to Nick, too. "Nick. Good to see you." His gaze traveled to me. "I don't believe we've met."

Nick put a hand on my back. "This is Tara Holloway, my fiancée."

The man's smile became even broader as he shook my

hand then clapped his hand on Nick's shoulder. "Congratulations! Now, what can I do you for?"

"Any chance they can take a look around?" Bonnie asked. "They haven't yet decided where they're going to live after they get married, but I think next door to me would be the perfect place."

The man chuckled and took a step back. "Come on in. My wife's around here someplace. She can point out the so-called features. But I can tell you about the equipment and systems. We had a new AC unit installed two years ago. Replaced the water heater six months back. It's still under warranty. Everything else is in good shape." He turned his head and called down the hall to his wife. "Hon? We've got someone here to see the house."

"Already?" came an excited voice. The wife appeared a moment later, wiping her hands on a kitchen towel. "Why, hello Bonnie and Nick. How are you? And who is this?"

Introductions were exchanged again, as were offers of congratulations on our pending nuptials.

"So happy for you two! You'll make a lovely bride and groom." The woman started back down the hall, waving for us to follow her. "I'll take you on the grand tour. We've been empty nesters for a while, but now both of our kids are married with homes of their own. We're ready to downsize to a garden home or condominium." She stopped at the first room, a small home office with French doors and built-in bookshelves and cabinets. "Lots of storage in there. Not sure if you bring work home with you, but it's a quiet place to get things done."

From there, she led us into a sizable living room with a fireplace and wide windows looking out onto a covered back patio and shady yard. "Plenty of space in here," she said. "Plus you can keep an eye on your kids from here if they're playing out back."

Our next stop was the kitchen. While not as large as Bonnie's or my mother's, it was still plenty big enough and had a comfy breakfast nook. The wallpaper in the adjacent formal dining area was a bit out of date, but it would be easy and inexpensive enough to replace it.

"The bedrooms are back here," she said, leading our five-person parade back across the living room to another hallway.

The master bedroom was sizable, with windows overlooking the front yard and a separate garden tub in the bathroom. It was the jetted kind I'd always dreamed about. And when the woman threw open the double doors that led to the master closet, I gasped in delight. *Have I died and gone to heaven?* The closet was a walk-in, four or five times bigger than the closet in my town house, and featured built-in shelves and shoe racks. For the first time ever, I would actually have enough room for all of my clothes.

"Uh-oh," Nick said. "She'll never be happy with a smaller closet after seeing this."

The other bedrooms were sized well, as was the shared bath. The house had plenty of space for a married couple, a kid or two, and a few furry pets. Still, we weren't ready to buy a house now, were we? I mean, we hadn't even set a wedding date yet.

As the couple walked us back to the front door, the woman asked, "When's the big day?"

"October second," Bonnie answered for us, turning our way. "I planned to mention that to you later." She looked at me. "Your mom called your family church in Nacogdoches and the pastor said that's the first date they had available."

The man and woman exchanged a glance.

I raised my palm. "It's not a shotgun wedding, if that's what you're thinking. It's just that things have been crazy busy for both of us at work so we left the planning up to our mothers."

The woman smiled. "And I take it they want to see you two married off ASAP?"

"Of course!" Bonnie cried. "The sooner they get married the sooner I'll be a grandma."

Nick put a hand on her shoulder. "One thing at a time, Mom. One thing at a time." He shot me a wink to let me know it might not be all that long before he'd be thinking of children, too.

I whipped out my phone and ran a quick Internet search. Sure enough, Mercury would be in retrograde on the day of our wedding. Madam Magnolia had been right about that. I only hoped she wouldn't be right about the chaos. After everything I'd been through the last few days, all I wanted was some peace and quiet and normality.

Turning to the couple, Nick asked, "How much are you asking for the house?"

Their price was more than fair. Besides, mortgage interest rates were low, and we'd be able to use the tax deductions home ownership provided. I could tell by Nick's expression that he was sold on the idea.

He turned to me, cocking his head. "You want to talk about this and get back to them later?"

"What's to talk about?" I said, reaching out to give his hand a squeeze. "Let's do it."

Coming soon. . .

Get your

Death, Taxes, *and Pecan Pie*

while it's hot!

A special Tara Holloway e-novella before the series concludes—with a bang—with:

Death, Taxes, *and a Shotgun Wedding*

Available in November 2017 from St. Martin's Paperbacks